Penshurst Publishing   First Edition - December 2015

ISBN   978-0-9734452-8-2

For Judy

Other Skylines

A collection of short fiction

By F. Bradley Reaume

Murder on the GO

Chapter One

Too many stories have nice neat endings. It's the Hollywood touch. Symmetry is big - you know, the main character says the same thing at the end of the story as he did at the beginning - only at the end it's imbued with layers of meaning.

Most real stories don't have endings, they just stop being interesting.

"This train is westbound. Express to Oakville with stops at Oakville, Bronte, Appleby, Burlington, Aldershot and Hamilton," crackled the familiar voice through the public address system. "Departure in two minutes."

A steady stream of commuters bound for home filed into the double decked train cars. Most passengers headed for their usual spots where they met friends, co-workers, or train acquaintances they'd come to know simply by sitting in the same spot day after day for their commute.

Humans are creatures of habit. Some people chose their seats because the exit doors of a particular car lined up with a preferred stopping position at their home station; others because they liked the view.

The cars were filling quickly and people were beginning to gather in the doorways. The ride to Oakville was only 25 minutes and the runners, those people who wanted to avoid the inevitable parking lot chaos in Oakville, were willing to stand for the entire trip. Many of them had been sitting in front of computers all day anyway.

Rail commuters into Toronto almost all work in the few blocks just north of venerable Union Station where Government of Ontario or 'GO' commuter trains ended their run on several different lines into the city. Some commuters linked up with the subway system but most simply walked to their final destination.

As a center of finance, numerous bank towers dotted the core of Toronto. Insurance companies lined one avenue, joined by hospitals, and government buildings. Two universities also filled up much of the central core. Add retail outlets, hotels, restaurants, entertainment and cultural facilities, a growing number of residential high rises and Toronto was pretty much complete. Though you'd never know it from all the construction cranes.

Most of the thousands of daily commuters into the city center worked between Yonge Street, Toronto's traditional main street, and University Avenue, it's triumphal boulevard. Though there hadn't been much to be triumphal about in years, since the last Blue Jays World Series.

Homeward bound train passengers settled in for the trip, chatting with friends, joking on various topics of the day and discussing the news, sometimes national, always personal.

Fred Deeter was heading home for a bit of rest. He was sifting through evidence collected so far in his investigation of a double murder at a Toronto restaurant sometime before the victims had been discovered that morning. Forensics had yet to issue a full report. The case was likely to be his last active case, as the Toronto Police Detective had been recently assigned to the cold case department.

Police referred to the cold case department as the dead end of police work. It was a mix of their black humour and an acknowledgement that police careers often ended with detectives assigned to ponderously wade though files, reading and rereading evidence that had led others nowhere. It was thought that their experience might trigger something in the case review that had been missed.

Now, with improved scientific methods, primarily DNA evidence and computer file sifting, cases could be reopened with some hope of success. Deeter had toured the basic cold case facilities and been introduced to the large volume of case files but had not yet chosen one to pursue.

The politics of police work meant that he would likely be given a moderately old, high profile case to investigate. At the same time he was going to have a few other files open at any one time, so he could add to the information on file and perhaps find a new path of investigation that might lead somewhere.

The police detective had been volun-told to request the cold case department. It was partly a favour as he was still recovering from a gunshot wound, suffered on an arrest some months ago; and partly a place to park him as there was some concern he was a marked man given his connection to that arrest.

Deeter had just returned to the force after a brush with a terror cell which he had helped to bust while investigating a murder. The murder itself had been fairly routine but he had taken two shots to the stomach while arresting a Syrian man for doing the deed. He was unaware that the murder had a deeper and more sinister aspect as the associates of the Syrian suspect were not interested in their countryman speaking to authorities. They took him out at the arrest in a blaze of gunfire that nearly killed a few bystanders and laid Deeter up in hospital for several months.

The Royal Canadian Mounted Police, the closest thing Canada has to a federal police force, took over the case in the wake of the shooting and were able to neutralize the terror cell which had authorized the hit.

The RCMP relayed to the Toronto Police that they believed the terror cell's mastermind was still under cover. Still, they were pleased that they had cleared away the growing cancer and set back the group in terms of recruiting, training and materials the cell had acquired. It was apparent that the dead Syrian was probably a dupe, someone recruited to the local cell, likely by another low level player. The murderer had been apprehended not far from the scene. It was the dead man's own brother.

Deeter's 15-year police career had been peppered with successes, mostly due to his ability to recall strange bits of information at the right time. On a couple of cases he had taken a logical leap where the evidence pointed and then looked backward for supporting evidence. It had worked often enough to cement his reputation within the department.

This counterintuitive approach had worked wonders, but he always operated on the premise that he was wrong and his investigations were simply closing potential doors. His approach had sent him on a few wild goose chases.

He was confident in his unconventional approach, but not so fixated on his theories that he couldn't abandon them when common sense provided the push. He knew he had to let his theories mature before presenting them to brass. More than once he'd gone too early and more than once he'd been wrong. Even computers were dependent on the data base they worked from and the quality of the search parameters they were given.

One time Deeter had remembered the colour of a witnesses eyes, a fact that put the witness in a different location and one that had altered the investigation. On another case he plucked from his mental files a small detail of an older victim's high school days and that had led him to uncover a small lie by a witness, which eventually broke the case.

Det. Deeter seemed to possess a data bank of arcane information that held in the face of new information, made things stand out to him that didn't square with other details he had retained. He was looking forward to the cold cases as a bit of therapy and a chance to exercise his powers of recall. He had a few old cases of his own that he wanted to give another go.

However the discovery of two bodies in a downtown restaurant had landed on his nearly cleared up desk as a going away present from his boss.

Knowing it would take forensics a few hours to provide a rudimentary file on the case Deeter had conducted the usual interviews of crime scene regulars and victims' relatives before retiring for the evening to review his notes.

Whenever he took the train to his suburban home, he made the 20 minute walk down to Union Station from Toronto Police Headquarters on Bay Street north of College. The walk and the ride were good therapy and gave him a chance to clear his head.

He lived in suburban Burlington in an older home just west of that town's small downtown core. He used to make the drive when his work hours were less predictable, but recently he'd been commuting by train anticipating the more regular hours of the cold cases he would soon be working.

The double murder had taken place in a mid-town restaurant on Church, just south of Bloor - a bit off the beaten track. The owner and a waitress had been found in the morning with head trauma in what looked like a robbery gone bad. Locals had been interviewed and forensics officers were working on toxicology and prints and were looking to establish the cause and probable time of death.

Unlike many of the commuters Det. Deeter didn't like to speak to friends on the train. However, like clockwork he always sat in the same section to be closer to the door. He wasn't a runner when the train stopped but he did figure he might as well shorten his walk, especially on bad weather days. Besides he was a bit claustrophobic and being a sardine, even for a minute or two while the crush near the exit thinned out, was uncomfortable.

Deeter rode the train often enough to be familiar with several of the commuters. The same people occupied the same sections every day. In the mornings when he rode the train Deeter saw the same two young women sitting together. They were obviously friends. One was on the husband hunt and the other was apparently trying to find herself by regularly, radically changing her hairstyle and style of apparel.

Two older women sat nearby. One always had a cup of commuter coffee and a Hamilton Spectator while the other flipped open a laptop and stared at it much of the way in. They looked like bank employees. Three students sat in the car but did not converse or even sit together. Two of them listened to portable sound and lugged large kit bags while the other, a young woman, travelled in with an older man, probably her father. She too seemed to be carrying much more than a laptop in her large bag.

Deeter often wondered what these people were carrying that was so important. When one or two people a car had a large bag they could be stowed and were generally not an issue. However, when more than 50 per cent were carrying large bags, or backpacks or computer cases on steroids, things got a bit tight and uncomfortable. There was simply no place to store all the stuff people brought with them. The cars were added to the system in the 1980s when all anyone needed was leg room. And even that was a bit of an issue.

On his way home Det. Deeter pumped his tired legs up the stairs to the train platform, enjoying the exercise even if he didn't enjoy the effort. The smell of oil and diesel fumes grew stronger as he pushed through the scuffed and scarred door, still swinging from the person in front of him. He headed down the platform to the second car from the front of the train. It would line up with the exit stairs at Fairview Station in Burlington. He could cross the bus loading area quickly and find his car to head home. His home was nearby in suburban terms but as there was no direct way there, he was looking at about a mile walk. He took his car.

He darted into the train car, turned into the lower seat section and found an aisle seat in his usual four-seat section. He always chose the aisle because it afforded a quicker exit and more legroom. Less claustrophobic.

Sitting down, he looked around the car, taking stock of his surroundings, an old habit from his police training days. Familiar faces meant that he was on the right car. Like many commuters he was always acutely aware of checking to see if he was on the right train. While the trains were always on the same track, regular riders never checked the listings and once in a while the schedulers would mix it up. This was especially true of those who rode sporadically as they understood the routine but failed to account for changes.

Today he saw a few regulars, a crown attorney he had often dealt with who got off in Oakville, another young guy in the IT workers' uniform, dark pants and a light coloured hooded sweatshirt. Ever since the tech revolution, the train, once the domain of shirt and tied office workers, was now more likely to carry a young, rough looking computer expert who had refused to let their student days go.

Companies needed these people so badly they had let their dress standards drop to where employees had to merely arrive clothed. Most of them dressed like students and particularly scruffy ones at that, with torn jeans, ripped tee shirts adorned with fading pop culture logos. The employers reasoned that the public never saw this ragged army of the screen, except of course when they arrived and departed from their work.

The train also gave refuge to a few hard workers or hard livers who couldn't keep their eyes open after a long day, and who drifted into the unflattering facial expressions of mid-afternoon sleep.

He nodded at the Crown attorney when they met each other's gaze. The young lawyer probably only knew him as a police detective or maybe by a case where he'd been called as a witness. They both settled back into their seats with the lawyer snapping open a brief case and pulling out a thick file to read.

Deeter was holding his little notebook. It was small enough to tuck in his pocket. He liked having it handy when he was thinking about a case. Sitting on the train was valuable as it offered 45 minutes of nothing to do but ruminate. Deeter could sift through cases in his mind, consult his notes and scribble down things to check out, people to speak to or ideas that occurred to him.

Sliding into his mental reflection Deeter was interrupted by a loud snort and the accompanying movement from one of the sleepers. Everyone on the train looked at each other and smiled. They enjoyed the spectacle partly concerned that they too had done it at some point or another.

Deeter remembered the times when he had been soothed to sleep by the rocking of the train on the tracks at the end of a week of 12-hour shifts. Then there was the one time he decided to stay after work and catch the Jays game with his wife. The game had gone back and forth with many runs scored and many pitching changes on both sides before it went into extra innings.

A real estate agent, Charlotte Deeter had had a wonderful month, and as a reward had been given tickets to her company's private box. Several other agents and their spouses were also on hand.

As much as he enjoyed baseball, and leaving the stadium before the end of the game was an anathema to him, he knew he'd never make it the next day if they didn't leave. On the ride he fell asleep, and as his wife was unfamiliar with the train stations she didn't rouse him until the final Burlington station approached, one station too late. They had to take a connecting bus to give them a lift back to the previous station. That cut into to sleep time.

Deeter liked baseball – he especially liked amateur baseball, mostly because he had played amateur baseball. He was a big fan of the pro game before the 1994 strike that shut down the season and cancelled the World Series. The strike ended it for him. He stopped playing slow pitch a few years later and concentrated on Old Timers hockey, which he still played year round.

Deeter stared at his note book while the last few riders ran to get on before the doors closed and the train started on its way to Oakville. The final announcement of the train's departure echoed in his ears, the doors slid closed and the train started moving.

Almost 25 minutes later the train neared the station in Oakville as one of the sleepers cleared his throat, startled out of his sleep. Deeter looked up from his notebook at the commotion. The man stretched his neck, held too long in the same position. He must have been deeply asleep. He was more agitated than most sleepers, looking wildly about and clearing his throat loudly before settling back into his seat and closing his eyes.

A few commuters got off. People often rose from their seats a little in advance of arrival at the next station to avoid the crush of commuters. Some got up to change seats if their group of four were all still sitting and a nearby section was empty. The extra space was a comfort at the end of the day.

In the four seat section behind the man who had woken up so abruptly there lay another sleeper wedged against the window. Deeter looked up briefly to stretch his neck before returning his attention to his book. As he did so the man stirred slightly and shivered before going quiet again.

Oakville West came and several passengers went. At Appleby so many commuters had exited the train that there were some unoccupied seats. Deeter scribbled notes in his book. He reminded himself to speak to crime scene investigators in the morning about the double hit. It looked like a hit with two victims. He would have to sift through the factual evidence and compare it to the statements received at the scene to determine where the investigation should go.

He had already assigned some of the background investigation to members of his team. They needed to quickly get a handle on financial and familial situations and start probing for soft spots in the web of relationships of everyone who appeared to be involved.

The crime looked like a robbery on the surface but nothing appeared to have been taken. Could be the robber was scared off. Possibly there was something else to be found, a crime of passion, a deal gone bad or a hit on one of the victims. Police were conducting interviews this evening. There were always several paths leading the investigation and they needed to be walked in order to zero in on potential perpetrators.

Tomorrow he would sift the statements, review the forensics report and figure out an investigative direction. Deeter figured the case would be largely wrapped up after a few weeks of his time. Then it went to the Crown's office to determine if there was a case for prosecution.

Deter had received bank records and financial statements just as he was leaving the police station. A quick look through those had provided nothing substantial. He had done the first round of interviews with the victims friends and family, the delivery man who found the bodies and other restaurant employees. He had not had a chance to speak to the restaurant owner's wife who had not responded to calls nor been found at home. That alone was not unusual as people had busy lives that often took them out of touch for hours. Again, nothing jumped out at him except the fact the restaurant had been planning to open a suburban location. One of the locations being considered was Burlington.

He had seen the bank records both personal and those of the business.

There were a few unusual things, including regular substantial payments to a Doctor Archibald, but everything else appeared to be normal as part of the expansion.

The Blue Dome was a niche eating spot as one of the few restaurants specializing in trendy Mediterranean cuisine. Lots of olive oil, pasta, tomatoes and feta cheese. Sort of a Greek and Italian fusion with some north African elements added. The fare wasn't Deeter's favorite but a lot of the weight-conscious professionals loved it.

"Speak to Dr. Archibald. Speak with victim's doctor re: health problems. Speak again to nearby storeowners. Speak to forensics to see if they have anything to go on," Deeter mumbled as he wrote down instructions to himself.

Then his cell phone murmured with a message from the beat investigators that the restaurateurs' wife had arrived home.

A youngish man with a hooded sweatshirt rose from his seat two sections in front of Deeter, put a book into his backpack, slung it over his shoulder and moved past Deeter to the exit. His action caused other people to rise and begin making ready for their exit in anticipation as the train chugged into Fairview Station. A bit more space opened up as people began to crowd the exits waiting for the doors to open.

Deeter clipped his pen to his notebook and slipped it into his inside pocket. This was his stop.

The train stopped and the doors opened. A woman screamed. People started to pour out of the car, some of them momentarily shaken by the scream. The crush of people anxious to get home soon had them moving again. Deeter looked back down the car. Standing two four-seat sections past where Deeter had been sitting, a woman was standing over the man who was asleep, wedged against the window, who Deeter had seen shiver slightly at Oakville station. The woman held her hand over her mouth, horror in her eyes, and she was shaking.

Passengers looked over. One young man bent down to rouse the sleeping man who had slid far down in his seat. He shook him once to wake him before he recoiled as the shifting body revealed its secret.

As he pulled the sleeping man's face away from the window, his face revealed a trail of spittle trickling down the man's face where it had been turned towards the window, his pants were wet and the smell of feces wafted through the air.

The commotion spread and the train continued to regurgitate its passengers. As those nearby the stricken man started to move away and those in the doorways strained to see back to where the commotion was, while at the same time being swept from the train, Deeter pushed his way back through the exiting commuters and dodged into an empty seat as people exited. Someone had pushed the emergency strip.

People exited in a hurry for the parking lot, standard commuter reactions to the end of a long day. GO conductors waded against the human stream to get to the stricken man.. Deeter identified himself as a police detective and quickly made a few phone calls as the emergency response took control of the area.

Chapter Two

The one-time sleeping man, Edward Smythe–Rodgers, was sleeping no more, at least not in the traditional sense. Smythe-Rodgers had entered the big sleep. Sort of like REM sleep but without the possibility of regaining consciousness.

It looked like a heart attack or a massive stroke. After all, Smythe–Rodgers was middle aged, overweight, a chronic smoker who worked a demanding job in Toronto's financial district.

"These things are never simple," said Toronto Police inspector Paul Kronos into the phone. He had called Deeter at home. Only a few years from retirement Kronos was a stickler for his detectives showing up at the office for their morning meetings, which took place at exactly 8 a.m. Metro police detectives referred to him as Father Time.

"Division just told me he died of strangulation from acute anaphylaxis," Kronos said.

"Sir, I know I'm going to the cold cases but I was on scene, let me have this one. It may turn out to be nothing, just natural causes but the train left from Toronto, which means if it's murder, it probably occurred there."

"If it is a murder. I thought you yourself saw him clear his throat and shiver after the train stopped at Oakville."

"It's gotta be treated as suspicious. How does someone who is highly anaphylactic come into contact with the substance that will kill him without there being something left behind? Unless of course it is removed by the killer."

"They are checking during the autopsy to see if he ingested anything," Kronos said.

"Yes sir, I did see him, but he must have come into contact with the nuts or whatever it was at some point before or during the trip. What else could give him that reaction?"

"I'm trying to get you this one, however, our 905 counterparts don't usually get interesting cases and they are hanging onto this tight."

"I thought that there were supposed to be procedures to work together on these cross-jurisdictional things?"

"Yeah, well, there are," said the Inspector. "I bet if I played that angle the 905ers might fall into line. It might mean a temporary team of detectives from all jurisdictions, though. You live out that way. You can speak their language. It might work."

"That means I've gotta carry these guys through the Toronto police department?"

"Yes, you can take charge through the force of your personality," said the Inspector. "I've gotta set this up. Just remember the double murder in the restaurant is your priority. You can let the guys in the burbs do the early grunt work on this one."

Deeter set up a meeting with Peel Detective Ted Marlowe. He played along and did a recognizable Bogart.

"With your name you should be a detective," deadpanned Deeter over the phone.

"That's right, shweetheart," came back the jovial and practiced reply.

Deeter and Marlowe met with Halton detective Charlie Bridgewater. On meeting Marlowe, Detective Bridgewater took the bait and Marlowe managed his stock response.

Marlowe and Bridgewater were experienced and had varied backgrounds. Bridgewater had been on the force for 15 years and was involved in some high profile local homicide cases - usually public domestic executions or business deals gone bad.

A little younger but with substantial experience, Marlowe's background was in financial and white-collar crime.

"You know: computers, internet, banks, fraud, that sort of thing. All the fun stuff," Marlowe explained. "I haven't actually seen blood in 12 years. Other than my own that is - some of those paper cuts run pretty deep, you know."

"Well the Smythe–Rodgers funeral is today. I think we should be there," said Deeter.

"I've already taken the liberty of setting up a police presence," said Bridgewater. The others looked skeptical. "Well, the funeral is in Burlington and Halton cops have to be scheduled as far in advance as possible. Union rules, you know. Anyway, when the body was released I asked the family and then put in a request for officers."

"Plain clothes?" asked Deeter.

"Well, uh, no, actually. I just requested a surveillance unit to take pictures and generally check out the event. I guess you're right though, plain clothes would be better."

"That's right shweetheart, wouldn't want to scare anyone off now. So call off your boys Louie, we're taking no chances," deadpanned Marlowe, as he gestured to the phone.

All the initial investigative plans were laid. Bridgewater and Deeter would attend the funeral in addition to the photo unit. Marlowe was to begin an analysis of Smythe–Rodgers financial background as well as pour through all the statements of witnesses. The train car had been sealed and names had been routinely taken of those people who were present at the time of death. However that many people had simply walked away from the scene when the doors open. The initial forensics report showed no unusual substances were present on or near the seat which Smythe-Rodgers had occupied.

Already appeals for witnesses had been broadcast through the media and by GO Transit officials.

Deter suggested they arrange for plain clothes officers to ride the train a few times to see who the regulars were who rode it, but who had not come forward with a statement.

Chapter Three

Marlowe figured the double decked car had 126 seats and usually carried additional standing room passengers. If they could identify 130 or more passengers they stood a good chance of speaking to everyone who was in any proximity to the dead man. Already police had statements from 120 passengers and a few more people had called in after hearing a media appeal.

"One guy is adamant he had nothing to do with it. He said any DNA we might find was simply his chewed fingernail that he flicked on the floor," a police constable told Marlowe. "I'm not sure if he's more upset that the DNA could prove he's a murderer or simply disgusting."

"Anything else I should look at more closely?" asked Marlowe.

"Yeah, a few. The people in closest proximity had the most to say. Nobody knew Smythe – Rodgers and nobody was familiar with him as a regular rider. However, he lived in Burlington and had extended family there. One guy, a Peter Daniels said he had seen him on the GO before but usually when he took a much later train."

"Well we found a monthly pass in his wallet so we don't know what time he got on the train, but it looks like he was a regular rider. I think we're still waiting for forensics on all his personal effects."

"There were a few other things," said a young constable who had joined the detectives to provide a report. "The screaming woman, Mary Mithers, was sitting in the same four seat section as the vic but diagonally across from him, she said he appeared to be asleep when she got on the train. The train car was her regular – she works at TD – but she hadn't seen the vic before. It was moderately full when she arrived taking the seat because it was on the aisle. She said she liked the aisle for the extra space it gave her for her bag."

"What the hell do all these people carry in their bags? Everybody under 30 and every woman on the train always carry bags with them," said Deeter. "Some of them are huge and really make for a space problem when the cars are full."

"Are we finished now?" asked Marlowe. "Someone has issues."

"The other two spots were filled," added the constable. "It's in the report."

"Give me the short version," said Deeter.

"One was the guy sitting beside him, the guy who pulled him away from the window. He gave a statement that evening. Didn't know Smythe-Rogers, hadn't seen him on the train. Said he was a regular rider but not every day. Other than that, about 70 people were sitting upstairs or on the landings of the car at each end. They all told basically the same story - general confusion at the discovery and a desire to get away from the train and get home."

"What about the guy sitting across from him on the window?"

"Haven't found him yet. They are checking security tapes."

"There are only 54 seats on the lower level and only really about four or as many as 32 with any real proximity to the vic. Most of the spots are accounted for. You should probably read all of them but there's not much there."

Marlowe nodded and took the big folder of witness statements back to his desk.

He first read statements from those who were present but who were not real witnesses. From experience he found that the least likely person sometimes had a telling little tidbit to share.

Chapter Four

The Smythe–Rodgers funeral was a dreary affair. The church was a little pioneer building in downtown Burlington. One of the oldest Anglican churches in the area St. Luke's still clung on to a tiny churchyard and small cemetery just west of the city centre.

To Smythe–Rodgers' credit he had arranged his plot long enough before his need that he secured one in the small churchyard. However, many on hand felt the debit to his bank account must have been large to afford such exclusive company. Still others wondered if very young pioneer influenza victims from the early 19th century were really all that exclusive a company to keep. In any event the church yard was now very pretty and the old church and its environs had a certain cache among the local urban suburbanites.

There appeared to be no family battles in the Smythe–Rodgers universe. Colleagues were all respectful, if a little distracted that they were away from the trading floors and had to turn their cell phones off for an hour. Several people left the service briefly while reaching into their breast pockets. Everyone pulled them out as soon as the service was over and the casket was being positioned at the grave site.

Police discreetly took photos of the mourners at the graveside ceremony.

"Okay shweetheart, you'll want to know more about the black boyd," said Marlowe as Deeter and Bridgewater entered his office in Mississauga. It was a good central place to meet.

Deeter smiled lightly. Bridgewater mumbled something starting with "Shweetheart" but quit. "I've gotta work on that. Gotta watch some of those Bogie movies."

"The black woman is interesting," said Marlowe, pointing to a photo of a youngish black woman about 35 years of age dressed in a very expensive suit. "A few witnesses have her giving coupons out in the concourse to passengers as they were heading for the tracks."

"Yeah, so."

"It appears the coupons were very unusual. The writing on them was extremely small save for the headline that said 'Save 25 per cent on GO and TTC passes'. One witness still had it deep in his brief case and forensics said it had peanut essence all over it."

"You mean a person handing out flyers at Union Station happened to know the victim, who was also allergic to nuts, and handed him a flyer covered in peanut oil? I think we gotta find this woman," said Deeter.

"Already done Fred. She works part time for Metro Promotions. She was handing out the coupons as part of a promotion. She didn't know the vic. She said she had a huge bunch of peanuts in a net bag resting at the bottom of her coupon box. She said it was something to eat while she waited between trains. She only attended the funeral as she felt her desire to snack on peanuts was to blame."

"It's an accident? I don't believe it. Something here doesn't add up."

"You could be right Fred, I spoke to the vic's family. They were aware of the allergy but described it as moderate only," said Bridgewater.

"What about forensics?"

"Well they ID'd the guy who flicked his fingernail. So we can be certain of two things. He was on that train at some point and he has a bad anti-social habit," said Marlowe.

"What about the vic's business dealings?" asked Deeter.

"No, go back to forensics. It appears as if peanut oil was injected into Smythe-Rogers' leg, just above the ankle. The lab guy said it was a deep injection, consistent with a stab rather than a controlled insertion of the syringe. It also appears to have happened while he was sitting as there is no sign that he walked on the leg after the injection."

"Okay, so he was injected on the train. That would account for his death."

"So he got a short dose first to slow him up, and then at some point on the trip received a second dose by injection? Was that the cause of death? And nobody saw anything like a stabbing injection?"

"Right, it was the cause of death and so I've doubled up with the seatmates he had in his section. Nobody saw anything that could be construed as a stabbing attack. According to the lab it appears to have occurred from directly in front of him, potentially the person sitting across from him or someone with access to his lower left leg, just prior to his getting on the train."

"And that person remains unknown."

"Yes, we are checking security tapes and have officers on the trains trying to identify him."

"And financials?"

"Well we have the vics' records. He was involved in corporate loans and investment banking with a Schedule Three bank downtown."

"Schedule three?" asked Bridgewater. "Refresh my memory, please."

"That's a bank with a special charter. Schedule threes have no branches and are almost exclusively lending institutions only with some corporate and investment interests," explained Deeter.

"So who's on his client list?" Bridgewater asked.

"Well, a veritable who's who of corporate Toronto. However, most of the dealings were small. It's almost as if the big boys used our vic for small potato deals, either cultivating him in case of need or simply playing him off against the bigger players. According to company officials they had started to charge for deals that did not materialize as the time lost was costing them quite a bit. Seems they knew they were being used."

A survey of all of Smythe–Rodgers clients yielded little, save an unusual number of repeat customers whose deals often flamed out. A few leads would be checked out but they were not promising. It was nagging at Deeter that he was missing something.

A lot of information had crossed his desk on the Smythe – Rodgers case and as the days went by he was getting pressure to lighten the load on his investigation.

"You've got other cases Detective," pointed out Inspector Kronos. "Those victims deserve your attention as well. Toronto cases are what we pay you for. Investment bankers in the burbs are not high on our list."

"It was a pretty public murder," said Deeter.

"Or accidental death. It may just as easily have been a fluke or an accident, notwithstanding that somebody apparently stabbed him with poison. Hey, maybe it was suicide," said Kronos. "Anybody look for a note?"

"I'm not saying you should stop your investigation. I'm saying move on and give everything on your plate the attention it deserves. The two suburban guys can keep things going while you catch up here."

Deeter left the room and headed toward his desk. He was deep in thought, walking with his head down and eyes watching the floor.

"There had to be something I'm missing," he thought. "Perhaps the Inspector was right, he should put more emphasis on the double murder he'd been reviewing when Smythe-Rodgers died. At least that was murder for certain."

"Old Father Time got you down, old boy?" said one of the other detectives looking up from his desk.

"No, it's not him. I just can't see something that's right in front of my face."

"Many people call it 'the floor'," said the detective still at his desk.

Deeter telephoned Bridgewater and Marlowe suggesting another meeting to compare notes later in the week to wrap up their side of the investigation.

"You got the talk too, eh," said Bridgewater. "My Inspector said I should reduce my involvement."

"Yeah, Marlowe said the same thing when I talked to him," said Deeter. "He said the Toronto guys could handle it, after all how many investment bankers get offed in Burlington and something about this being the end of a beautiful friendship, shweetheart."

Chapter Five

Deeter went back to his notes on the twin restaurant killing. Then he went back to the crime scene.

The restaurant had been in business for many years and had a loyal local clientele. However, few people knew of it who did not live downtown, stuck as it was on a little side street off Church, up near Bloor a couple of kilometers from the financial district but worlds away in terms of familiarity with the downtown financial set.

The restaurant's kitchen had all the usual pots and pans hanging from ceiling racks. There was a huge plastic two month 'wipe and write' scheduling board used as things in the business changed rapidly. The days were filled with reminders of deliveries from LCBO, soft drink suppliers, food vendors, meat suppliers and the like. It listed big parties who had booked reservations. It also had the staff schedule on it and even staff birthdays and other sundry bits of information.

Deeter had looked hard at this schedule. He took a photo of it on his cell phone. Suppliers who had come in early in the morning of the murders confirmed all was well prior to the Labatt representative who dropped by at about 9 am only to find the bodies.

Both victims were found with blows to the head but there were no signs of struggle. The apparent murder weapon was about the only thing out of place. A heavy iron skillet lay on the floor near the bodies. Those bodies appeared to have toppled off high bar type chairs after being struck. There were no prints on the skillet save those of the kitchen clean-up crew.

Deeter wondered how two people could be whacked without either hearing their assailants. The blows to the head must have happened at virtually the same instant, or he thought, been at two different times entirely.

The handle of the skillet had been wiped clean and only the rim of the cooking surface revealed any fingerprints. Those had belonged to the cleaning staff who washed pots and dishes at the end of each night. Those people had been spoken to and had alibis.

Deeter remembered in passing, one of the cooks said that the restaurant was supposed to be opening a suburban location. A light bulb went off. He decided to speak to the restaurateur's wife.

"Hello Mrs. Arleche I just wanted to go over a few things with you."

"Thank you Detective, I am happy to help but still not quite myself, this has all been such a shock. I've been over everything I can think of with other officers. They wrote it all down."

"Yes I'm sure they did, Mrs. Arleche but I wonder if you can remember anything else? Was there anything unusual about that day?"

"Well no, I mean there were always things scheduled, deliveries being made," but nothing has come to mind and believe me I've relived that day and others before it many times trying to see if something comes to mind, but nothing does."

"How much time do you spend at the Blue Dome?"

"I used to be there a lot as a backup waitress, and I still go in on short notice, but we have a wonderful and reliable staff. I haven't been needed there much in the last few years in that way. I do go in sometimes to do spot inventory as I do the books and like to keep track of what we have on hand and what we need. My husband did most of the ordering, especially the perishables. I handled the management side on the regular orders, cleaning, deliveries and such."

"I understand your husband was going to open a second location in the city," said Deeter.

"No. Well yes. It wasn't firm yet. He wanted a second location. One of our best customers was pushing for it. At first it was going to be uptown, better for our old clients who had moved that way. Then it was going to be in the suburbs. My husband thought there would be as many former clients living in the suburbs as well the reputation of the restaurant would not be drowned out by all the other upscale places there are uptown."

"Who was financing this expansion?"

"Well, my husband has . . . had a number of high profile clients. Let me get the papers. I just saw them yesterday somewhere." She went to a desk and started rummaging around. "It was some of them who pushed for the second location. He had reservations because he was very involved in the day to day operations and knew he couldn't be in two places at once.

Mrs. Arleche returned with some papers. "Here is what you're looking for. Doctor Martin Archibald was the main backer. He was already a 20 per cent owner of our first restaurant. Marty is a long time friend of my husband. He was one of our first customers. He was going to put up 33 per cent I think, yes it says that here," she pointed to the papers. I think he was going to approach some of our other regulars to see if they wanted a piece of his part of the pie."

"An Edward Smythe—Rodgers of Friedrich-Barnes was hired to find another 33 per cent and we were in for the balance."

Fred Deeter caught his breath. Edward Smythe–Rodgers was involved in securing part of the financing for the venture. The owner and a waitress were dead. And now Edward Smythe–Rodgers was dead. But there appeared to be nothing else to tie the two cases together - even the causes of death were significantly different.

Deeter was again confused. Was there a connection? Who was this Dr. Archibald?

He remembered something from the reports he had read. He took his leave of Mrs. Arleche. Returning to his office his suspicion was confirmed. The restaurateur and the waitress had both died from asphyxia - in the case of the two restaurant victims apparently due to the blows to the head which induced bleeding which upon which the unconscious victims choked.

But, he thought, what if they had been whacked on the head and then asphyxiated by covering their faces once they were unable to defend themselves? Was someone trying to disguise the killing to make it look like a robbery when it was something else?

He checked his own notes. Mrs. Arleche had an alibi. She had been in Burlington for several days running including the day of the murder. She was meeting with a local commercial realtor regarding potential locations for their suburban restaurant. She had shown Deter her GO Train ticket stamped at 2:35 p.m. at the Appleby Station in Burlington for the ride back to Toronto.

"Deeter, we have something interesting about that banker. Detectives said that one of the passengers on the train called in and said he distinctly remembered that the vic was on the train and appeared asleep when he got on. He said he was one of the first people on the train and he wondered how the guy could get on and get comfortable enough to close his eyes that fast. There was apparently another guy sitting in the same section who got up as he arrived to sit down. He was described as young guy with a backpack."

Deter remembered the youngish man who had gotten up just prior to the discovery of Smythe-Rogers death.

"Forensics just confirmed, Smythe-Rogers died from acute allergic asphyxia."

"In his brief case they found a few pages of notes regarding a restaurant that he was helping to finance - the same one where the double murder took place two days before. Looks like your two investigations might become one."

"I'd really like to find the witness who sat across from Smythe-Rogers on the train. That person might be able to confirm when he got on the train."

"Yeah, we thought the same thing though he appears to be one of only a few people who we've not been able to track down. Given his appearance we thought he might be a computer worker, they are notoriously relaxed in their appearance, or perhaps a student. We're working those angles."

Deter figured it was time to pay a visit to Dr. Archibald.

He arrived at Archibald's office and was ushered into an examining room to wait for the doctor. After a few minutes a 40ish man swept in and introduced himself.

"Yes, it has been a very difficult week. First my friend Gabriel Arleche is killed and then I hear Mr. Smythe-Rogers who I have dealt with on a number of business deals has died suddenly. What can I help you with Detective?"

"I understand you were committed to help finance the restaurant expansion into Burlington?"

The doctor's eyes darkened for a moment. "Yes, well, it wasn't firm that it was Burlington but that's where Gabriel and his wife seemed to be leaning. I was pushing an uptown location. It was easier for Gabriel to handle both if they were in the same city."

"You were close friends with Gabriel?"

The doctor smiled. "Yes, we were childhood friends. Our families were quite close. Gabriel's parents started the restaurant and my parents were in the produce trade. They all lived on the same street and my parents had a booth in the St. Lawrence market for years. My sister runs it now."

"You were a backer of the Blue Dome. How profitable was the restaurant?"

"An excellent question, detective. I had loaned Gabriel $50,000 which we agreed gave me 20 per cent in the equity of the business should it have to be sold - Gabriel figured he could get $250,000 for the sundries and good will. However I was not included in profits unless they were substantial, only then would I receive a dividend in addition to steady repayment of the loan. Gabriel approached me to loan him an additional $100,000 to finance a second location, saying it was a 33 per cent interest and I would be entitled to a third of the profits."

"You must have wondered why the first loan didn't entitle you to profits?"

"No detective, the first $50,000 was a loan to a friend. The percentage of equity was Gabriel's idea in case the building burned down. He was trying to protect me. The $100,000 was a business proposition. But that appears to have died with Gabriel, I'm afraid."

"Mrs. Arleche thinks the deal is still on. She was scouting business locations and keeping appointments with property managers even on the day of the murder."

"Well until then it was on, I suppose, we hadn't firmed up anything at that point. I knew that she was interested in the Burlington location as Mr. Smythe-Rogers had interested investors who lived there. They needed that additional investment to put the deal together."

"You said you were in for $100,000 and I understand Mr. Smythe-Rogers clients were in for $100,000 leaving an additional $100,000 for the Arleche's. However you say they already owed you $50,000?"

"Yes."

"Have you spoken to Mrs. Arleche since the murder?"

"I passed on my condolences. I was a childhood friend of Gabriel's and did not really know her. I spent time with Gabriel in his restaurant. I have been a regular there for years and would see her there on occasion."

"You attended the funeral?"

"Of course. Though it required a bit of juggling of my appointments to make it. I didn't stay for the reception as I had to get back here."

Deter left the doctor's office and went to the offices of Friedrich-Barnes. Soon he was elbow deep in financial records and other files.

It didn't take long to see the trail. He put in a quick call to Detective Marlowe in Mississauga.

"There's some funny business with our vic - Smythe-Rogers. He's discovered that the owners of the restaurant we're skimming money from the operations which appear to disguise the profits they were making. According to their deal with Dr. Archibald that meant that they didn't have to turn over a dividend to him as a partner in the business. In his investigation of the business deal for expansion Smythe-Rogers caught on to the skimming as the profits did not seem to be properly accounted for."

"Any evidence he told anyone?"

"Not yet. But I wonder if the doctor can account for his whereabouts on the morning of the murder."

"Smythe-Rogers might have even mentioned it in passing or as part of their business arrangements as he could reasonably believe that the doctor knew and that was how the Arleche's were paying back the money he loaned them."

"If that's the case, the doctor is a prime suspect."

"It all boils down to who knew what? And when? Only that can help determine the timeline and who would want to take out Gabriel and eventually Smythe-Rogers."

"Well it's safe to say that Smythe-Rogers' investigation likely kicked off a chain of events. But who would he have told first? I'm guessing Gabriel. If his notes are to be believed he thought that the Arleche's both were in on the scam and the scam was really to make it easier to pay back the doctor."

"But if the doctor did not know . . . If Gabriel did not know . . . .But apparently the doctor did know."

"Would Mrs. Arleche have killed her husband if he confronted her?

"Maybe, but not likely. They could say it was her idea that the payback amount was part of the operating costs. They would have worked it out."

"Would the Doctor have killed Gabriel in a confrontation once he knew he was being ripped off."

"Maybe, but only if Gabriel stuck by his wife's accounting choices."

"And what about Smythe-Rogers? What's the motive to kill him?"

"Well, there is motive if you believe that he had not yet told anyone about the apparent skimming. If he threatened to tell the doctor and the Arleche's were unhappy about that, they have motive. So it appears that whoever killed Smythe-Rogers likely had nothing to do with Gabriel's death."

"What about the waitress? Could there be some sort of triangle here?"

"Maybe, but we've encountered no evidence of it. Though she did have a restraining order on her ex-husband."

"That's a lot of 'maybes' what we need is concrete evidence."

"So go out and find it."

Deeter looked at Smythe-Rogers' appointments book and found he had cancelled a meeting with Gabriel on the morning of the murder.

"Drinkwater, you got anything on the Smythe-Roger's case?"

"Ahh, so happy to hear from you too," said Drinkwater into the phone. "I do know that our vic was in Burlington earlier in the day of his death."

"Yeah, well, he lived there. What did he do? Grab a coffee on his way into the city? Tell me something I don't know."

"It turns out I know who to talk to. I found out he met with a commercial real estate broker around noon looking for potential locations for a restaurant."

"How did you figure out he was even there?"

"Security cams have him getting on the GO Train westbound at about 11:25 a.m. Knowing the restaurant angle I asked around about anyone looking for a commercial restaurant location and found out he met with a broker. He had a woman along with him. They arrived in a very nice Porsche."

"She wouldn't have been about 5 foot 2 with long brown hair and answer to Maria?" asked Deeter.

"Yes she did and was. You obviously haven't been keeping me up to speed detective."

"Well, I called you. Anyway, it appears that our banker vic and a double murder in Toronto on the same morning are connected."

"You knew about our vic searching for an investor for a restaurant. Turns out the owner of that restaurant and a waitress were murdered the same day as our vic. Looks like I'm the new lead on this case."

"My inspector will be so pleased."

"I'm going to need to look at those GO Train security tapes. Just curious, does Smythe - Rogers travel with anyone on the train?

A quick call to the property manager in Burlington, with whom Smythe-Rogers and Mrs. Arleche had met on the day of the murder, revealed that Mrs. Arleche had brought along a friend to their meeting, described as a potential investor in the project. That friend matched the description of Smythe-Rogers. Mrs. Arleche had arranged the meeting, not Smythe-Rogers. She had been driving the Porsche.

So the banker had cancelled a meeting with Gabriel where he was likely going to address the financial skim, to instead meet with his wife regarding potential locations for the new restaurant?

Deeter was intrigued. That seemed odd. Who did Smythe-Rogers tell about the skimming? If he asked Gabriel to meet, did Gabriel let Smythe-Rogers know he knew about the skimming?

What mattered, thought Deeter, is who knew what, when? Knowing that would strongly suggest the likely killer or killers.

Deeter again visited Mrs. Arleche.

"Mrs. Arleche I have uncovered evidence that the restaurants accounts were being skimmed."

"Skimmed? How? I did the books and everything seemed fine to me."

"It appears that at least $4000 per month was coming off the top before profit and loss were calculated."

"You say, $4000. Precisely. That's not skimming, that's the amount I took to pay back our operating loan each month. I do the books and frankly I hate to owe Martin Archibald any money. Since he helped us he was leaning on Gabriel for favours, extended hours for his own events, and more than the usual number of favours a businessman might do for a friend and loyal customer. I wanted to get him paid back ASAP. I figured as long as Martin was getting his money back he would be happy."

"Did Dr. Archibald know about this arrangement? After all he was supposed to get a percentage of the profits over a certain amount, and amount that might not be reached given the payments were taken off the top."

"You would have to ask him. Certainly, I took the payments to him off the top. It isn't profit if you are paying back a loan. It's part of the cost of doing business."

Did your husband know about your approach to accounting?"

"Ahhh, yes. Yes, of course, though we never spoke about it much."

"I understand you met with Mr. Smythe - Rogers on the day of the murder regarding the restaurant expansion."

"Yes, we were scouting out locations in Burlington. I drove there in the morning, looked at some locations before picking up Mr. Smythe - Rogers at the GO station just after noon. We had a meeting with a commercial realtor scheduled for 12:30 p.m. I dropped him back at the train station at 3:20 p.m."

"What kind of car do you drive, Mrs. Arleche?"

"A Porsche - a present from my husband a few years ago."

Did you know that Mr. Smythe - Rogers cancelled a meeting with your husband at the restaurant the morning that he went to Burlington with you?

"No. I didn't know that. I called Mr. Smythe - Rogers and asked him to attend the meeting as I had had trouble arranging it for several weeks. The broker told me he had some recent information for me that required a fairly quick decision. So I made the arrangements."

"I understand that Dr. Archibald favoured a Toronto location?"

"Yes, but he didn't have one and he hadn't ruled out a favourable location in the west end. I went to the meeting to see what new properties might be available - we still had to have the Doctor on board as he was to be a part owner."

"Was the Doctor aware that payments to him were coming off the top of profits at the Blue Dome?"

"I understood that Gabriel had told him as much."

Deeter was confused. Was Gabriel able to explain away the apparent skimming and was that enough to stop him worrying and get back on track with the new venture? If so, Smythe-Rogers must have spoken to Dr. Archibald to be sure that the arrangement was known to him as well.

After all, mulled the detective, it was the Doctor who was apparently being financially damaged by the accounting and who was also in line to drop another $100 large on the new restaurant.

Chapter Six

Deeter went to train officials and began the painstaking task of going through all of the video security tapes. The camera was situated in the door of the train and was angled to view those who entered the car and had a sidelong view of the length of the lower section of the car. The view beyond 15 feet was pretty fuzzy through the convex pinhole camera lens.

He saw Smythe-Rogers get on the train in Toronto at 11:25 a.m. He saw him get off the train in Burlington Fairview station at 12:15 p.m.

He went to the tapes of a trip at 5:19 p.m. the express to Oakville with stops at individual stations further down the line west of Oakville.

There was no evidence of Smythe-Rogers getting on the train in Toronto however there was a likely lump in the seat he had occupied. Deeter was familiar with many of the other passengers as their statements had been taken. He even saw himself, a bit bored, scribbling, gazing into space and scribbling again. He noted the reaction of passengers to the stirring of one sleeper and then a lesser reaction at Smythe-Rogers brief stirring.

Nothing seemed out of place. The only notable moment was when the young man who was sitting across from Smythe-Rogers packed up and left his seat prior to the train reaching Oakville. His motion had caused the victim to start from his slumber.

Just before he got up to leave the young man, had bent forward in his seat as if grabbing at his pack the then stretching to his full height. His hood covered his face for the entire trip.

A look through the documents showed there was no interview of this guy. In fact he seemed to have been ignored or gone missing. Moments after the first passenger abandoned his seat to make his way to the door the young man reached between his legs, moved upright again, stood and moved away from the seating area, with his head down.

"Is that the moment that Smythe-Rogers was injected?" thought Deeter.

He went back further on the security tapes. Deter found that Smythe-Rogers was already on the train and apparently asleep for most of the trip from Burlington. There was tape of him moving slowly along the platform in Burlington, then boarding the train, sitting down and apparently falling asleep as he is slouched down and did not move for long stretches.

The train left Fairview Station as Smythe -Rogers began to drift off. At Appleby Station a young person with dark pants and a grey hooded sweatshirt entered the train, and though it is virtually empty, he sat down immediately opposite Smythe-Rogers, an unusual choice of seat for two people who do not know each other when most of the seating areas are unclaimed.

Deeter eyeballed this person, he did not appear to be the same guy sitting across from Smythe-Rogers when the train pulled into Oakville on the return trip. The clothing was different enough to notice. This second young man was not particularly tall, in fact he was a bit short and slight. The security video suggested he was wearing tailored pants, all together too well fitting for the average computer worker or student. The dark gray hooded pullover was an odd match to the tailored pants and what appeared to be dark dress shoes.

Deeter could feel the beginnings of a theory.

However, when he looked at the security video he could see the Porsche drive up to the station house at Fairview, Smythe-Rogers get out and make his way a bit unsteadily to the station. The security camera caught the Porsche leaving.

"So Mrs. Arleche had dropped Smythe-Rogers off at the train station the day he died," Deeter thought. "Why wouldn't she have just given him a lift back to Toronto? It appears that she traveled back to Toronto in her car. Had she exposed Smythe-Rogers to whatever gave him the allergic reaction? If she had what took her so long to get back to Toronto, as police assigned to break the news to her of her husband's death did not encounter her until she arrived home well after dinner, he wondered.

Deeter ran, and reran the security tape showing Smythe-Rogers getting on the train. Everything appeared alright as he boarded. Only the young man sitting with him at Appleby seemed odd. Deeter scrolled through the security footage from inside the train car several times. The two did not appear to converse and Smythe-Rogers in fact never appeared to wake once he settled into a nap very soon after getting on the train at Fairview Station. The young man kept his head down and his hood over his head.

Deeter decided he had to follow the security footage for the entire trip. Shortly after leaving Appleby Station the young man leaned forward as if looking for something. He popped upright with something in his hand, a book maybe, which he transferred to his left hand and then leaned forward again. He popped up again and started to read his book.

At Oakville West and Oakville the car fills up, though not to overflowing. In the throngs at Oakville the young man gets up and moves off the train. He can be seen walking through the underground concourse to the buses. The train makes its way to Union Station in Toronto and passengers disembark and the train refills with commuters for the trip back to the western suburbs. A young man in dark pants and a hooded sweatshirt eventually comes and sits across from Smythe-Rogers who has only moved a bit in the entire trip from Oakville, by this time he is twisted slightly against the window.

Deeter watched this several times noting nothing overly strange. The two hooded young men were probably not the same person, though they did not look very different. The first one seemed slighter than the second, and the first one, steadied himself on the seatbacks as he exited the train. The second one, walked purposefully to the seat across from Smythe-Rogers.

The second man slung his backpack under the seat but made no effort to retrieve it or anything in it until he was preparing to exit the train in Burlington. The first young man made two moves towards his backpack, the first one, to retrieve a book which he reads with his head down.

"That's a woman, who exits the train in Oakville. She is wearing tailored pants but has a dark grey hooded sweatshirt over her blouse and is wearing the hood up," Deeter said to himself. "It certainly looks like a woman the way she grabs the seat backs even though the train is stopped. Deter noted that more often than not the women touched the seats on the way by, but the men simply walked off the car."

"She goes to the buses. Did she bus back to Toronto. Is that why she was late?"

Deeter called forensics. He asked a couple of questions. The forensics team promised to take an additional look at the body.

Deeter then reconsidered the evidence from the restaurant.

Forensics had determined the time of death as sometime around 8 am, a couple of hours before the bodies were discovered. Tests suggested the victims were bashed on the head with a heavy skillet more than once and both asphyxiated likely due to blood and fluid.

The crime scene photos did not give any additional clues except the waitress' body was further from the bar area although still near a bar stool. However that bar stool seemed to have been placed near the body as it was not in its normal position at the bar. According to Mrs. Arleche the restaurant often served singles at this location which overlooked the kitchen. The bar stool would not have been there, but closer to the bar, especially as the restaurant was closed.

Deeter surmised, it appeared as if Gabriel had been sitting at the bar and had been attacked there falling forward on the bar and then sliding off to the floor. He had slight bruising on his forearms and his chin and cheek, likely from hitting the bar. That squared with forensics.

Deeter wondered if the waitress had come into the room to investigate the noise and been similarly attacked while standing up. She fell where she was struck and the chair was placed near her to make it look like she fell from the chair. What would be the advantage to the killer in creating that scene? thought Deeter.

"Someone would have had to sneak up on her from behind, either when she was speaking to someone in the room or investigating Gabriel on the floor."

Did it look as if they were killed at the same time? Yeah, thought Deeter, that was the assumption by investigators. It appeared they had been attacked at the same time, suggesting a surprise attack by more than one assailant.

"What was the waitress doing there at 8 am?" wondered Deeter aloud.

Her family had been interviewed and Deeter went through the file to review the notes.

She was a single mother, divorced, and her ex-husband was under a restraining order, limiting his contact with her. He lived in Woodbridge, north west of the city, and worked as a machinist in a north Toronto machine shop. He was at work the morning of the murders, corroborated by his time card and two witnesses who said he usually arrived for his shift just before the 7 am starting time.

If he wanted to kill his ex-wife he would not have had the chance to kill Gabriel in a sitting position unless he killed him first. He also had no motive to kill Gabriel. His alibi checked out, he appeared clean, thought Deeter. However, he rarely completely dismissed any potential suspect from his considerations.

Other restaurant staff said they would occasionally go into the restaurant early to collect paycheques, especially if they weren't due to work for several days. Gabriel was usually there in the early morning after he had gone to the produce markets and made his daily purchases. His presence at the St. Lawrence market the morning of his death was corroborated by those vendors he usually dealt with and by his purchases.

"So," thought Deeter, "somebody wanted Gabriel dead and likely the waitress was just collateral damage, in the wrong place at the wrong time."

"So who had motive to kill Gabriel?"

The phone rang. It was Mississauga Marlowe. "Got your note about the hooded guys on the train. We still can't find the one that got off in Burlington. And I never knew we were looking for one that got off in Oakville."

"Yeah, I need you to go into the financials and put together a motive through the skimmed accounts, the proposed new restaurant and potentially the doctor. He seems all too innocent in this. You see his explanation of his motives in the notes. It's all very logical, that he loaned the money to a friend, that additional investments were business oriented, but it doesn't ring true somehow."

"I've got nothing to tie him to the murders but somehow I think he's involved. I haven't yet looked for any real tie between the good doctor and Mrs. Arleche. He claims to have not known her well. She refers to him as a family friend using his first name. Perhaps she knew him better than he lets on. Can you check both of their financials for evidence of a tryst?"

"Sure enough Shweetheart, I'm on it."

"Hey, and we need something more concrete to tie Mrs. Arleche to the Smythe-Rogers murder. I think I have her on the train with him in disguise. I've got someone looking into train station footage at Oakville. And then there is a similar looking person who travels with Smythe-

Rogers westbound, leaving just before he is discovered dead. The bus drivers don't remember anything specific about passengers coming from the eastbound train so I can't even be sure the potential suspect even got on a bus."

"Right now she was the last to see Smythe-Rogers alive. She arranged to meet with him that morning as Smythe-Rogers cancelled an appointment with Gabriel. She got him to meet her in Burlington to discuss a potential restaurant location, somehow slipped him some allergen, and once he was on the train going eastbound to return to Toronto, she got on the train at Appleby Station, injected him with allergen to finish him off. She got off the train in Oakville and disappeared. I'm guessing she caught a bus back to Appleby Station where she retrieved her car. He remained on the train going into Union and then stayed on it returning westbound where he eventually asphyxiated and was discovered dead as the train pulled back into Burlington."

"While it looks like her on the train in disguise, I am looking at security tapes to see if I can catch a glimpse of her in any station she might have travelled through. She did have motive to kill Smythe-Rogers, especially if the repayment scheme was not widely known and she believed that he was going to tip off the doctor about the repayment terms - and that the doctor would be angry. I have strong circumstantial evidence but something more concrete would be good."

"We could round up the usual suspects and see if one of them says anything interesting," said Marlowe.

"Yes, a good plan. Let's nail down everything in sight - financials, security tape movements and any communications between the principals in the case."

Deeter collected the security tapes from GO Transit. There were two glimpses of the person who sat on the train opposition Smythe-Rogers but neither proved anything. There was no definite appearance of Mrs. Arleche anywhere, as Deeter suspected she removed her disguise after leaving the scene of the crime.

Closer scrutiny had a series of very short phone calls, probably texts, between Mrs. Arleche, Smythe-Rogers, Gabriel and the doctor. Everyone appeared to be talking to everyone else.

Gabriel's cell phone was gone. Smythe-Rogers cell phone was similarly gone. Warrants had been issued for both Mrs. Arleche's phone and the doctor's. All too predictably Mrs. Arleche's phone had been allegedly broken and replaced two days after the murder. She had enquired about taking over her husband's phone but told that she needed it to have it assigned to her number.

The doctor's cell phone was recovered by detectives but the messages did not provide anything substantial. He had texted Smythe-Rogers a number of times regarding several business deals including the proposed restaurant. He also messaged Smythe-Rogers regarding the trip to Burlington to scout real estate. He had texted Mrs. Arleche saying he had an open mind about a suburban location but he still strongly recommended a north Toronto space. He also contacted Gabriel asking for a meeting the morning of the murders, before his office opened, but was told by Gabriel it would have to be another time because the restaurateur had another engagement, presumably his visit to the markets and the scheduled meeting with Smythe-Rogers that would soon be cancelled. Gabriel said he would not be there until later that morning.

"But he was there, early. Why would he say he could not meet until later? The waitress would have only taken a few minutes, tops, assuming she was getting her paycheque. It can only be the Smythe-Rogers meeting. Could there be another meeting, something that would take longer?"

"It couldn't have been Smythe-Rogers, he was on his way to Burlington. Or was he? When did he change his plans. What train did he catch again?"

Deeter checked his notes. Smythe-Rogers had taken a 11:30 train to Burlington for his afternoon meeting with the commercial real estate people and Mrs. Arleche.

"At that point Gabriel was already dead."

Deeter arranged to have both Mrs. Arleche and Dr. Martin Archibald come into the police station for interviews. He arranged with Halton Detective Charlie Drinkwater to conduct them, as he had never spoken to either one of them before.

Drinkwater introduced himself to Mrs. Arleche and got right down to business.

"Quite frankly, Mrs. Arleche, there is a lot of evidence that points to you as the killer of your husband Gabriel, the waitress Anna Scott, and Mr. Smythe-Rogers. This will go much better for you if you tell me the truth.

Lies of any kind are smoking guns to a Crown prosecutor."

She nodded and sat up a little straighter in her chair.

"I understand, but I didn't kill anyone."

"We understand you had arranged for a meeting with your husband at the Blue Dome the morning of the murders, to explain the apparent skimming of business accounts."

"No, I could talk to him any time why would 'arrange a meeting' at that time? I wanted him to clear the air with Martin. So I asked Gabriel if he would be there and then let Martin Archibald know he could meet with him if he wanted. Is the doctor saying he didn't go?"

"Mrs. Arleche; the doctor said he tried to get a meeting with Gabriel but that Gabriel declined citing other commitments. Are you suggesting that Dr. Archibald knew about the skimming and wanted to meet with Gabriel about it?"

"Yes, Mr. Smythe-Rogers had found the way I kept the books and broached the subject with Mar . . .Dr. Archibald. I told my husband it would be better for him to meet with the doctor, as they were good friends and explain that the payback came off the top of the profits. I said he could blame me if he wanted to and try to get the doctor to agree with us, or failing that agree to change the bookkeeping to show profits ahead of payments to his loan."

"Dr. Archibald was more likely to be less angry with Gabriel if Gabriel could pretend innocence and blame me. I don't know why he killed him, and poor Anna," she began to cry.

"Why didn't you tell investigators of your suspicions when you first spoke to them?"

"I don't know. I was in shock I guess. My little plan to pay back our loan quicker was jeopardizing our chances to expand the business and if Mart . . .Dr. Archibald was angry enough he could put our business in danger - especially if he insisted on all his money back."

"And then I heard about Mr. Smythe-Rogers' death. Well I didn't know what to think except that having been with him for that meeting with the commercial real estate people I looked to have something to do with it."

"Mrs. Arleche, when did you arrive back in Toronto?"

"I got back midafternoon. I was too upset to drive so I stopped for a while to clear my head. As I left the station after dropping Mr. Smythe-Rogers, I heard on the radio that there had been a double murder in a restaurant near Bloor, and prayed it wasn't ours. I pulled into Appleby Station and tried to phone Gabriel. He didn't answer his phone. Then I received a phone call from a Toronto Detective saying there had been an accident with Gabriel and I should return home immediately. I knew something bad had happened so I did my best and drove back to Toronto."

"Did you contact the doctor?"

"No, I didn't know what to do. I was so upset that I dropped my cell phone somewhere and lost it."

"I see. There is evidence that you went on the platform. Were you wearing a coat or sweater?"

"I was there. Mr. Smythe-Rogers was a bit unsteady so I walked him up to the platform."

"Why didn't you give him a ride back to Toronto?"

"I offered but he said he was going to the financial district and I was heading home, uptown. He said it would be easier for him to take the train and he said he had a monthly pass so he it wouldn't cost him anything. He did complain the Porsche was a bit small and uncomfortable."

"I had no idea the doctor would be so mad. How could he kill his best friend?"

Then Drinkwater met with Dr. Archibald.

"Hello Doctor. I'm detective Charlie Drinkwater from Halton, part of the joint investigation in this case.

"I understand you tried to meet with Gabriel on the morning he was killed?"

"Yes, but he said he was unable to meet me, frankly I wondered if he was having a liaison on some sort, he was obviously meeting someone else but didn't say anything specific. I was shocked when I heard later that he had been killed."

"You had recently found out that he was manipulating the books. Didn't that make you angry?"

"No actually, as I explained to an early police inquiry, I loaned Gabe the money as a friend, he needed it or his business would fail. He is an old family friend and besides I liked him and his restaurant. I often conducted business meetings there and Gabe was very accommodating before I loaned him money and after. If I was concerned why would I consent to a business loan of another $100,000?"

"Perhaps you withdrew that offer after you found out about the scam and demanded your money back. Perhaps you went to the restaurant in spite of what Gabriel had told you? Perhaps you struck him with a skillet in rage?"

"Is that what killed him, it must have been a heavy blow and I'm not that big a guy as you can see." He held out his arms to make himself as large as possible. He was not a large man, about 5'6" and fairly slightly built.

"I told you I understood his desire to pay me off quickly. Sure it was a bit of a surprise to find out that was how he was conducting his books but it made a lot of sense. Paying me off was part of operating expenses. I could see how profitable a well run restaurant could be, that's one of the reasons I was interested in an additional investment."

"Detective, I couldn't have killed Gabriel because I wasn't there and I didn't have any motive. I wanted to speak to him regarding the north Toronto location. When I heard that his wife and Mr. Smythe-Rogers were scouting locations in Burlington I was concerned as I thought we had established the major advantages of the second Toronto location. That's what I wanted to meet with him about."

"Damn it," said Deeter who was watching behind the glass. "Both seem to have airtight stories. Circumstantial is huge but there is no motive. All we can do now if sit and wait. See what these two do in the next few weeks."

"Hell, the Doctor had a weak motive to kill Gabriel, and Mrs. Arleche appears to have had no real motive to kill Smythe-Rogers and both appear to have alibis for those murders. There is nothing to tie them together, expect perhaps a little bit of familiarity that Mrs. Arleche has for the Doctor."

"It is awfully curious how everyone's cell phone except the doctor's goes missing in the couple of days after the murder," said Drinkwater. "But all we have is coincidence and conjecture and cow farts."

"Bogie never said anything about cow farts, at least not on camera," said Marlowe. "I think all we can do now is wait in Casablanca, and wait, and wait, and wait."

Deeter filed his paperwork on the investigation and dutifully moved into the cold case unit full time. Mrs. Arleche's story checked out as there was security camera footage of her car parked at Appleby station for about an hour.

Several months went by during which Deeter received a monthly report of the activities of both Mrs. Arleche and Dr. Archibald.

Both seemed to move on with their lives. Mrs. Arleche sold her family home and moved into a modest condominium just outside of downtown Toronto. She ran the restaurant but was making efforts to sell it.

Dr. Archibald continued to practice medicine, continued with various property deals and moved his dining preferences to a Thai place very near his office.

"There hasn't been any evidence that they have even communicated," said Deeter into the phone. "Our guys have been tracking them fairly closely, but only for a few days here and there, police resources being what they are. If they were spending time together regularly we would have seen it."

"I've been through Archibald's financial dealings a few times. It seems he used Smythe-Rogers firm a fair bit on the front end of business deals. They were paid fairly but never included on the back end of the deals if they went through, and more often than not they did not," said Marlowe.

"Could there be any motive there for the Doctor to want Smythe-Rogers dead?"

"Nothing that I see. Everything is above board. If anyone might be a bit pissed off its Friedrich-Barnes whose employees were doing a lot of legwork for Archibald deals that went nowhere. But that is par for the course in banking finance."

"It's a bit of a tangled web. Mrs. Arleche has spent some time with the commercial real estate agent from Burlington. Apparently he called her a couple of weeks after the murders just to formally exclude her from interest in the Burlington restaurant venture as other clients were interested in the same property."

"She drove out to Burlington one day to meet with him and he ended up having dinner with her. They have met downtown on two occasions since. There doesn't appear to be anything there that existed prior to the murders."

Months had gone by and Deeter began to let the cases go cold. Police resources had been slowly pulled from the case and he was only getting the most basic financial info on Dr. Archibald and Mrs. Arleche.

He had almost moved on when, while sitting in the lobby of the Royal York Hotel during a break in a conference on police cold case investigation, he unexpectedly spied Mrs. Arleche walking across the lobby. He was about to get up and try to catch her when she was met by Dr. Archibald.

Deeter watched keenly from across the lobby wishing he could hear their conversation. The Doctor bowed slightly, smiled thinly, and said something. Mrs. Arleche held out her hand as a greeting, and demurely dropped her head. She said something, nodded with a thin smile and took her leave of the doctor. It looked like nothing other than a chance meeting.

Deeter took some notes to add to the case file. Sometimes what appears to be random chance is anything but. And then there are times it really is random chance.

He reviewed security tapes of the Royal York lobby. On a hunch he went to the same day the previous month, then the same third Thursday of the month. He went back a few months and hit pay dirt. The same scene played itself out three months before and three months before that.

Evidently the good doctor and grieving widow had reason to meet every three months and exchange a short word.

Deeter checked and found that Mrs. Arleche had continued to make the $4000 monthly payments to the doctor to cover his investment. The payments were transparent in the financial record, in the form a cheque every month. So why the clandestine monthly meeting?

He tried to make sense of it. They do not have any contact that could be seen by anyone watching - no visits, no phone calls and only a monthly cheque mailed to complete a business deal. However, they do arrange to meet every three months in the same public place, with the appearance of happenstance - they exchange a minute of conversation and depart. What is going on here?

The bits and pieces of the case were still flying around Deeter's mind but were having trouble sticking to each other. He went to bed still thinking about it and woke up having moved past any consideration. Then out of the clear blue sky he got it - what if they were casually checking with each other about any police surveillance or pursuit of the cases?

What if the two murders were unrelated in motive but only related because the murderers knew each other? What if Mrs. Arleche had murdered Smythe-Rogers for the doctor, while the doctor murdered Gabriel Arleche for his wife?

It appeared that they both had alibis for the murders they might have had motive for and had some vague connection to the murders they did not have motive for, thought Deeter.

Mrs. Arleche was possibly on the train when Smythe-Rogers was killed with an injection of allergen to his leg. She had no motive to kill him. Doctor Archibald had requested a meeting with Gabriel the morning he was murdered but had no apparent reason to want him dead.

So, was Mrs. Arleche's motive the funny accounting business? Was Gabriel angry when he found out? Was Gabriel having an affair with Anna, the waitress? Was Anna the prime target and Gabriel just collateral damage?

Certainly Mrs. Arleche could have disguised herself on the train and been the hooded person sitting across from Smythe-Rogers. She could have gotten a syringe from the doctor filled with peanut oil. It is possible that Mrs. Arleche exposed Smythe-Rogers to peanuts to weaken him first which would provide the opportunity to finish him off. Leaving him on the train was an effort to make it seem he had died with a different set of passengers making any investigation a dead end. Who was the second hooded passenger? Perhaps merely a co-incidence?

Did the doctor go to the restaurant to kill Anna with a bash to the head and then a pillow to asphyxiate her before doing the same thing to

Gabriel who happened upon the scene, or perhaps the other way around. Did he trade the murder of Gabriel for the murder of Smythe-Rogers? After all, Smythe-Rogers was apparently fairly upset with him and his less than fair dealings.

Now, how could he prove it?

Deeter arranged for another interview with Mrs. Arleche and went over the detail of the case before citing evidence that Dr. Archibald was having an affair with the waitress, Anna. He had no such evidence.

"Did you have any knowledge of this affair, Mrs. Arleche?

She blanched at the idea saying that she had no idea something like that could have been going on.

Then Deeter arranged to video tape the next scheduled meeting at the Royal York. As she had previously Mrs. Arleche wandered across the open space at precisely 12:35 by the overhead clock. Slightly half way across, Doctor Archibald seemingly crossed her path and they engage in a few moments of small talk.

However, this time when Mrs. Arleche spoke to the doctor he looked visibly upset, shaking his head. He exchanged what appeared to be a few sharp words and they both depart with a nod and a handshake. It was evident that Mrs. Arleche handed Dr. Archibald a note when she shook hands with him, the surprise of something in her hand was evident when he shook it.

That was enough for Deeter to think he was on to something. He dove back into the case, now a year cold, with an eye on the likely doer of the deed and a look to assign motive to the opposite party. In a trade off the motive would be switched though the deed was in the other's hands.

Within two weeks of the latest meeting at the Royal York. Mrs. Arleche had her condo up for sale and was preparing for a trip to Italy, one Deeter suspected she had no intention of returning from.

Something was there. They had conspired to kill at least two people and three were dead. However, motive was murky. Both suspects ties to the murders were murky. Exactly why three people were dead was unknown.

Deeter figured he had time on this one. Eventually they would do or say something that would break the case. Or someone else would. Light always finds the cracks and exposes information and ultimately truth.

Deeter wondered if he should confront the Doctor and Mrs. Arleche with his knowledge of their regular meetings or if he should bide his time and let the tumblers of information fall into place.

Then it hit him. Mrs. Arleche had claimed she returned to Toronto by train to the initial investigators. She had told him she returned by car after taking some time to compose herself.

Something was not right. More and more Deeter believed in the theory that each of the killers had done the other's dirty work. However, he still couldn't definitively assign which one of the potential killers had killed which one or two of the potential victims.

With such a mess, no Crown Prosecutor would take on the case, there was too much reasonable doubt and it was spread all over the place. The evidence was entirely circumstantial even if it heavily suggested the involvement of both the doctor and the restaurateur's wife.

Deeter was at a loss. Murder had been committed, but he could not begin to determine by who and for what reason. The regular meetings between the two apparent conspirators had ceased as Mrs. Arleche had left the country. The commercial real estate broker from Burlington had flown to Italy and spent some time with her, but he had only stayed two weeks.

Dr. Archibald had continued his business deals through Friedrich-Barnes investment bank, though now he paid them an hourly fee for their expertise.

Deeter still kept in touch with Detectives Marlowe and Drinkwater. He saw Drinkwater around town once in a while and even dropped in on him at Halton Police Headquarters, tucked in behind the large and auspicious looking Halton Regional Municipality Building just off the QEW.

Given its location and its suburban look it had more than once been mistaken for a shopping mall, though one curiously devoid of commercial signs or advertising. Even Deeter was taken aback at the size of the edifice when he first visited. it seemed to be a virtual hive of government activity - much of it appearing pointless but very much of consequence to those inside the hive - and the police were only one sub-section of the nest.

Marlowe remained a phone contact and one he tapped on several occasions investigating cold cases as his computer savvy and experience was valuable. He never did drop the Bogie bit, but that was part of his charm.

Deeter usually tried to figure which movie Marlowe was using as his source material, but let it slip quickly. He certainly watched the old black and whites a little more closely when they came up on late night television.

Occasionally he would hear a snippet of Bogie's Marlowe that sounded like Marlowe. It struck him that many of the old movie plots were as plain as real life but just as complicated as the Arleche - Archibald case. There were no momentous plot lines, no grand plans, just a slice of everyday life that had gone bad. And when they went bad it was often needlessly complex and full of coincidences that could never be nailed down - things that just presented a fog of motive, a wisp of reason, which quickly blew away in the whirlwind of events.

- END -

Heartbeat

It's getting colder every day now. The sun just isn't as strong. It doesn't heat up the air. The time for jackets and sweatshirts is coming soon.

A funny thing happened in early October, at the last baseball game of the season.

I decided to go to the game - I kinda like it when only the diehards are there. I got to the stadium and was walking through the half empty concourse, working my way to my seat. It's a lot of concrete trying real hard to be warm and inviting - you know, all the banners, most with optimistic mid-season slogans, all fading away for another year. As you know, we were out of it by mid-August and officially, mathematically cooked just after Labour Day.

Without the usual throngs of people standing shoulder to shoulder the concrete was more obvious and it just seemed a bit dusty and forlorn. It might have been the cool air.

"Last game of the season," I was thinking, "at least for these guys." Of course I was looking forward to watching a few playoff games and some quality baseball on television but I wanted one more taste of summer.

It had been a bittersweet year, from the hopeful days of late June and July, to the inevitable slip in August and disappointment of September. We had some good players but they couldn't carry the team for a whole season. August showed our weaknesses. I smiled in spite of my melancholy, for the past season, hopeful for the next.

"I don't know why I came today but it feels significant somehow," I consciously thought, even mumbling some of it under my breath, like I had to say it aloud for it to have any meaning.

Alone except for my incoherent mumbling, I walked to my seat in the most roundabout way possible. There weren't many people in the park as the game didn't matter, the last one of another unsuccessful season. I went to my usual seat, lonely amongst the smattering of humanity scattered around the stadium like the floating debris of an ocean ship wreck.

I've had these season tickets for years. In fact I had them in the old stadium too, and had been assigned these seats in the switch over. I share a pair with a group of friends. We all chip in to pay for them. Seventh row, seat five and six, just inside third base and outside the dugout. It's not usually hard to find someone to go to the game with, either one of my two sons or another among the little group that shared the tickets. Today however, my phone calls had led to nothing, only crickets.

I remember thinking that after this game, after I left the stadium the seats would remained undisturbed through winter hibernation. As I reached my row I looked along its length preparing myself in ritual for passage into the game. Excuse me, pardon me, sorry, excuse me . . . over and over again. I felt like Bugs Bunny but without the fear of being chased by Elmer Fudd through a theatre. Today, that passage into may perch was unnecessary.

Still I went to my own seats rather than just sit down somewhere convenient. I liked to sit in my seats rather than take advantage of the multitude of empty seats that had come to pass as the teams played out the string. It's all about perspective. I can't meaningfully compare things I see in the stadium if I see them from a different angle, no matter how slight.

Only an old man sat anywhere near me and he was engrossed in his scorecard, looking like any other cloud on the grey overcast day. He stood out only because there was no one else around. Kinda like a fire hydrant, there but unnoticed, like a city dwellers' neighbour. I guessed that I had seen him before if he held seasons tickets but he sat a couple of rows down and a bit over - enough to be lost in a crowd of a mid-season game.

The grey clouds tried to crowd out what little blue there was in the sky and a feeble light managed to get through. Despite the overcast, a ray of light fought through long enough to cast a shadow of the old guy's head across his scorecard. He adjusted his scorecard so the sun shone directly on it and he seemed to study it a bit more closely.

The game started but I found that I kept turning my attention towards the old man. After ambling down the row to get some soda I was closer to him than my own seat so I sat down on the edge of a seat behind him, expecting my presence to be only temporary. I tried to strike up a conversation.

"Goddamn shortstop," he spat. He hadn't been speaking before I moved closer so I figured he must have verbalized his thoughts for my sake. I guess this was conversation. You know, friendly banter between patrons. I smiled to myself.

"Lucky for him I ain't the official scorer."

His venom was amusing so I spoke a quiet defense of the rookie. "Smith in the Herald says his speed allows him to make more plays than any other shortstop in the league."

I followed my most sacred principle of human interaction. Always quote some-body else, then you can disagree with yourself with no loss of face.

"AAARRRGGGHHH, don't matter none if he can't make Little League outs.

"But he accepts more chances than . . . "

"Yeah, yeah, but he don't know when ta hang on."

I shrugged. I considered going back to my seat, perspective and all that, but the old man provided something new. The game continued and I switched my attention to the field. The teams had changed and the shortstop in question was up at the plate. Before I could direct a comment on his not inconsiderable batting average the old man spoke, as if he knew he was interrupting my thoughts.

"And he hasn't got the strength to hit even one out," he paused, as if waiting for me to catch up. "And his on-base percentage is the worst in the league for a leadoff man."

Insult to injury. I felt as if he were talking about me.

The man at the plate managed to beat out an Astro-turf assisted bounder. My companion clapped hard, "Attaboy!"

After the scattered cheering stopped I asked him who he liked.

"On this team or in the league."

Afraid of a tirade against fan voting for the All-Star Game I directed my inquiry to the field. "The only guy who can play at all is Grieves out in center. He's got all the tools to be a great one. He's young so he'll get better. He's fast, has a good arm, good base runner, he can hit with power and average and adjust to situations. He has maturity to make the right play at the right time."

I agreed with the old man's assessment of Grieves, a bit of a no-brainer. However I questioned his singularity of choice. He shook his head, "Nothing but bodies around here until the farm teams can produce players around that center fielder."

"Couple a years," he answered my unasked question.

I was beginning to wonder what kind of man I was talking to. He could read my mind and he was knowledgeable enough to be outspoken. It suited him. We sat in silence as the next batter fought off some pitches and then slashed one past a diving third baseman. The ragged crowd struggled to their collective feet with a cheer as lusty as many a much larger crowd could muster.

The shortstop on first had taken a big lead and was approaching third as the outfielder retrieved the ball. A frantic coach waved the runner home and the fielder threw. The crowd continued to scream encouragement as ball and runner sped toward the catcher who looked like a cornered animal, constantly adjusting his feet and angle of his body to field the throw and get into position for a tag. The umpire stuck his head into the collision like a fan on the edge of his seat. His hands went out, palms down, and the score was tied at one.

The crowd roared and the old man smiled. The smile was practically a laugh, like the residue of a particularly well-told joke.

"It'll be a while before we see that again," I broke the silence. The old man blinked and without moving turned the joy into glass, a mere reflection of the previous moment. He sat down slowly.

"Don't need ta hear that, can feel it in here." He thumped his chest. "With the new rules catchers have to treat the play at the plate just the same as a play at third. They need to get behind the plate, field the throw and drop the tag in front of the plate - the old way of blocking the plate and taking the throw out in front won't cut it anymore."

The rest of the side went down quietly as did the visitors in the top of the seventh. The crowd rose to stretch. The old man just sat there with his fist back on his chest and a faraway look in his eyes. I tapped his shoulder.

"You all right?"

He shook his head, "Yeah. Well, I don't rightly know." He looked into my face. "The season's over."

It sounded like a death knell, like a big dusty book falling on a big dusty table, in a room with only a single bare bulb.

"I've had two heart attacks before but I bounced back both times. It's a wonder what two weeks in the southern sun can do for you."

He took a deep breath and motioned back to the plate, "Now it's our turn," his words rubbed together like anxious hands. "Can't see how there can be a pitchers' duel in this cool weather."

Sure enough the batter hit the second pitch into the left center gap for a stand-up double. The meager crowd roared and settled back in anticipation. The silence expanded as each batter went down with a whimper.

"I can hardly wait for next season." The old man looked at me. "It'll be that long before I get over this one."

I felt like a child watching an elder contend with something religious. The old man sought to contemplate and wonder about parts of the game that I couldn't begin to dream.

The game wore on and the old man became less vocal. He was eating peanuts with the speed of a rat coupled with the rat's attention to his surroundings. A pile of peanut shells formed around his feet and became so big that he looked planted in the stadium concrete.

The top of the ninth produced a run for the visitors and a 2-1 lead. The first batter of the bottom of the ninth produced no noise from the home crowd save the old man's coughing. He pounded his chest some more and settled down. The next batter worked the pitcher and was rewarded with a seeing-eye single between first and second.

He was replaced with a pinch runner, a call up from the Double A farm team. The farmhand looked confident on the outside but his nerves were evident.

The defense brought in a relief pitcher and the new runner danced around trying to outrun his nerves, while the reliever warmed up. Once the pitcher moved to the rubber to resume the game the runner stood as still and nervous as a teenager at his first high school dance. The batter went down on four pitches, the fourth a mighty swing and a miss. Some of the crowd started to leave but the old man only rose to watch the final out. I reluctantly pulled myself up to join him.

"I wonder how much they'll want for these seats next year?" I commented.

"Doesn't really matter anyway - had 'em so long I don't really think about it." He looked ruefully at the perch. His attention went back to the field. I watched him cross his fingers.

I had to smile - all that knowledge about the players and the game and the old guy still believed in luck.

"He's going ta steal on the second pitch," he said without looking at me. The pitcher wheeled and threw. The batter checked his swing and the umpire did not move: ball.

The pitcher made ready again. As he looked to check the runner the runner took a short lead but was edging toward a larger one. Once the pitcher looked away the runner took off. The catcher had no chance and the runner was safe at second. The man at the plate had swung to protect the runner so the count stood 1 and 1.

"You were right!"

The old man merely nodded without looking at me.

The next batter was pinch-hitting to get the platoon advantage. Just the sort of thing a manager worried for his job would do, in a lame attempt to keep it. Surely not all his questionable decisions of the season could be erased by making an obvious one in the final meaningless game.

The old man remained standing so I joined him. It was nice to stretch the legs before leaving the stadium.

On the next pitch the batter tried a drag bunt but the ball rolled funny and seemed to hit something, changed direction, and went foul. The infield moved in a step at the corners and the pitcher threw again. A full swing produced a massive connection that was foul ten feet from the plate and screamed into the stands. It bounced among the hard concrete and molded seats as some kids raced along the empty rows trying to anticipate the ricochets in an effort to retrieve it. One of them tripped and went down hard. A moment later the winner held the ball up signaling an end to the race.

"Great change-up," I marveled.

"If it hadda been great he wouldn't a touched it."

I nodded in concession. The certain awe I felt for this old man was tempered by his gruffness.

"Well," I thought, "if you weren't gruff you couldn't be old."

The next pitch was a fast ball. Even from our position you could see the batter's eyes get wide and the bat twitch before he brought it around to meet the ball. He fouled it straight back. The next pitch was a ball: 2-2.

The pitcher set again and threw another fastball with a season's final effort. Right then things slowed down like movie disaster sequences. The batter swung slowly and the ball rocketed into straight away center field. The old man put his hands to his chest and coughed, he wavered for a split second and fell forward.

I saw him out of the corner of my eye and for a moment of slow time waited to watch the ball, but I knew where my duty lay. I jumped the seat to get down to his row too late to catch him before he hit the hard seats. But I grabbed his shoulder before he could tumble into the row in front of him.

The crowd cheered lustily as I wrestled him into his seat. The old guy merely moaned still holding his chest. I glanced up and time has asserted its normal flow with the batter rounding third as his teammates met him at the plate happy to celebrate the walk off homer to end the game and the season. Their enthusiasm was more play acting, as it was nice to win but the win really meant nothing. The batter reached the plate with a rueful grin that said volumes about the thrill of a game winning hit in the context of a poor season suddenly ended.

I waved to the usher who had already summoned first aid. The old guy had a bleeder on his forehead where he had struck the seat in front of him. The sparse crowd made it easy for paramedics with a stretcher to remove the old man. There were a few gawkers among the fans that made their way past our seats and up to the concourse. In fact by the time they were ready to move him there was nobody left save a few of the morbidly curious. The paramedics took him down the stairs below the stadium where they continued to work on him.

I trotted after them now more interested in the old man than the game. After all it was over. The old man - not yet. After minutes of pacing I was called to his side.

"Thanks for waiting around. I'm all right but this is the best one though. Come see me in the hospital," he looked to the attendant, "At the General. We can talk about next year. My name is Frank Baal." He extended his hand with his elbow resting on his chest and turned it into a little wave as he was slid into the ambulance.

Somehow I knew I'd be around to check on Mr. Baal. He knew things about the team, about the game, that I didn't even know I didn't know. I wondered if I could get my season's tickets next to his for next year. I started to work out how I might make that happen - the others in my season's ticket group might notice the slight change, two rows down and a dozen seats over, but they likely wouldn't really care. I made a mental note to get more info from the old guy about his ticket arrangements. In fact sitting behind him might be better. As long as I could speak to him during the game - it would be good.

The attendants closed the ambulance doors.

"Why is this the best heart attack? The other two must have been doozies," I asked the attendant.

The stadium attendant looked at me, like I knew, "Always on the last day of the season. It's more the timing than the severity. Last couple of years he hasn't made it past the fifth. At least the game is over, he'll be less agitated that way. It's getting so regular our supervisor reminded us to be ready before shift started."

He nodded to the driver and the vehicle started moving. They went slowly through the nearly empty concourse and I heard a gruff far-away voice rattle, "Don't turn on the siren. It'll scare me half to death. I'm all right. Where did the homer go out? How much did it clear the fence? Did anyone pick up my scorecard?" The ambulance turned the corner, was reflected in a patch of sun on its way into the parking lot and was gone.

- END -

Cannes - Con

Part One

It's a movie set. Strewn about are all the usual accoutrements of movies, a couple of large camera rigs on gyroscope platforms, racks of costumes, actors in groups waiting around, lighting rigs and people with clip boards. And actors.

The director stands up, spreads his arms and yells, "Cut." Very movie-like, cinema-esque even.

A camera rig directly in front of the director pulls up and moves away giving the director a full view of the set.

He surveys his domain for a moment, turns to his left and yells, "Print it. That's a wrap. Wrap party tonight at Mario's – 9 p.m."

The director then turns to his right to address a person standing beside him. "Well, we did it, and we're under budget."

"What budget?"

The director moves into his trailer followed by his right hand man. He takes a glass and pours a drink.

"Hey it's cheap Scotch – but it's Scotch," he looks at the bottle, "well at least it's from Scotland – Poughkeepsie is in the Highlands, right?"

He lightly tosses the empty bottle in the garbage, where it takes its place with several other empty bottles.

"Yeah, the Illinois highlands, I think."

The director holds the glass up and looks through it to the light on the other side.

"Do you know that 'Scotch' was the single biggest line item expense in this film."

"As an accountant you'd know that."

"And so much more," said the director. "But no, I'm not an accountant anymore, after today. Now I'm a director – slash – producer - slash - accountant. Much bigger deal, and the studio executives love it."

"How do you know?"

"Film is all about money, Gary, money coming in, and money going out. How much did you spend? How much did you make? The execs will love it when they hear how much I saved on the budget of this master . . . blockbu . . . er, ah, I mean profitable venture."

"How much did you save then?" asked Gary.

"Well considering the average budget of a serious film in Hollywood is over $100 million. I saved . . . um," he counted on his fingers, "about $100 million."

"So you shot your epic for about the cost of toilet paper on any other movie."

"Now Gary, that's so negative. It's about the cost of Scotch on any other movie. Anyway how else could you afford to own 10 per cent?"

Chapter Two

It's Mario's Restaurant and the film wrap party is underway.

The director slash producer slash accountant and Gary pull into Mario's parking lot, which is dark, in contrast to the very lit up restaurant.

Gary and the Director jump out of the aging Ford Taurus, the Director puts on a baseball cap with the logo of his production company, a logo of two quotation marks surrounding an empty space, underscored by " " Productions. He ties a sweater around his waist. Gary takes off his light jacket revealing a Boston Red Sox jersey. He throws his jacket into the car.

They move from the car and make their way into the restaurant.

"Frankie and the Zipper said they'd meet us here," said the director, looking around the parking lot before ducking inside the building.

"There will be a studio big wig here according to my agent. Remember, its director – slash – producer - slash - accountant."

They enter the bar. Loud music envelopes them. Immediately a young woman comes up to director.

She grabs him by the arm, "Ed, I hope you don't mind but I gave the deejay a list of stuff to play." Another young woman walks up – "Oh, and here is my friend Amanda."

"Nice to meet … hey, weren't you in the crowd scene?"

"Yes, the crowd scene when the soldiers leave," said Amanda, "the crowd scene when the soldiers arrive and the crowd scene at the end. And I was in other scenes as member of a various backgrounds. I even had a line.

Amanda gathered herself together and turns to one side, "I remember Antonio, mama."

She remained in character a moment and then turned to Ed with a smile.

"Hey that was good, I'll look for it in the dailies."

Then Fred and the Zipper glide up to the group.

"Now why don't you introduce me to your friend, Ed?" said The Zipper turning to the young woman. "You look wonderful, and I saw the dailies already. It was a cinematic moment, your line was."

Amanda smiled broadly and said, "You really think so?"

The Zipper moved quick, offered to get Amanda a drink, and they walked off together towards the bar.

"It's about time you got here," said Fred. "I hardly know anybody. I had a ton of trouble getting past the doorman and I'm the star of the picture. What did you pay him with, as much beer as he could drink and permission to annoy?"

"This party is the second largest line item in the budget. And his pay is the largest line item in this party."

Ed's agent Caroline approached, shepherding a studio executive. The studio guy had a young woman on his arm.

"It's about the horror of war and the effects on a small town during the strange period in Italy between Nazi occupation and allied victory. It's a serious film," said Caroline, making quote marks with her fingers when she said "serious film."

"I understand you wrapped under budget," said the studio man. "Very impressive."

"Yeah this party is one of the biggest expenses in the film."

The studio man laughed.

He and Ed stood back and surveyed the whole crowd. "Yeah, we're still shooting actually. That's why we're in an Italian restaurant and everybody was asked to come in their shooting costumes."

A closer inspection of the party goers showed a number in army gear, some wounded people and a number of period touches.

Ed pointed to several camera locations. My lead actors are scheduled to do a scene in the middle of the party. We'll get a few more shots. There are a couple of small dialogue pieces that will be shot and then the cameras are shut off and the party transforms into a . . . . party."

Chapter Three

The phone rings in a very messy office. While the sound can be heard, the location of the phone is a mystery.

A beep signifying voice mail, then, "Ed this is Caroline. I have good news and good news."

Ed picks up and grunts.

"Ok, at your request," she said, "first the good news – the first prints of 'As You Were' are complete and will run in limited release in several art house cinemas in LA, Chicago, New York and Toronto starting about a month from now. That gets you into this year's Oscar contention. The better news – 'As You Were' didn't get into Sundance (then with a hint of anger) Bloody Redford said it wasn't alternative enough – this is about the Italians being introspective about war – how much more of an alternative interpretation is there?"

"Anyway, the better news is that Cannes called less than 24 hours after I Fed Ex'ed them a print. You're in, in fact they want to make 'As You Were' the Day Two feature. I think the timing is good."

"That's great," Ed said as he reached over for a cigar. He waved it around and then replaced it in his cigar humidor for re-use. "What's the timing?"

"Ed your tickets are all set," said Caroline.

"Okay that too. First, what's so great about our timing on the Festival?"

"I think we're a bit ahead of the curve on war introspection stuff - that and they were desperate for a Day Two Feature in English. We told them we aren't springing for sub-titles. All the Europeans understand English anyway and without them it gives it a bit of an in-your-face Hollywood feel."

"Okay . . . Timing part two. Tickets? Who else is going?"

"Studio guys insist upon an entourage. They've provided four tickets for you and your group. LA to Paris – Paris to Nice and a hotel which I am trying to upgrade for you – you leave tomorrow."

Ed – "So it's the timing – not the art – or the deal?"

"They said the timing. I say timing. Give me some time and I'll work up a little press for you. I'll let you know once you've arrived."

Chapter Four

Ed in his Taurus pulls into a suburban driveway. Gary is outside watering a bald patch of lawn.

"Sprinkler system can't reach this spot – gotta do it by hand," said Gary.

Ed surveys the brown grass and dirt, "Looks like you've been doing a wonderful job."

"Hey I'm busy, who knew we'd get two weeks of stifling heat?"

"In the middle of summer?"

Ed changed the subject. "I have to go to Cannes."

"It's just inside the door – on the left, " said Gary, gesturing toward the house.

"The Film Festival"

"That's a kinky sort of description – well there are magazines if you require."

"In France – the Film Festival in Cannes."

Chapter Five

Ed and Gary buzz into a highrise condo. Ed pushes the button.

"Hello" squeaks a voice from the wall speaker.

"Fred, it's Ed – let us in."

"Us? You bipolar or something?"

"Gary's here too."

They arrive at Fred's condo and tell Fred the news in his living room.

"Cannes? Tomorrow? I can't – I have . . . " he trails off.

"Fred it's a once in a lifetime opportunity. Star treatment – shit you were in the bloody movie – practically a lead role," said Gary.

"In terms of screen time maybe – but as the designated extra – it hardly qualifies as a role. I played 53 different parts."

"Such extraordinary range. I give him two thumbs up," said Gary.

"The actual range is about what you can do with make-up and clothes," said Fred. "I was bearded three times, mustachioed twice, bearded and mustachioed once, in heavy makeup 22 times and had my face obscured by lighting, clothes or camera direction 30 times. I looked as you see here only once when I played the guy in the phone booth during the German retreat at Monte Cassino."

Chapter Six

Ed, Fred and Gary drive to a baseball park. There is a game going on, slow pitch.

"There he is," said Ed. "Playing right field. He loves this team."

"Evidently they don't love him, "said Gary, noticing that the Zipper was wearing an off-colour jersey that was a bit small.

"They are always calling him up to play."

"Hey Zip, hey Charlie." Ed waved to catch his attention, but couldn't seem to. Then a ball was hit and Charlie moved to field it. It bounced off his glove and he picked up the ball.

"Charlie! Chuck, Chuck, over here, over here!"

Charlie saw Ed and fired the ball to him. Ed was standing well out of play.

The team all dropped their heads to their chests in unison on the field when Charlie, aka The Zipper, fumbled it, lifted their collective gaze as he picked it up to throw and then dropped their eyes again when he airmailed the throw out of play.

Ed stuck up his hand and caught the ball.

"We at least he's accurate," he said.

"Does what he's told, too," said Gary.

After the game Ed beckons the Zip to join them.

"Chuck, Zip-man, I need you to come to Cannes with me."

"Caen? Why are you going to Caen. I thought your film was about Italy."

"Chuck, the film is showing at the Cannes Film Festival and I need to have a group of associates with me."

"Are we threatening people?"

"No. My agent said it just looks funny if the producer/director/ accountant is all by himself, he, I need a group of people attached to the film to accompany me."

"But I can't let these guys down," said the Zipper tugging at his shirt.

"I think if we asked nice they'd provide your airfare."

Part Two

Ed, Fred, Gary and Chuck the Zipper are on a plane, the red eye to Paris, France.

"I can't sleep on planes," said Gary. "I'm going to be a mess tomorrow."

"We're supposed to land at 8 am and then get our flight to Nice for a landing at noon local time. We don't have to do anything the first day except settle in. The film's distributor has paid for our hotel and will cover expenses incurred while promoting the film - food, a party, some clothing. We aren't supposed to sleep until about 9 p.m. so we can make a quick switch to French time and be ready to go the next morning. There will be events and likely a bit of press."

"So we can do what we want the first day?" said Chuck. "Just don't sleep until 9 p.m. Got it."

"Easy. We can check out the festival, some culture, local sights and get us some grub," said Fred.

The plane landed they made a smooth transition to their flight to Nice. Eventually the boys disembarked in Nice and went to the baggage carrousel. Bags start to drop into the carrousel.

"I always tie a bit of red plastic to my bag handle so I can more easily identify it in these places," said Gary, who looked down the length of the baggage carrousel in expectation.

His gaze drew the looks of his friends. Every bag had a red plastic tie, the airlines baggage claim ticket affixed to the handle.

"See, there it is," said Gary. Oblivious to the airline ties he moved toward the moving baggage display and grabbed a bag with two red ties on it.

The entourage reached their hotel without incident, save their difficulty speaking French to the cab driver, their inability to pay the fare in Euros and their complete lack of understanding that they had been taken for a circular and expensive ride through more than one city in the south of France.

"Well, I think we handled that well," said Fred as the cab pulled away from the hotel. Just then a computer bag slipped off the moving cab and crashed onto the street, tumbling just a bit before coming to rest.

"Good think I invested in the high end computer bag," said the Zipper, moments before a car ran over the bag, another ran it over and then a third squashed it entirely.

"When is our big screening?" asked Gary.

"Caroline said the Festival wants to make "As You Were" the second day feature," said Ed.

"Cool."

"It's actually not so great. The big films are at the end of the Festival and so the press and all about the big stars rolling into town midway through the Festival. Still there isn't much else for the Festival to do than show movies so we are up - and likely have most of the press attention to ourselves."

"So is the first day tomorrow?"

"No its the day after, so we are up the day after that. It gives us a bit of time to become acclimatized. Carol got a break on the rooms by coming in a day early and leaving before it's over. We're here for six days."

"Let's get us some grub - I'm starving."

Walking along the waterfront the boys spied the Cafe Roma, a large restaurant with a big patio section under a large awning. They perused the menu board, shrugged and went in.

They were seated and a stack of menus were dropped on the table almost sliding off - with the waiter saying "Excusee, une moment."

Ed made a face of disgust. Chuck looked at the menu and made a similar face of disgust. Fred, was watching a middle aged woman at a nearby table with a dog sitting on a chair and he made a face of disgust.

"Well boys we aren't in Kansas anymore," said Gary.

"I'm not even sure there is a Kansas anymore."

The waiter returned and jibbered something in French.

"Pardonee, no comprendee, le lingo. Je suis Francaise?" said Ed.

Waiter - "Oui."

Charles cut in, caught the waiters attention and started rubbing his stomach. "We are a-hungry - can we get le food?"

"For crying out loud Chuck of course we can get food, it's a freaking a restaurant."

"It's a cafe," said Chuck. "I was just trying to see if our waiter would switch into English, Ed, as its fairly obvious from your language skills that his English would likely be much better than our French."

"It's obvious from your language skills that his Chinese would likely be better than our French."

"I knew I should have brought the phrase book," said Gary.

"Okay I got this," said Fred, "it's apparent you guys are outta your element. "Monsewer, que est-ca steak tartar pour la tableau?

Waiter with a smile. "Mais oui, coming right up. To drink?"

"Ah yes, umm, quatre dece Heniken, s'il-vous plait," said Fred. The waiter nodded and left.

"Well that worked out nicely."

Immediately several waiters crowded around the table putting down opened bottles of Heniken on the table two at a time until the table was covered with open beer bottles.

"Yes Fred," said Charles, "I agree, that worked out very nicely."

Charles grabbed a beer and began to pour. "Look, If I fill the glasses right up we get through 6 bottles."

"There are 40 bottles of beer here. Are we expecting company?" asked Ed.

Gary turns to a nearby table - "Que, esque ca ce amie un Heniken?"

The four youngish women at the table look a bit quizzically at him, two turned away with expressions of disgust. But one laughed.

"I am a friend of Heineken, merci," she said with a grin.

She took the beer and turned to her friends. "Voulez tous amie le Heniken?"

She says to the boys table. "Merci, trois Heineken, sil - vous plait."

Gary handed her three more.

She took them with a smile. "I am Jennette. Are you here for the Festival?"

"Mon amie Gary, et Charles, et Fred, et Ed. Ed is une movie, er, un cinema director. Le garcon is entreed avec le Festival."

Jennette and another girl smiled. "Tout Francaise estque terrible."

"Francaise ne pas du uno languageo," said Gary.

"Really I might not have known. Perhaps we should speak in English."

"Le cafe est infected with Americans," said a second girl at the table.

Jennette looked a little horrified and at the same time sympathetic with her friend. "My friends were not expecting this. They are Danielle,

Simone and Brigitte."

Realizing they had far too much beer Jennette spoke to the cafe maitre'd and managed to give out about 24 Heinekens creating a favourable impression of the Americans and giving Ed an opportunity to plug his film and where and when it was playing.

"Put that on the promotions budget."

"We have a promotions budget?" asked Chuck.

"We do now."

"Ed, I'm surprised you aren't filming this for use in the trailer."

The boys got their dinners but barely notice the raw hamburger as they are so hungry and somewhat captivated by the youngish women.

"Now what?"

"First we have to wake Charles," said Gary.

"We should take a stroll along the boardwalk so you can familiarize yourselves with the town," said Jennette. "It's the least we can do to repay you for the Heinekens.

The group rose to leave - with Ed picking up the tab, scowling all the while, not because of the money but because he was unable to think of a way to use the experience as part of the film. He was beginning to get the kernel of an idea.

They walked through the streets to the boardwalk taking note of various media camps and one red carpet line-up for a major movie release.

A media person spied the group, consulted a clipboard holding a number of photographs and came to interview Ed, who was speaking to Jeanette and was exactly as pictured in the reporters notes.

"Monsieur, when does your film screen? What can you tell me about it for tomorrow's paper?"

"My film, 'As You Were' screens tomorrow at this cinema. It's an anti-war picture, comic, dramatic and deeply disturbing as it details the confusion that occurred during the Nazi retreat from Italy in 1944."

Jennette looked at Ed with renewed respect.

"Of course my distributor will have made sure your office has a copy of the media guide."

"We do, but I must say it is very limited, no video, no still photos and a very austere package. Is the film in black and white?"

"We did the package that way on purpose," said Ed, "to make a point, a point about the austerity and sacrifice of war and occupation. The film is not in black and white - that was going to be too expensive . . . . I mean, it would have cost us dearly in terms of accessibility to our audience and cut into our actors ranges."

"Can we get a photo of you and your group? I assume these people are with you and are associated with the film?"

"These guys, gentlemen, were all actors in the movie. Fred played several non-recurring roles?"

"Yeah, I was killed 14 times in various make-up."

"These girls are actresses who I am considering for roles in the sequel. The follow-up film is similar in scope, detailing the end of Vichy France and the brutality that occurred once the oppressed majority were able to turn tables on Nazi collaborators."

"My photographer would like a few shots."

A scruffy bearded guy with a large camera rig stepped forward and started directing. He lined up the group, shot them in various ways - surrounding Ed, girls on one side, boys on other, mixed up and with the Cinema in the background.

"What's the proper spelling of everyone's names?"

The reporter and cameraman left.

Jennette looked at her companions and began to nod. "We would very much like to see your film. Where can we obtain .. . . billets?"

"Why don't you all accompany us to the screening? It appears as if you are all now part of the entourage."

Jennette looked at her friends. "That would be wonderful."

"You'd better come in the aspiring actress look. Frankly, I'd like you to make an impression, get two of you to dress like you're going to the beach and the other two to dress up as formally as much as they can. I'll arrange limos. The contrast should ensure us some press."

They made arrangements to meet at the hotel before the screening. Chuck was walking asleep. He was bumping into people, constantly falling asleep and having to be woken.

The girls took their leave of the boys as the guys had to return to their hotel as the witching hour of 9 p.m. was approaching. They had all had a number of beers and were a bit punch drunk from lack of sleep.

"I can't push this guy much longer - he's too heavy."

"We're almost back to the hotel."

Gary was pushing a sleeping Chuck along on a baggage carousel. It had the name of a hotel on it, one that was not theirs.

Chuck was asleep in the hotel suite and Gary had returned the carousel. Ed, Fred and Gary remained awake in the suite's living room drinking.

"Hey lay off that stuff, eh?" said Ed. "Our expenses are not unlimited and we have to be at our best for tomorrow's premier."

"What are we wearing?"

"I've been thinking about that. I'm going in military fatigues. You and Fred are going in impeccable suits, and Charles is going as a beach bum to mirror the girls. We need to adopt outrageous attitudes, but not obstructive to the press. Charles and myself will sign any autographs that are offered. You two in suits refuse autographs but encourage photos and photos with fans - speak to them in a formal sort of way. You need to be incredibly aloof but quietly accessible. I'm going to act like it's all below me and boring - accepting autographs but refusing to speak. Chuck is supposed to be soaking up the attention, like he's the star of the show."

"What about the girls?" asked Gary.

"Hopefully they come dressed as I wanted. I am hopeful that they will be a bit star struck and nervous with the press - they love that stuff."

"You are rolling the dice here, anything could happen," said Fred.

"Bingo, I'm hoping something will happen to get us more press - hopefully good press but anything is better than nothing."

"I have a bad feeling about Zippo back there; he crashed much too early, he could have trouble adjusting to the time change."

The girls arrived at the hotel a bit early.

"Are we taking a limo?" Danielle asked.

"Oh yeah, three limos," said Ed. "Gotta make a big impression. Well okay its one limo with three trips. Charles looking like a beach bum, you Danielle in the swim suit, Brigitte nicely dressed and Gary also in the full penguin. Half of us on the first go round, then Fred, Simone in the swim suit - you are looking good, and Jennette in the second and then I'll come through last. We are supposed to meet the limo just outside, we are only a couple of blocks from the cinema, it will pick us up in turn - that is if Caroline has done her job."

The group exited the hotel and almost immediately the limo arrived.

"Once you arrive take care to linger for photos and with the fans," said Ed, "move slowly through the red carpet crowd. There might not be many of them as we are not well-known stars, or better put, not at-all stars. But the French don't know that. Acting people, that's what this is about. Act like stars and you'll be one. Let the whole group gather together before we enter the cinema."

The first group entered the limo and was whisked away.

The car arrived and they slowly got out, lingering to increase the tension. As the car door opened two young women shrugged at each other, threw down their cigarettes and screamed on cue. Caroline had arranged for a few of her acquaintances to scream at the appropriate moment and rush in for autographs. The press took the bait and rushed in for photos and the few French film-fans that were on hand moved in for a closer look.

Gary was first, looking the elegant Euro-star, he slipped out of the car, shrugged his jacket back into place and moved toward the first autograph seeker. While he did that, Brigitte, also well dressed got out of the car and moved beside Gary, speaking in French to the fans who want to converse. Gary tried to look cool, but didn't quite pull it off. He looked like a cross between confused and shell-shocked. The French took it as an American movie star look and closed in.

Danielle, then exited the car, wearing only a bikini, she caught the crowds interest immediately. Gary was forgotten - and then Chuck exited the car, stifled a large yawn and playfully reached towards Danielle with a big grin on his face. The crowd lit up and autograph seekers went wild, ignoring Danielle but keying on Chuck.

Having dropped its last passenger the limo pulled away and in a few moments was back to disgorge Simone, in a bikini with a see through wrap on. She caught the crowd's attention like Danielle. Then Jeanette exited the limo, unseen through the shaded windows and started mingling with the crowd - she was the most natural of the group and most looked like she might be some minor movie star. Then Fred got out, smiled broadly and moved slowly up the red carpet, signing autographs and nodding to fans, holding his hands slightly apart and flicking his right forefinger as if clicking a camera. He got into a few fan selfies.

The car left and was back quickly with Ed. He was in full camo-military garb, of an undistinguished nation. He slipped a riding crop under his arm and waved lightly at the crowd with a short armed flash of his opened hand - the others all rallied round him and they glided into the cinema building.

After the film Ed, Jeanette and Charles were positioned behind microphones in the press room to answer questions.

Reporter - "Miss Jeanette, were you even in the film?"

Ed jumped in, "Allow me to answer that. Jeanette's scenes were mostly cut in the editing room as her performances were so strong they overtook the story. This is not the final commercial cut of the film, in its released version I will likely restore some of her scenes as her character is central to the sequel that is already beyond the planning stages. And of course, if the market bears it, there will be a Director's cut, with multiple extras, released in the future."

"I have very little experience," said Jennette, "but I have complete faith in the vision of our auteur producer and director. I will be happy to shoot more scenes for the sequel and happy also if they do not make the final cut. My film career is entirely his to shape."

"Some of the scenes appear to be shot on an epic scale, but lack wide shot depth. Was that on purpose or was it done to reduce costs?"

"It is a product of my vision for the story," said Ed. "Most of the partisans and simple country folk do not know the bigger picture of the war - their information is limited - all they see is the local soldiery pulling out and abandoning them. That is the epic scope within the narrow focus. Of course it also saved us some money that we could put into other aspects of the film, expanding party scenes, special effects etc,"

"I didn't see a lot of CGI, stunts or other special effects," said a reporter.

"They are there. All of my actors do their own stunts. For example when you see one of the actors crash into a table in the party scene, it is the actual lead actor doing that for authenticity. The table top is obviously real and not a prop-style table. Broken furniture and broken bones cost money. It's all done for authenticity, in the service of the viewer."

"What is your focus on regarding the film's scope, story and take-aways?"

"The scope of the story is immense," explained Ed. "I invite the viewer to take away from the film what they see, hear and feel. We are presenting an epic within the slim confines of the lives of a few characters. The comic scenes are there for a reason - they enhance the characters as more than cardboard cut-outs and they breathe life into a tragic time in human history."

Gary leaned over to Fred, "Holy shit can he lay it on."

"There is a rumour that you shot this film for what was described as 'no actual money' is that true?"

"I can assure you lots of actual money was used, more than I would have liked, but I had to remain authentic. Shooting costs were what they needed to be - we took extra shots where necessary and didn't scrimp on effects. It is true I am an efficient film-maker. I don't believe in being lavish without reason, or extra expenses just to pad the budget into something that seems impressive."

"I see here that you've listed yourself in the credits as Director / Producer / Accountant - that is highly unusual," said another reporter.

"Yes, I believe the producer should have a strict eye on the film's budget and costs as the success of any movie in the end comes down to it financial performance."

The group left the press conference and returned to their hotel. There were a number of messages awaiting them.

Ed grabbed them and started to read aloud. "Let me read some of these to you all. 'Congratulations on a great opening - Caroline.'

'Heard there was a strong reaction to your film - Charles - by the way I told you so, you owe me a drink.'

'You are beyond 30 days owing on the camera rental - please call our finance department with payment arrangements.'

'If I don't get my money in one week, I'll sue the shit out of you - it's likely the only thing with value that I can get my hands on."

'We subbed out the period music for something a bit cheaper - I think you'll like the new feel it gives the film - Sound Editor Joe Schmoe - the pan flute is very emotive."

"We'll enough of that, just some business issues to contest in court. Tonight we party."

"How are we doing that?"

"By finding a party to go to and using our new celebrity status to get in."

Chapter Seven

The entourage scoured the city but it took a phone call to Caroline to make arrangements. They gathered at the door of an exclusive club - restaurant, just off the beach in Cannes.

Fred talked to a door man and pointing at Ed, "He's the producer - director of 'As You Were' a film which premiered today at the Festival - and has had great feedback from the press so far."

The doorman consulted his sheet and let them in. SAS they passed he stuck out his hand.

Chuck shook the offered hand.

"What a lovely fellow that doorman was, very friendly," said Chuck to Fred once they got inside.

Once they adjusted to the dimly lit club - with the throbbing music and very low light they realized they were surrounded by well known and recognizable faces.

"Holy crap, everyone in the place has a familiar face."

"Even you Fred," at least to me and anyone who watched the Entertainment News tonight.

Fred and Chuck eased into the room and joined in conversations.

"I'm just here to be seen by the right people," said one very young woman. "My agent says I have to have a bit more presence."

"I'm most uncomfortable here," said another starlet. Looking at Charles, she said, "It's always middle aged money coming to speak with us to get us to make more money for them. It's disgusting."

Starlet One looked at Chuck, "Not like you sir, I saw you today at the festival press conference. Your film has had good reviews."

"Not my film, though I am associated with it and had an acting role."

The starlet laughed, "You are more than an actor?"

"I was an advisor to the director and took an active part in the production," said Chuck.

The starlets were all of a sudden more interested. "Oh, do you have another project you are working on?" asked one.

"Yeah, I'm trying to find the drinks." Chuck looked around. "Can I get you girls something?"

Just then a roving waiter happened by with champagne flutes. Chuck reached for a few and handed them around. A few of the starlets looked at Chuck differently.

Over to Fred who was engaged in conversation with a movie producer type.

"We used a little CGI - tried to keep it to a minimum - you know the cost?" asked Fred.

"Yes, I know, the cost of CGI is the disbelief, the disengagement of your audience. Too much CGI and you lose them."

"We used it mostly to save money. Invest a little in CGI but save a lot on actors, sets, action sequences and stuff."

"It's about the art of cinema and the cinematic experience."

"It's about the budget and the product."

"A very pragmatic approach," said the producer, "but without wonder who would attend a film?"

"Without CGI who could afford to make a picture?"

Back to the starlets. Charles had rounded up a tray of drinks. The girls took the drinks, with their eyes on other groups, as if he was a roving waiter.

"Not sure what everyone wanted but there is some choice here," Chuck said. "Please take one."

"Weren't we just talking to you?" asked a starlet. "And you're a waiter?"

"Yes and, er no. We were just talking and I'm not an official waiter, I was just being helpful."

"Oh." She turns to her nearest companion. "He's just being helpful."

"Well that's awfully nice isn't it. I wonder if he'd be nice and get us some hors d'ouerves?"

"When in Nice . . ." said Chuck.

"I think he made a funny - except we are in Cannes."

"Our film is in the Cannes . . . .In Cannes, or in a bottle or jar . . . it doesn't matter."

Ed sauntered by Chuck with two starlets - one on each arm. "We're going to find a cosy corner to talk about the sequel."

"What about Jennette, Danielle, Simone and Bridgett?"

"They are already in the cozy corner. Anyways Caroline called, said we have another round of press tomorrow. The film has been picked up by Net Flicks and a Russian film distribution company. We are already in the black. It appears the sequel is a done deal."

"Wow, things happen fast in Cannes."

"That's what I was thinking," said Ed, moving into a section of couches where Jennette, Brigit, Simone, Gary and Charles had gathered. Charles appeared to be asleep, as he had not adjusted to the time change.

Jennette noticed the two starlets that Ed brought back to the group. She gave Ed a dark look.

"You know, you should be speaking to studio executives while you have the chance. Fame is fleeting," she said.

Ed looked ruefully at the starlets. "You are right. Problem is I don't really know anyone. Can you point out a few of the Euro famous and come with me as I do the rounds?"

Jennette smiled. "But of course." She took him by the arm, scoped out the room and began walking.

"There is Fernando Iglasias," star of several big Euro-films. He usually plays the good looking but socially awkward up and comer."

"Mr. Iglasias," she said. "I am a big fan of your films. I'd like you to meet the director to today's feature "As You Were". Ed and Fernando shook hands. "Tell me are the films written specifically for you or have you been selected through a screen test?"

Iglasias at first seemed stunned by the attention and struggled to continue listening to the conversation nearby that he had been peripherally in on - but the question caught his ear and the introduction of Ed stifled the earlier conversation as the knot of people nearby listened in.

"Nice to meet you Mr. Ed," he looked somewhat confused at the one name introduction. "Oui, Mademoiselle, the parts have been written for me. Though I am becoming a bit typecast. I am looking for a part that breaks the mould."

"Perhaps Ed's sequel could provide that."

"Perhaps, he fished around in his jacket pocket and pull out a card, handing it to Ed. This is my agent's number please call if you are interested."

Ed took the card graciously, but was thinking he could never afford the high price of a well known star. Jennette asked Iglasias about his co-stars and working arrangements, as if fishing for how he might work together with the other actors on Ed's sequel.

Ed was beginning to think that Jennette might be the best thing about this whole trip - she had the looks of a movie star, a head for business and seemed to glide into her role as a producer as if she'd been doing it all her life.

Jennette turned, bade farewell to Iglasias and moved Ed away. "We don't want to faun over him or talk too much. Just a bit of back and forth, show some interest and some knowledge of his background, fish around a bit and then we are off.

She steered Ed around the party, making introductions where she knew the face and using that to get Ed introduced to several Euro movie producers and studio men. Ed could never have managed it on his own.

After an interval with the group allowing for other party guests to come up to them, and several did. Jennette insisted the group leave. She had found another party for them to attend - a pre-screening party of a German film that was scheduled to be screened the next day.

They entered the new party and Jennette managed to squire Ed around it as well, collecting him several cards and introductions and conversations to be had later.

"Well, I'm not sure if you are a movie star, or a producer, or my agent," said Ed. "Caroline will be a bit pissed when I tell her what's happened."

"Just tell her that her original arrangements got the ball rolling," said Jennette.

"Which do you want to be, actress, producer or agent?"

"I wouldn't mind being all of them to try and get to know the business. Surely your calling card of being able to produce films very cheaply . . . inexpensively, is opening some doors. You might want to think what you would do with more of a film budget, what you could do that would enhance the profitability of the movie."

"Probably enhance a few scenes but use most of the money on promotion," said Ed.

"I hope that doesn't mean doubling your Scotch budget."

"No but it might mean a bottle of two of actual Scotch, bourbon is not good for the soul."

"I've heard it cleans the soul, or at least the soles," said Jennette.

Ed put in a call to Caroline explaining the successes at the parties, the new connections he'd made and the value of Jennette.

Caroline promised to meet with him after he returned to discuss how to make the best use of everything. Ed asked Jennette if she could come to the States to be a part of the discussions.

"Yes I can," but I have to take care of a few things here first and we will have to discuss money and contracts.

"No contracts until we get to that stage. But I will make sure that Caroline arranges for your flights, hotel and anything else you need while you are there. Frankly I'm thinking of exploratory talks regarding the sequel, your place in it and your future with " " Productions. It seems to me that everything is changing and becoming more expensive, and I will need some time to adapt to that."

The boys got on the airplane to fly home.

As they enter the plane, the film action freezes with close-ups and bullet points fading in explaining their future fate.

Fred shot three commercials for French fast food chain Quick Burger playing the same tourist character who finds a level of comfort in Quick Burger and its menu.

A snippet of the commercial - "Ah, a Burger Royale please s'il vous plait." Turning to his 'wife' and 'kids' - and speaking in awkward French with an

American accent. "It's a taste of home right when you need it."

Back to the plane. Charles sits down heavily and immediately drifts off. He didn't adjust to Euro time. He gets back in time to join his baseball team for a game. Never more awake he makes three of four great plays in the game and is lauded as MVP by his mates who generally seem please for him, if somewhat puzzled by his success and hyper-wakefulness.

Gary wins best supporting actor award at Cannes and is signed to a supporting role in a Paris art movie as a French mangling tourist that the stars of the film keep running into.

There is footage of him accepting his Palme du Or and attending a party with Bridget, who is more interested in the photographers than he is. There is a gossip tabloid showing them splitting though they were never a couple to begin with. Then a clip of Gary in a Parisian art house film, standing in front of Notre Dame asking a young couple in broken French where Notre Dame is and when does the game start.

Ed is seen stuffing a few cokes from the plane into his pockets. Then he is seen in earnest discussions with Iglasias and Jennette in a New York office - with a view to the harbour. There is a gossip tabloid on the table showing Iglasias and Jennette as a couple.

Ed is shown sitting in the director's chair, filling the screen. As his boom chair is moved away the camera moves in and it's a scene between Iglasias and Jennette.

"But I had to be nice to the Nazi scum or we would starve," said Jennette demurely. "I gave them this wine, that grandpa makes, to keep them happy."

She is seen filling a wine bottle with wine from a vat. "We all had to fight them in our own way."

"You call giving them what they wanted fighting?"

"When half the command has dysentery whenever the Resistance asked us to tie them up, yes, I call it fighting," Jennette said with a smile.

"I knew the Resistance caused some shit, but I had no idea."

- END -

The Room

Chapter One

The paint on the metal door was chipped, repainted and chipped again. It had been green once, then red and now it was a sheet metal grey. The door took a lot of abuse as angry players had kicked it, pushed it, and slammed it. It was dented in several places. The lock had been replaced more than once, as had the metal door frame which contained it.

Going through the door, the floor was covered by a rubber mat. The walls, cinder block, repainted several times. It smelled. Actually there were two distinct smells that varied by the time of day. A bleachy, formaldehyde, chemical clean in the early afternoon and evening or a stale beer and sweat odour most of the rest of the time.

Today it was a neutral smell, the smell between the smells, as the midday cleaning was giving way to several hours of use by sweaty bodies with sweaty equipment. Officially it was ventilated. Unofficially it simply shared air circulated from other similar rooms. the smells were mingled but they were similar enough that it made very little difference. Sort of like blending different bourbons and expecting something more refined than harsh, scratchy taste of all bourbon.

Those who weren't use to it would wrinkle their noses, make comments about it and otherwise draw attention to the aroma. I suppose even the best Scotch has the same effect. For anyone who was used to it, it simply did not exist. It smelled like a locker room, if you took any notice, because that's what it was.

To the initiated, the locker room is a sanctuary, an oasis of camaraderie before and after a game. A game, once finished, joins the great parade of historic sporting events that make up a competitive life.

Most of these events, and the micro-occurrences within them are forgotten, with a torrent of truths removed and remembered. Some of the games are remembered specifically. They are dominated by a play or series of plays that define them. Some of the events, and the lesson they implant are never forgotten. Some gain mythic status within the peer group - shedding details, streamlining events into a narrative that makes a point - or something. Some are even life changing.

They all begin and end in what is simply referred to as The Room.

The Room has a stature that a bench or a dugout does not, nor cannot have. While those areas are similarly all about the team they are not private like the Room almost always is. And when it's not - as in some old arenas where the walls are thin, where the walls do not ascend to the ceiling, where the ventilation system channels sound, the room isn't The Room. It is only as a complete sanctuary for the team that The Room holds its power.

Eddie pushed open the door and slung his equipment bag through first, its weight dragging him along behind it, while he manoeuvred his stick through the opening behind him in a practiced movement. Once as a youngster he had caught both ends of his stick on opposite sides of the door frame, denying his own entrance and getting a huge laugh from his teammates. They called him Doorman for about a month before it trickled away with a few smirks. Eddie had learned from his older brothers not to fight back against such things as the mere acknowledgement that the slur hurt was sure to fuel the life of the insult. Still, he never heard the word without a wincing memory of his turn as an object of derision.

As usual he was among the first to arrive and his spot, kitty corner to the door, at the farthest reach of the room, was of course, unoccupied. He would have been shocked to see it filled even if he was the last in. He was a corner man. He slung his bag on the floor, wedged his stick behind the wooden bench, removed his coat and sat down. The rink was cold but the room was almost imperceptibly heated. Just enough to take the chill off but not so much that it would be uncomfortable when the team came in after a heated contest ready to transform back into suburban dads, burned out corporate commandos, nine-to-fivers and never off the clock small business owners.

Wednesday night hockey with the boys was a ritual for Eddie, one that he had stopped enjoying on the ice as his skills had diminished, but one that

131

he could not give up just yet. He had gone from working on his game, and trying to get better to simply trying not to get worse relative to his teammates who were aging as well, just not all at the same rate.

Eddie unzipped his bag. It resided in the trunk of his car between games where the winter temperatures served to neutralize whatever additional sweat he added each week. Of course the sweat froze and lost most of its power during the week it was packed away, only to emerge again, mid-game while Eddie was fighting in the corner for the puck. A secret weapon of sorts but one that only had an impact on newbies and those players who would not likely go to the corner to challenge him anyway.

He took off his street clothes, and put on his base layer. The fabric was cold. He slipped his feet into his frozen skates and sat. A couple more players arrived. They nodded to each other. Once in a while there was a 'hey' or a crack about Eddie always being there first.

Once his body temperature and the equipment he wore had found a happy medium Eddie took off the skates and proceeded to don his armour. He had the best shin pads money could buy, a newish pair of well padded pants and an ancient, quality set of elbow pads and light shoulder pads.

His skates were old. As comfortable as slippers they were neither particularly expensive nor did they sport the latest in skate technology. But man, were they comfortable. It was an important distinction as in his youth he never had well fitting skates and had endured the agony of taking off tight, narrow fitting skates from feet that had numbed to the cold. Once the laces were loosened and blood began to flow again, his feet would rapidly warm providing an exquisite mix of pain and pleasure.

That pain was excruciating, and exquisitely exclusive to cold weather skating. It only lasted a dozen or so seconds and then rapidly diminished through pain, discomfort and stiffness into an echo of the initial shock of feeling.

The room began to fill up, everyone arriving in much the same order as they did every week. Some came alone, others in pairs. They all went like lemmings to their usual spot on the benches. Some of the best spots were reserved for those long time users who claimed them in the distant, ancient past and would only give them up when they stopped playing. If such a player missed a game his spot would remain open.

Rick was sitting under the No Smoking sign, pulling on a cigarette. The jokes had long ago been made, the irony commented upon and now only the most ardent non-smokers would take a deep breath and shake their heads. It was sort of obligatory. They did it every week, with the same slow side to side motion, the same 'tsk' under their breath, and the same glance at a sympathetic teammate for validation of their disapproval.

The boys got dressed in their own time. Each with a ritual of how they best readied for the game. It was an opportunity to ask and answer some of the week to week happenings as the talk slowly morphed into discussion of the game and their opponents.

"The guy with the red helmet, watch him. He scored two of their three goals last time we played them."

"That big defenseman, with the yellow flash on his gloves, likes to wind it up but he can't get back fast, so play for the fast break on his side if he does it. Just shoot it up the boards hard. If the winger is there it's a breakaway."

"These guys have a good goalie, he's an asshole, yeah, but he's pretty good. Remember, you've got to get him moving. His side to side is a bit shaky."

The last skates were being tied and the Zamboni sounds were far away. Jeff, a wiry and quick skating winger, not too tall with a wave of wiry hair that only got tamped down by a sweaty helmet, always sat beside the door. He pulled it open to see how much time was left in the ice cleaning operation.

"Once more around."

"Okay," said Eddie. "In a shocking move we'll go with the usual lines and pairs. I think everyone is here tonight."

"No, Jim's not here again."

There were only a few weeks that went by where someone wasn't missing - work, wives, kids, and various events often supplanted the weekly hockey ritual. In fact, players knew what the alternative line-ups were in virtually every case of someone missing. It almost didn't need to be said, except it was said so that there was no confusion. Years before making an assumption had led to the boys playing one short after the first shift change on the fly and ultimately a goal against. Never forgotten.

"Pete you go to center tonight - in Jim's spot. We might need you to double up with a few shifts on D, if Dougie runs outta gas."

"You always say that and I never run outta gas," said Doug.

"Why do you think I say it?"

Pete suppressed a grin and nodded. It was a common change and Jim was perhaps the most notorious member of the team for missing games. However, he'd been on the team for more than a decade and he was particularly skilled - so nobody complained too much. Plus when he wasn't available there was more ice for the centres.

Eddie knew you had to keep your centres happy as they were the major scoring threats. Lose one and the team suffered. It was difficult to replace a top player as they all already had as much ice as they wanted. So the centres always got extra ice if one of the forwards was missing. He also had to keep the defensemen happy as the good ones were at a premium and most guys didn't like playing defense. The team usually only went with four D and sometimes only three.

Jeff got up and started out the door. That was the cue for everyone to rise and head for the ice. They skated across the rink, dropped water and extra sticks and then a few pucks to warm-up with. They circled the ice a few times shooting against the boards and against Gord, their goalie. Some took a few leg stretches on the ice, Jeff always used the boards like a ballerina at the rail.

Nobody said anything, all the jokes had been made, all the laughs wrung out of the rituals.

The ref blew his whistle. The extra pucks were quickly dispatched to the bench, the teams lined up and the game began.

Chapter Two

"Well, we called that one eh?"

"Nice move on that asshole goalie. I love shutting his pie hole."

"Getting a goal on him early is the key. Once the shutout is gone he plays a lot differently."

"Good move on the inside to the boards, Pete, their D wasn't expecting that. It opened up the two on one."

Pete nodded with a smile, it was his signature move to fake to the open side of the ice as he moved up the boards, and then sneak inside near the boards. Defensemen never expected it as the space between them and the boards was small, but it always worked. So well in fact that virtually no defensemen had ever caught on, despite being beaten with it over and over. His own teammates only vaguely understood the play - having witnessed it but unable to figure out how he did it. It was all in the defenseman's balance, as soon as he put his weight on his leg near the boards to start to shift into the middle Jim put on the fake and used the defenseman's momentum against him. It was subtle but the defenseman tipped it off every time.

"Ah, 3-1 is a big win on these guys. We didn't give them many chances."

"Yeah, their only goal went in off my shin pad," said stay-at-home defenseman John. He was a big guy, a ponderous but fluid skater, a remnant of his youth, and he had the balance of a pyramid. He had never gone down.

The cooler was wheeled around and everyone who wanted one, scooped a beer.

"Oh boy, that tastes good."

"So who's going to the pub?"

The usuals signalled their intention with John adding his voice, "I'm in tonight. I don't have to get up early tomorrow, gotta meeting in town."

There was a knock at the door and everyone holding one, tucked their beer out of sight. A sign, pitted and old demanded that the dressing room was not sullied by smoking or beer, but that really meant don't make a mess and don't linger so the next team has to wait for the room. The door opened and a head stuck through.

"Hey, our goalie is caught in traffic, can your guy help us out? He said he'll be 15 minutes late but you never know."

"Yeah, yeah, I'll stay," said Gord as he grabbed his upper arm and shoulder pads to put them back on. It was common that goalies were asked to do double duty. "I'll meet you guys at the pub once I'm done."

The boys kibitzed about their upcoming week. A few lunch meetings were organized and minor family doings probed as they stowed their gear for another week.

The last few beers were tossed across the room to the thirstiest and the boys began to file out. A few of the younger guys took showers, thinking they might run into Miss Right at the pub, but the majority only wanted to get there, and besides with their street clothes on they were good to go, save for wet hair. It dried quickly in the sub-zero temps on the way to the pub.

Another week over, the ritual not yet fully complete, the boys left the room as they came into it, in ones and twos, making their way to complete the ritual.

Chapter Three

"From the low scoring team with the asshole goalie to the high scoring team with no goalie."

A week had passed and the boys were coming in again, banging the door on the back wall, as the door stop had long ago broken off, giving the resulting whack a distinctive boom and echo as the door hit it.

"So we play them a bit different, eh. It's not hard to outscore these guys with the sieve they have in net. They must really like him, to keep him all these years."

"He started the team. It's going to take a palace coup to get him to move on. Or at least a serious injury."

"I thought he was already injured, that's why he's so bad. He's been injured for five years."

"We still have to get it by him at least six times to ensure a win. Gordo's a rock but these guys fly and can put the puck in the net - look at their goals scored."

"They might score a bunch of goals but they aren't getting them on me," said Gord.

"Yeah, we beat them 5-4 and 7-3 the last two games. We just gotta bottle them up a bit. Four outta do it."

"Okay, four. I love shooting on this guy," said Jim. He was tall, fast, sneaky with the puck and had a very hard shot with a flash release. "It's really all about their D - if we get chances to shoot we'll be fine. If they shut us down it's a bit tougher to score."

"This is the team with that dirty little bastard winger," said John. "He's always sticking somebody, usually me in front of the net or on the back check behind the play. I'm going to drop that guy one day."

"Yeah, yeah, how many times have we heard that? If you're gonna do it be subtle or you'll get suspended and won't be able to play for a couple of games. Playoffs are coming up and we need you."

Jeff opened the door. "It's just going off the ice," he said as the Zamboni noise changed to a lower, more distant pitch.

"Usual lines guys, we can go two centres and three sets of wings or one of the D can swing forward. You guys decide."

Eddie knew the D would stay back. With only four of them it meant more playing time than moving up to the forwards where the addition would mean three full lines. He usually gave them the option though.

"One of these times I'm going up," said Dougie. He could play. He was big, fast, smooth and very skilled. Probably the best player on the team, he was a natural defenseman but craved a bit of goal scoring glory just to cement his unspoken supremacy.

"Why bother, you end up inside the buttons most of the time anyway," laughed Pete. "Hell, I thought you were a forward for the first two years I played on this team."

"I was. It's just that the D was so bad I had to go back and help all the time. Then I just decided to line up there, it saved me a bit of time getting back."

Jeff rose. The rest of the team rose with him and made for the door and the ice.

An hour later the door whacked against the back wall in a lopsided rat-a-tat-tat and the boys trooped in.

"Dammit. How could we lose to that sieve. I can't remember the last time they beat us."

"Ah, we were crap. Everyone was trying to cash in and was shooting wide. We gotta play our game. Pass it around, make the plays, open up the net. We made him look like a champ tonight."

"Fricken 4-1," he sat down heavily. "We were all over them."

"Except when they were all over us."

"Gordo played well. They musta had 50 shots."

"Yeah, and 40 of them were from inside the crease."

"I did the best I could boys, ya gotta help me out."

"You were great Gord. We just sucked."

"Hey toss me one," Shawn made the catching sign. He snared it with a gentle softening sweep of his arm.

"It was our chance to jump up. The Kings dropped their game too."

"It's all about the playoffs, finishing second gets us a good set up in the round robin."

"I guess. I just hate playing pissy like that. Playoffs start in two weeks. If we play like that again we'll be playing spoilers pretty quick."

"Sometimes we just need a bit of a reminder to play smart."

"Just remind Jim to play - hey Jimmy are you able to make it during the playoffs?"

"Yeah, I already told Marie that I have to make every game until the end of the season. And you know, I told her that I hate to miss those meetings with the kids teachers," he laughed and took a big slug of his beer.

"Well, that's good. Gordo, you okay until the end?"

"Yep. Us goalies can't be missing games. I'm there - here - where ever we play."

"Who's going to the pub?

"I'd love to but not tonight," said John. "Gotta head into the city for an early meeting in the morning."

"Me either," said Pete. "I'm heading into work right now. System's wonky and I gotta reset it. I'll be at it all night."

"Hey, at midnight my divorce is final, I'll be closing the place."

"Well who could miss that," said Ian. "I'm in for that."

"Hey, if Ian's there then so am I, who would miss that."

"Hey John, I saw that little poke even if the ref didn't. You guys even now?"

"No. I gotta do that a lot more before I'll even feel better. The little shit gave me a big grin after I did it to him. I guess it's game on."

The boys started to leave in ones and twos, most making their way to the nearby pub.

Chapter Four

Eddie stood outside the door to The Room. The kids trooped up through the main doors and alongside the rink. He could see them coming for a bit before they got there - it gave him a moment to formulate an individual greeting. He liked to gauge the kids individual moods to get a feel for the game to come.

"Hey Coach Ed, where'm I playin' today?"

"Don't know yet until I make sure everyone I'm expecting gets here."

Connor slipped into the room, wheeling his bag after him, pulling it quickly before the door closed on it. Inevitably the bag slipped sideways as Connor cut the corner too tightly. It came off its wheels, getting dragged into the room. Connor was the most average kid on the team, and the best choice as a swing man to fill in where he was needed. He could play offence and defence equally well - not at a high level, or he would have claimed a more fixed role, but well enough to be counted on in a pinch.

"I think we're only missing one," said Ed to his assistant coach, Tom, standing beside him. "My own Wednesday night team is always missing somebody and we usually are too."

"It's nice to have a full team, but if we are missing certain players it's not the end of the world," said Tom with a laugh. Tom was pretty easy going - he just did whatever Ed asked him to and was happy to let Ed carry the main responsibility for the team. He refused to carry a whistle in practice saying Ed was the only real authority on the ice.

The two coaches thought remarkably alike and were almost always on the same page. They coached their kids' team to ensure the boys, all the boys, had a good hockey experience. Ed could remember vividly some of the crap that went on in kids hockey when he was young and was determined to make the experience better for the kids. The team played at a select level, meaning the kids from the local league were especially selected to this team to play extra tournaments. They also practiced together once a week and played a number of exhibition games to get ready for the tournaments.

Select hockey was an opportunity for kids to play at a higher level without the over-the-top competitiveness of intercity hockey. Stories of shorting the bench, sitting players for missing practices where rampant at that level and Ed was determined not to let his desire to win, trump his belief in fair play. It was a tough juggle as some players and families took advantage of his nature to miss practices and complain about ice time, referring to minutes played as if they had a stop watch on it.

Ed took the view that the best and most committed players got the better positions and opportunities, though he rarely did anything other than simply roll the lines - except in the final minute or two of a close game.

Aidan was walking quickly up the aisle. "Hi Coach."

"Hey Aidan. You ready to play?"

"Yep," he said, matter-of-factly. He disappeared into the room, a faint 'Aidan!' echoing out as the door shut.

"You know it's their room now. It used to be full of parents, siblings and coaches. I like it better now that it's their room and we only go in at the beginning and end of the game for a few minutes."

"I like that. It's a good sign."

Tom and Ed watched the game on the ice as their team suited up. They really weren't watching as fans. It was more a distraction as they thought about their approach to today's game and the boys in the room.

Ed took a deep breath. There was five minutes left on the clock. It was about 15 minutes before game time. Any last minute equipment issues needed to be dealt with and then he would give his pre-game talk. Usually it was about specific concerns he had in their play. Occasionally it was a serious pep talk or attempt to motivate them. He never really knew if it worked or if they thought he was a bit crazy for caring about hockey so much.

He asked his son Marko what the kids thought about the talks. Marko declined to be interviewed. Ed took that as support for his effort. Marko would have given him a head's up if his advice was not appreciated. At least he thought he would.

Ed put his cold hands in his pockets and nudged open the door with his shoulder.

It was the noise that first hit him. It was the same every week. A lot of boys, yapping to beat the band and some just screeching about who knew what. Ultimately they were still pretty young. Some younger than others.

"Shut up. Why do you guys scream like that? You sound like a bunch of 6 year old girls." That quieted them down.

"My sister is six." He ignored that.

"How much time coach?"

"About 15 minutes," he said. Apparently they hadn't figured out that he came into the room 15 minutes before every game.

"Okay guys, I need to talk to you about our last game and something we coaches noticed that you guys need to work on."

The Room settled down. Only a few tears of tape coming off the roll and of Velcro being ripped and reset broke the quiet.

"Once you take your shot or make your pass you gotta head for the net. If I pass it to you Aidan, what are you likely to do with it? You're going to pass it back to me or you are going to shoot. Either way, once I pass it, I need to get closer to the net."

"Defense. We have to get the puck away from the front of our net. If you just shoot it to the boards or into the corner it gives us a chance to regroup, especially if we are chasing the puck around. Don't put it directly on their stick. To the low boards or into the corner. It's safe, and likely our forward is going to pick it up or at least challenge for it."

"Now who's ready to play?"

A chorus of "Me, me," invaded the room.

"Who's going to win the races to the puck?"

"Me, me."

"Who's going to work hard when they're on the ice?"

"Me, me."

"Who is going to skate hard and get off at shift change?"

The "Me, Me," was noticeably weaker. The buy in simply wasn't there for skating hard and getting off the ice, for playing only at the highest level they could muster. They still all measured their ice time in minutes and seconds and not in effort.

"Okay, boys, I'm holding you to that. Bring it in - Wolves on three."

Everybody gathered in the centre of the room. "One, two, three - WOLVES."

It echoed through the room and was even heard outside by their opponents. Ed made sure one of his assistants held the door open just as they were about to shout out their name - it helped the other teams realize what they were up against.

The game was an exhibition against their cross city rivals the Bears. They were working up to the third of their four tournaments - this one an overnighter in Ottawa.

The kids loved the overnight tournaments - they got a chance to live it up a bit at a hotel, eat out, hang out with their teammates and play four or five games of hockey. Tournaments were special. They were a little self contained season. For a team that was struggling, a good showing in a tournament made up for a lot of crooked numbers in the loss column. For hockey players there wasn't much that could beat it.

The old tradition of mini-stick games was fading as hotels cottoned on to the source of the noise and restricted the games. As the kids got a bit older they were less inclined unless they had a dedicated space. Sometimes even parents joined in - only to sheepishly back off when more players came. Some small games still broke out and the more enlightened hotels actually catered to the mini-stick games by setting aside meeting rooms for never ending contests.

The Wolves trooped out of the room and stepped right on the ice. Ed went on last carrying water, pucks and his game board. It was a tradition with him, he loved the feel of the smooth, perfect ice, and the sound and sight of players making their warm-up laps trying to avoid him by as little as possible.

"Around hard twice," he yelled, constantly amazed that the boys never understood that he would not give them the pucks until they had warmed up a bit, and he had reached the safety of the bench. The smart ones timed their circle to coincide with his toss of the pucks on the ice.

Chapter Five

The boys clomped back into the room. A satisfying, if not well executed 4-1 win. It could have been 8-1, or 8-5 or even 6-0. That was the nature of the lack of quality execution.

The team took the room. This year Ed and his assistants had left the kids to their own devices for a few minutes before going in after games. It gave them a chance to talk about the game without coaches hovering.

It was amazing what the kids knew. They were on the ice and they had a different perspective than many of the coaches or parent spectators.

There were a few confrontations and an occasional blunt comment - but the boys were learning how to chastise without rancour, how to motivate without pointing fingers and how to deal with group kinetics.

Once in a while reports suggested they called each other out in the sanctuary of The Room.

"Okay, let's go."

Ed and his two assistants entered the room. Immediately the high spirits and noise level dropped.

"We won though," floated over the rapidly quieting room.

"You guys did win," said Ed. "But you know you didn't play your best game."

Ed detailed some of the highlights and lowlights of the game, praising his players individually where warranted and showing his disappointment with certain types of plays to the collective group.

"We are having trouble getting it out of our zone. We can't be weak on the puck. It has to come out when we have it and we are only a few meters away from the line. It's okay to lose it outside of the line - but a huge mistake to lose it inside."

"We're up for practice on Wednesday and then we're in Ottawa on Friday for the tournament. I think we play our opener mid-afternoon. Your parents have the full schedule."

Chapter Six

Ed left the room. He waited outside to say goodbye to each kid as they left and to kibbutz with parents who wanted to talk hockey.

It was a litany of "good game" or "Wednesday at the triple rinks" or "2 o'clock at the Main Rink." Only one parent wanted more from him today.

"Coach? Ed? Got a minute?"

He had had this discussion before. Andrew's dad was a pretty reasonable guy but he had never played the game so he was always trying to understand Ed's approach.

"No criticism, just wondering; why did you have the boys playing back in the second period? All the parents were screaming at them to go for the puck but they were all hanging back - I figured it wasn't an accident, but why?"

"It wasn't. It's probably better if you get Andrew to answer that question. That way he has to think about the tactic and the reasoning behind it. I always figure to get more buy in to things when the kids really understand it."

"Andrew isn't always as forthcoming as I'd like. I'm just trying to understand so I can reinforce it - I noticed he was creeping forward of their blue line a bit."

"Yeah, he was supposed to in the configuration that we were playing. We have several versions of it. It's meant to give the kids a bit of a breather, so they have more gas in the tank in the third period and can return to a heavy fore-checking style. I'm glad you figured it was a plan - perhaps you can pass that on to the other parents. The boys say the screaming from the spectators is annoying when they are playing according to our plan while having the parents yell out contrary instructions."

"Well, maybe you should explain it to the parents," he laughed.

"It's hard enough to get it through to the boys."

"Yeah, but the parents could help reinforce it when we talk after the game."

"Maybe. It's not a bad idea. I suppose I could send a little explanation around."

Most of the boys had only played house league hockey where the tactics were very basic, as coaches had enough on their plate with teaching basic skating, game rules and passing. Good players were often ignored as the weaker players took up most of the coach's time.

Select hockey offered the better players a higher level of understanding of the game and coaching at their level. Ed preferred coaching kids who had a high level of interest and capacity to learn. He found it frustrating to deal with those who were there at the insistence of parents or whose skill level was significantly below their peers.

"Well, a win's a win," said Connor's dad Brent, one of the assistants. "I sure would like to see them pass the puck more. It's hard for them to get past that house league style where the good players simply take the puck and go and never pass because they don't have any confidence in those receiving the pass. Either they can't take a pass, won't return one or aren't even in position for one."

"Well that's our job eh? Your guy made a couple of nice passes today."

"Maybe that's why I notice it. I pound on him all the time to move the puck. It's important to move it when the play dictates it, not when you run out of options."

Knowing his dad would stay until the last kid has left the room, Ed's son Marko learned to be the last out.

"Did you grab anything left behind?" asked Ed as Marko emerged.

"Yep. One of the kids left their practice jersey hanging up. I think it was Andy."

Ed and Marko started down the hall, "We'll find out on Wednesday. Whoever doesn't have theirs is guilty."

Ed remembered his own time playing hockey. His own father had been around the rink all the time but he only coached one year. He had played some high level Junior hockey and couldn't understand why the kids didn't get it or seem to care even, about getting better.

He had passed on most of what he knew to Ed and also fostered in his son a healthy distain for the over the top approach.

Ed could remember going to the rink almost in fear of making a mistake or not demonstrating complete understanding of a tactic. He vowed never to be that way and sometimes had to reel himself in when he started down that path.

In retrospect he understood how his own father could have had the frustrations he had as he had been anxious to keep teaching new things but kept getting caught having to go back and do remedial work with those kids who couldn't grasp the lessons. Ed had turned down two requests that he coach an intercity team.

He looked at Marko. The boy played the game very well. He played for fun and he seemed to enjoy coming out to the rink. That was good enough. It was a competitive game and that aspect of play always crept in. Sometimes Marko embraced it and other times he shied away. Marko had only once mentioned playing intercity but after a quick deflection by Ed it had never come up again.

"It's amazing I stuck with it for as long as I did," Ed thought. Eventually he had banned his father from coming to the games because the post game discussion was so painful. He could never do anything right it was always about the litany of things he did wrong. Understanding his dad in retrospect did not dim the distaste he had for his father's approach.

His dad would say he didn't have to worry about the good stuff he had to worry about the mistakes and difficulties. Deep down, Ed knew he was right, but his father didn't understand that perfection was not his son's goal. He just wanted to have fun with his friends.

Playing kids from other cities had no cache - who cared if you won and couldn't wear that win at school and swagger among the losers for the whole week?

Chapter Seven

Eddie carried his bag into the room. He still played for fun but he had learned to play for competitive fun, there was no joy in who you beat, unless they were long time rivals. The joy came from playing with his friends and gaining their confidence and winning or losing together.

And of course there was the joy of a well aimed shot, a smooth stick check or a perfectly placed pass. Those things brought satisfaction and sometimes a warm feeling of success that never went away.

Eddie headed over to the far corner. He opened his bag and took out his skates slipping them on with the laces still loose. They were cold, but that's how they always felt.

In fact he once played a few games in a summer league to fill in for a vacationing friend. When he first put his skates on they had felt so warm it was like someone had poured a hot coffee into them - it was most uncomfortable.

The boys trooped into the room and they went through the rituals. They played their game, a 6-2 win, good passing, solid goaltending and decent defence.

"Stupid mistake pinching in like that," said Doug. "I knew two steps in I was going to get beat, but I was committed. I couldn't even get a piece of him on the way by. I tried."

"That one's a gimme. Can't remember the last time it happened."

"Now it's the playoffs guys - I'll send around the playoff sked and it'll be posted in a day or two."

"Hey toss me a beer," Rick clapped his hands together, an unlit cigarette between his teeth. Gord, who always sat on the other side of the door from Jeff, was already filling one request and quickly tossed another one in Rick's direction.

"I don't know how you can smoke those things, especially right after a game," said Jim.

Gord's toss went wide and high and Rick made a heroic stretch to catch the can of beer, softening the catch to keep the beer undisturbed.

"Nice catch, and it isn't likely to fizz up either. I'm impressed," Jeff said.

The kibitzing continued for a few minutes. A few of the guys took a poke at Gord's throwing skills, excusing him because he was a goalie. A few others made plans for the pub. Rick had popped the beer without incident and taken a deep sip but just sat there trying to quell a little acid reflux, a burning sensation in his throat and chest.

"Hey, you coming to the pub Rick?" asked Doug who turned towards Rick just in time to see the cigarette fall from his lips and the beer can crash to the ground between is feet. Rick slumped down and sideways and his eyes rolled back in his head.

"Shit. Rick, Rick. Shit . . .he's having a heart attack," said Doug. "Crap, whatta we do?"

Jeff jumped up. "I'll get help. I gotta phone. I'll call 9-1-1. Somebody lay him out and pump his chest, just under the breast bone."

Jeff ran to the front of the building. These rinks were built of layers of cinder block and were notoriously difficult for getting cell signals through. As he ran he saw the rink manager just coming back to the office from cleaning the rink and parking the Zamboni.

He waved his hands frantically to catch his attention.

"We got a guy down - looks like a heart attack. I'm calling 9-1-1. Do you have a protocol in place or a set of defibrillators?"

"I got the defibrillator - what room?"

He sprang into action. Jeff was already talking to the emergency service and the paramedics were on the way.

He finished up and returned to the room. The rink manager was there with the defibrillator. Rick was lying down with his eyes open speaking to John and Pete.

"Wow, that hurt. I'm not feeling so bad now," said Rick, trying to get up.

"Crap these things have a bit of zap to them," the rink manager said rubbing the two pads together.

Pete gently pushed Rick back down. "The paramedics are on the way. Let's not take any chances."

"I think it was a dive," said Gord with a smile forced through a look of concern. "The throw wasn't that bad."

"Are you kidding, only a heroic save could have stopped it from going back into the ice chest ready to explode into the face of the next guy." Rick grimaced and clenched his neck to one side. "How long for the paramedics?"

"Hey, settle down Rick. They said six minutes about five minutes ago. I'll go out front and look for them said Jeff.

Just as he opened the arena door the paramedics pushed their way through. He quickly directed them to the right room and they flooded in.

"Have you zapped him?" asked one of the paramedics seeing the defibrillators.

"Yeah, just once. After that he started talking and wanted to sit up."

As the paramedics took Rick's pulse and listened to his heart they heard the story of his fainting and got his symptoms. They took his phone number and asked that someone call his wife as they were taking him to the hospital.

"Naw, I think I'm good, I just stood up too fast when I caught that throw," said Rick. He grimaced again. "Okay, maybe you're right. Getting checked out is a good idea."

The paramedics loaded Rick on a stretcher and started to wheel him out. As they did he stopped talking in mid-sentence. Once paramedic started compressions on his chest the other quickly manoeuvred the wheeled stretcher out of the room and into the arena lobby. It was pretty empty at this time of night.

They appeared to have stabilized him and quickly loaded him in their van and took off to hospital. Their lights were flashing but they ran silently. Jeff called Rick's home number. Jeff and his wife knew Rick and his family so he quickly explained what had happened to Rick's wife Elaine. He said he would go to the hospital.

"I'll go too. Yeah, so will I," said a number of guys when Jeff explained what had happened.

"There is no point of everyone going. I said I'd meet her there, so I'll go. She knows me. Dougie, you have your phone? I'll call you at the pub and let you know what's going on."

Jeff quickly finished changing and headed off for the 15 minute drive to the hospital. The rest of the team slowly changed into street clothes and made their way in ones and twos to the pub. Virtually everyone was there waiting for news.

They ordered their usual round of light beer, pizza and chicken wings and tried talking about anything other than the drama of what they had witnessed.

"I think Rick's wife is a teacher, at least she was going to teacher's college to qualify. She'd been an accountant or a CPA or something, before that."

"I wonder if the stink of the room woke him up," said Gord. "I really feel bad about that lousy toss."

"No matter what it was, it was coming," said John. "You can't smoke like that and not have consequences."

The boys tried to watch a hockey game on the pub's TV but they couldn't get past Rick's troubles - at least not until they got the call from Jeff.

They waited. Everyone had anticipated something from Jeff real quick. It hadn't come.

It was nearing closing time when the pub door opened up and Jeff came in. He had his head down. He made his way to the table.

Through the air, thick with expectation, he said, "Rick's okay, I think. He had another attack or fainting spell on the way to the hospital and other once he got there but they said he was stable. They were going to keep him a few days and do a number of tests.

"Holy shit."

"Good thing they got there as fast as they did."

"Was it a heart attack? Stroke?"

"That's what the tests are for. They are treating him and trying to isolate the cause. His wife seems pretty good. She said she's had this in her family before and knows what to expect. They said there was no classic signs of stroke, except for the fainting but they didn't want to say more without any test results."

"I guess that's good news. How long is he going to be in hospital?"

"Did he say if he was playing next week?"

"He wasn't doing a lot of talking," said Jeff. "I'm guessing we shouldn't count on him for a while anyway."

The boys chatted quietly, drained their beers and wandered home. Goodbyes were subdued.

Two days later, Jeff called Eddie at work.

"Hey, thought I'd better let you know first - Rick passed away last night. He had another big heart attack and died before they could take any action. At least it was quick."

"Oh boy," was all Ed could say. "Oh, boy."

He had known Rick for 10 years through hockey. Jeff had brought him into the team when they were looking for a few new guys to replace one guy who had married and moved away and another who had been transferred to another city. He had never seen him outside of hockey save for one time at Home Depot in the summer. They hadn't had much to say to each other in the midst of summer.

"How is his wife? You know them a bit, eh?"

"Yeah, he was an old neighbour of mine. We moved uptown a couple of years ago but we still socialized once in a while. His wife is nice - she and my wife do the Black Friday stuff every year. She's a teacher now, just got a full time contract in town, she was substituting for a couple of years."

"When's the funeral?"

"Don't know. Might not be one. Elaine is not keen on it, but said she might have a memorial service. I'll let you know if I hear anything. Can you tell the rest of the team. Don't want to tell them before the game on Wednesday - will be a shock you know."

Chapter Eight

John looked at the empty space on the bench. The room seemed much larger than normal. The talk was down.

"You know guys, Rick would have wanted us to go out and play hard. He loved playing and always gave his all," said Jeff. "We need to dedicate the rest of the year to his memory."

Jeff passed out a two inch wide strip of black cloth and a safety pin to each member of the team. "Just wrap it around your left arm and pin it in place, nice and deep into the jersey to get it on there good."

"Oh, man. I don't like doing this."

There was a murmur of ascent from several players. It wasn't putting the arm band on that bothered them it was the fact they had to wear it at all.

The room was silent save for the sounds of rustling cloth and 'owws' from pin pricks. Every guy took multiple glances at Rick's empty spot.

They trooped out, claimed a 3-2 win and trooped back in. There wasn't much enthusiasm.

"Hey it's a win."

"But it doesn't feel the same."

Ed wondered why there was no loss of skill on the ice as Rick's usual spot on the wing was filled without trouble. The only loss seemed to be the specific loss of Rick's face and his empty space in the room. He wondered if they were all so easily replaced.

"It's a loss guys, but we proved tonight the team goes on," said Ed. "Rick would have wanted us to push on, he never missed a game and I know he missed a lot of stuff other guys here might have chosen instead to make sure he was here."

The boys all grabbed their post-game beer. Pete wandered around to each guy delivering beer. He put the cooler in the center of the room so people could get their own seconds.

Jeff raised his can. "To Rick."

"To Rick," they all intoned, and took a sip.

"I spoke to Rick's wife Elaine last night. She asked me to thank everyone here for their words of concern and good memories of Rick. She said the team was important to him. He would often talk about things that went on in games on the ice but he rarely mentioned anything about The Room," said Jeff.

"That's cause drinking beer in soaking underwear isn't too exciting," said Doug, tipping his beer in Jeff's direction sitting in his underwear and shoulder pads.

"Maybe. She said Rick looked forward to Wednesdays and told her he was concerned that he was beginning to like the beers with the boys more than the hockey, he felt his age was beginning to erode his skills."

"Naw, Rick still had it. Any one of us gets fooled when a new guy swings down the wing, but we all adjust."

"Anyways," said Jeff, "I know what Rick meant by it. I love the hockey but The Room is every bit as important to me. I miss Rick and I'll miss this when it's time to hang 'em up."

"That's not going to happen for a while - God willing. To the team. To Rick. To the win." They all raised their beer cans in salute.

There was silence for a moment, broken by John asking, in an almost comically normal tone of voice, who was going to the pub.

The usuals assented. Then one or two others decided to join them at the pub. Like the week before, when almost the entire team went in expectation and left in hope, the team returned to the pub in mourning.

Chapter Nine

After the Wednesday practice the boys were spent. Ed had skated them hard wanting to build up their endurance for the tournament that weekend. He used the hard skating to hone their skating skills and to push their speed and endurance. They were never very happy with him and he tried to keep the hard skating fun with relay races, some shootouts with hard skating for those who did not score.

Ed was sitting on the bench at the end of practice as Tom was putting his shoes on. He thought on Rick's space on the bench, in fact right beside where Marko usually changed. He thought about losing Rick and flashed through how the hole would be filled on the team. Rick could be replaced, heck he could be replaced in the broader context of the team.

Then the awful thought of Marko's spot being empty struck him hard. He choked and gasped. He turned away. "That cannot happen," he told himself out loud as he crossed himself.

"But Dad, if I don't leave school early we won't get to the game on time," said Marko before seeing the stricken look on Ed's face. He mistook the look and corrected himself.

"I mean Coach Dad, Ottawa is a long way. When are we going to leave?" he grinned at his father.

"Yeah, I haven't thought about it much," said Ed, catching and righting himself. "We might go first thing in the morning so you won't go to school at all. We can leave here, get there and have lunch before the game - a light lunch and then dinner with the team afterwards. I think we've arranged a restaurant to meet at."

"No school at all, sweet."

"No school but lots of homework I understand. If you get it done on the ride there you'll have a much better time in Ottawa."

Marko made a face but did some homework in the car on the way to Ottawa. It was hard to concentrate through the building excitement and the jiggling car motions.

"Who do we play? Do you know the arena? Is that Ethan's car up there?"

Ed laughed. He loved Marko's enthusiasm and really liked the opportunity tournaments gave to the boys to create memories - maybe not specific ones but memories of good times, hard work and success on the ice, and the usual small time shenanigans that pre-teen boys would engage in - eating too much, drinking too much pop, swimming in the pool, lounging in the hot tub trying to look cool - and generally ignoring common sense instructions and their mothers' wishes.

The dads got it. There was a time for living and stretching the boundaries of everyday life. Not to the point of dangerous or foolish or even unsupervised. But instead of being with the boys they often held back at a distance, with one or two dads keeping a distant eye on mini stick games or tamping down the running around the pool with a sharp word.

The excitement in the room was palpable.

Ed wondered if he should try to cap it so they wouldn't burn out. He wondered if he did succeed at calming them if they could ever get the fire back. He asked his assistants who shrugged. They decided to let it go, they only had to keep it up for a couple of hours and could settle into Saturday's double header with a good night's sleep.

With five minutes to go in the previous game Ed entered the room. He hated when someone was missing. He had fixed his line-up and was expecting Ethan. Juggling it at the last minute was never a good thing.

He put his cold hands in his pockets and pushed open the door with his shoulder. The noise was incredible as the boys were at a fever pitch of excitement.

"Who do we play? Are they any good?"

"Okay guys give me the floor."

The Room settled down.

"You don't need your lid yet," he waved off a few kids who were donning their helmets. They could hardly wait to get on the ice. The room hummed with anticipation, almost as if the kids were plugged into the wall, jittery with electricity.

"We are playing a local team - the Kanata Kangaroos - don't ask," he said to his two assistants standing in the doorway.

"Kangaroos?" mouthed one of the assistants with a shake of his head.

Ed shook his head with a smile. "They better not be Waltzing Matilda all over us - where the hell does that come from?"

"We are playing Kanata. They play in a Select League in Ottawa. They are in last place. What does that mean?" he asked the team.

"We're going to win," said Nick, who always cut right to the chase.

"We might win, but these games, against weak teams are a test. It's a mark of a great team to not take anyone lightly. We cannot be overconfident. We have to treat this game as if it is against the best team we've played all year. Great teams don't just win because they are good. They win because they play well even when they don't have to. We cannot be selfish with the puck. We cannot try to do things that don't work against good teams or we will be in trouble. And once we hit the panic button we are likely to lose."

"In many ways this is a character building experience. These games are tougher to win than games against better teams. We have to force ourselves to play our best game against a weaker team."

The boys nodded sagely but Ed knew they didn't really get it. He hoped that his approach would help them focus on maintaining their in-your-face style of play and would help them focus on those times when they didn't do it, and the consequences.

The door opened and Ethan came through. His dad hovered in the doorway, "Sorry, sorry we got caught needing gas and couldn't find a station."

"Ethan!" most of the boys called, piling obviousness upon their obliviousness that he wasn't already among them.

"Ethan, get ready quick. Boys make some room for him."

Ethan settled into an already existing small slot between the two boys he usually sat between. They had called out his name the loudest when he entered.

"Of course the Wolves are going to fore check in their wolf pack. Of course the Wolves are going to feed on their mistakes. We are going to see the weakest member of their herd and put pressure on that spot, hard skating, good passing, quality shots. And please boys, follow your shots to the net."

"Once more around."

The boys all rose and started yelling, their enthusiasm spilling over. Ed couldn't contain them, so he stopped trying. He wanted to do their usual Wolf yell at the beginning of the game but they were not to be silenced. The room was electric and loud.

"This is the first game, do not take it lightly," he yelled over the noise. "We need to win in order to get to a final on Sunday afternoon. Go get 'em."

With that the boys spilled out of the room and onto the ice.

Even Ethan had managed a quick change and was with them fully dressed and as excited as anyone.

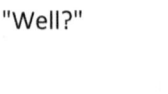

Chapter Ten

"Well?"

"You were right coach."

"We just thought we'd win." It was music to his ears. Something was getting through.

"Well it's a good thing we did win, at least if we want to get to a final."

"Boys. Coach Ed was right. And what's worse is you didn't listen or didn't believe him," said assistant coach Tom. "Thank you Marko for that late goal. Frankly, a 5-4 win is nothing to be proud of against these guys. We should have won 8-0. I hope you've learned your lesson."

"Gentlemen. Winning teams never take anyone lightly. Sometimes that is difficult to do, but you have to do it consciously. You have to put in the same effort you would against the best team you have ever played in every game - it's what winners do. You guys thought there was a party going on and you all wanted to go. You cannot win games by yourselves."

"Everybody grab a juice and put any garbage or recycling in the bins. We are a classy bunch and we don't leave the room a mess for the next team. We are meeting later for dinner. If anyone wants a swim, now is the time, as soon as we get back to the hotel. Tomorrow we play at 10 am right here and then 6 p.m. at the other arena - remind your parents. Please be here at least 45 minutes before the game."

Ed left the room, trailed by Tom and the defense coach Brent.

"You were right - right on the money. They took it too lightly."

"That team wasn't particularly good but they had a couple of kids who could really go. Both kids on their top line had really good shots."

"Yeah, well, bad teams are usually just heavy on the bottom end. That's really the difference, at what number in the pecking order are the players weak or inexperienced or whatever?"

"These guys barely have two decent lines but they do have a very good top group," said Eric.

"They may be in last in their league but that might mean that the other teams, and we play one tomorrow evening, are actually pretty good," said Brent.

"One game at a time guys. First we face off against Markham. They were in a tournament we were in earlier in the year - they didn't win it but I think they did pretty well, lost in the semi-final I think."

"Do you know who beat them?"

"Not sure - it was somebody we've never played. I think they played before us in the first game and won big against a weak team. It's hard to tell until you see all the results of the tournament games to know what you are witnessing in the early games," said Ed.

"We're already checked in. I'm going to stay and watch a bit of the next game - it's the team we play tomorrow at 6. We'll be around for a quick swim in an hour. I think the restaurant is a short walk from the hotel."

"Is everything out of the room?" asked Ed when Marko came out.

"Yeah, everything except Cliff and his dad. I think Cliff's helmet is broken or something is missing."

Ed wandered back into The Room. He had a little equipment repair kit. It came in handy.

The Wolves gathered the next morning in the room - trickling in one or two at a time. They were subdued and appeared serious to Ed as he watched them enter.

"This is going to be a good game, boys," he announced to his assistants as the last kid slipped into the room. "I've never seen them so determined."

Five minutes to go in the previous game and the coaches all entered the room. There was a low murmur of voices punctuated by an occasional loud word or two. The boys were all talking among themselves, in their lines or with their defense partners - Ed had insisted on a couple of changes to the usual parking spots in the Room early in the season, to encourage just this type of talk. The talk hadn't really happened until today.

"Wow, am I dreaming? Ed asked under his breath to Brent who was right behind him.

"Holy crap, this is unbelievable."

"I don't want to disturb them. Whatta think?"

"Let them go for a bit, pretty soon they'll stop as they realise we're in the room."

Sure enough one by one the conversations ended and the kids looked up expectantly. It was an entirely new thing for Ed who wasn't quite sure about himself in this new room. The cinder blocks were the same, the toilet and sink and showers were the same and there was even a bit more bench room than many arenas they played in. But the room was completely different. It's as if, as one, the boys had become much more serious about their game, their play and their team - or at least one of those things.

Ed was stunned. He expected a bit of a transformation when he saw the seriousness of the players as they entered the room, but this was something entirely different.

The room was crackling with fierce determination but it wasn't loud, it wasn't nervous. It was calm. They were holding their buzz in check. The boys all waited patiently for Ed to begin. He decided to let them wait to build up the tension and add power to his words.

Peter broke the spell.

"Coach we want to win. We all talked about being determined in our play. Everybody is going to do it."

"Well then there isn't much to say. Go play the way you all know how. Go Wolves!"

The boys trooped out of the room. Peter winked at Ed.

An hour later, they walked back in. There was little talk, but a noticeable swagger. The Wolves were the possessors of a 10-1 win. They had laid it on thick - heavy fore check, a relentless determined style of play, never giving up on a puck or a play and working harder than they ever had before.

Ed, Tom and Brent gave them The Room for a few minutes. They heard nothing. It was very quiet in that room and Ed wondered what was going on. Then just as he was considering it was time to enter, there came a mighty, glorious, unified yell, with "Wolves" gasping for air somewhere in the middle of it.

Ed was taken aback. He thrust his hands in his jacket pockets and pushed open the door with his shoulder just in time to see most of the boys still standing in the middle of the room - with huge, big grins on their faces.

"I'm sure no team in the history of hockey 'got it' as suddenly and as completely as you guys got it today," he said.

"Last night coach. We got it last night. We all talked."

"Well I am impressed. Very impressed." The assistant coaches nodded in unison.

"Wow. That was as incredible a display of hockey as it was a display of determination and dedication to effort. I don't really know what to say other than - let's do it again this evening."

That evening the room had changed again. There was a looseness among the players - a confidence suggesting that they knew what was required of them.

"Boys, this is the most telling game. After that display this morning I expect to see all the puzzle pieces fall into place. I've always said that playing the game correctly will result in good things but I understand that there are opponents out there who are trying their best and they will occasionally make great plays, get fortunate bounces and take advantage of the nooks and crannies of our game. What you boys demonstrated this morning doesn't guarantee a win but it makes a win very much more likely. Go get 'em."

As the team hit the ice Ed relayed his fear to his assistant coaches. "I've seen it before. Once you think you've found the formula you think it will all happen and you don't have to continue to push it. We'll see how they react today. Even though they had 'got it' they aren't sure how to 'keep it' yet."

Yet the boys managed another win 6-2 with a very solid display of hockey and of confident dominance. The game had been close through two periods but the Wolves did not panic. They played their game and eventually a few hardworking goals went in - and then their opponents were forced to open up to try and get back in the game and the Wolves were able to pop a couple of goals on odd-man rushes to cap the scoring.

They were in the final.

Ed had seen signs of complacency with the new approach, almost a faith that they would win no matter what because they had discovered the magic secret. It was only displayed by a couple of players but it was catchy and as the game wore on an entire line was floating like the win was theirs by divine right.

A confident team hit the ice for the final. It was a tough game 0-0 through two. The Wolves broke through with a goal on a deflection off a defenseman. Instead of redoubling their efforts some of the players stopped the hard fore-check, content to break up plays as they were developing in the neutral zone, looking for a good bounce or a break, but generally hanging back and trying to preserve the one goal lead.

Then as their opponents were changing, the ice opened up as the Wolves defenseman Ian grabbed the puck and started a hearty offensive rush. With all the Wolves sensing something big, Ian pushed into the offensive zone with a head of speed, he made a move on the defenseman but was cleanly poke checked and their opponents had a clear two-on-one break with only the Wolves other defenseman back.

He played it perfectly taking the pass away but the Wolves goalie anticipated pass too long and the shooter caught the short side with a quick release wrist shot. The game was tied.

With only five minutes left in regulation time the Wolves were stunned and they panicked trying to get the goal back immediately.

Two long passes were both intercepted and despite Ed trying to calm them down and get them back to playing a methodical game, they tried another long pass. It went for an icing bringing the face-off back into their end. Their opponents put on a play. Rather than try to win the face-off back to the point men for a shot, they pushed it forward, and four players crowded the net looking for a loose puck.

Ian lunged at the puck but was only able to push it away from the front of the net back out to a pinching point man. He wound up, took his biggest slap shot and one of his mates was able to whack in a rebound. They were losing 2-1 and their opponents were whooping it up.

There were only a few minutes remaining in the game but the frustration and shock was evident in the Wolves who kept trying to make miracle, heroic plays to tie the game. They weren't able to get much going and time expired.

An angry set of players marched back into the room. Some scowls, some tears and some looks of shock, graced their faces. The door shut behind them.

"I'd like to be in that room," said Ed. "I'm not sure how they are going to react. I think we need to give them some extra time on this one. "

The room was silent until Marko spoke up, trying to understand.

"How did that happen?" asked Marko. "One minute we are in control and the next we are scrambling."

"I'll tell you how it happened. Ian fucked up," the profanity hit like a bomb. "Ian tried to be the hero and Ian cost us the game by being out of position - two huge mistakes and both times they scored."

A couple of the kids murmured agreement. Ian had been in on the ice for both of the goals against. He had never been one of their strongest players.

Cliff took the assent as a license to keep piling it on. "He's been fucking up all season. He doesn't think about the team, it's all about him."

"Wait a minute. Nobody complained when he scored that late goal yesterday. Nobody complained when he got a winner against Markham in our last tournament, or when he made a great play to kill that three on one in the opener."

"All I know is Ian screwed up and we lost a game we were going to win," said Cliff, holding up a tournament souvenir glass. "And now I have this nice glass for my milk when I shoulda had a nice big trophy."

Peter stood up. "Enough. We all take the loss, we only scored one goal."

"Yeah, and that was enough to win, except for Ian."

Peter strode across the room and grabbed Cliff by the front of his shirt then used his forearm to push him back into the wall. With his legs bent because of the bench Cliff couldn't get any leverage and was in no position to fight back. He tried to push back on Cliff but without his legs under him it was no use.

"I said 'enough'. Ian is a solid player for us. He tried his best. This time it didn't work out. I can guarantee you Ian was trying to win the game - he was not trying to make a mistake."

Ian had his head down - listening. Watching the ground. He nodded. "I just did the best I could. I'm s-s-s-sorry guys."

Peter gave Cliff a final shove before turning around. "You have nothing to be sorry for, Ian, you tried your best. That's all you can do and all anyone can do. We win as a team and we lose as a team. It goes for everyone, don't let me catch you not trying. We don't have any issue with people who try. But if you are caught not trying I will be pointing fingers just like Cliff."

Cliff did not take his smack down very well. He considered taking a swing at Peter but the rest of the room was so cowed by the outburst that he wasn't sure he would accomplish anything except for defending his own honour.

Peter turned to him.

"Cliff, nobody is trying to lose. Don't take runs at your teammates. We are a team. We all get a part of a win and we all take a piece of the loss. Ian did his best. I'm not sure anyone else would have done any better or any differently in the same place."

"I don't like losing. We had that game in the bag."

"'Enough', I said. A one goal lead is not 'in the bag'. Get out of here, wait until the door is completely closed and then come back in, and we'll put this behind us. We are a team."

Ed and the coaches were completely caught off guard when Ian exited the room half dressed. He turned away from them, faced the door and waited as it closed. Then he took a deep breath and went back in. Silence oozed out. Then the hubbub started low.

The coaches entered. They saw the tension in the room. Peter was standing facing Cliff who was still leaning oddly against the wall. The boys all sat down grateful that the coach had broken the spell.

"I believe we made great strides on learning how to win this weekend," said Ed, who knew something important had happened in The Room. "I also think we learned that it isn't as easy as simply flipping a switch. I'm proud of you guys. You gave it your all and very nearly took home the hardware."

Cliff finished undressing so fast he was out of the room only moments after Ed finished his talk with the team. Ed knew something was up but never found out. Marko refused to be drawn into any description of what went on.

Chapter Eleven

"Rick is gone and here we are in the final. Elaine wanted to come by and watch."

Eddie cooked up a tribute for Elaine and cleared it with the other team.

The boys took their warm up and each managed a little wave or nod to Elaine in the stands as they swung by the far blue line. Then the teams lined up for the opening faceoff.

Rick's line mates got into position with Jeff at centre and Brent on the left wing. They left Rick's spot on right wing empty for the opening faceoff.

As planned the other team won the face off and took the puck back behind their net. They paused a moment while all the guys on the ice stopped in a neutral zone trap formation, two outside their opponents blue line and two more just outside their own blue line.

They turned to Elaine, and they touched their hands to their black armbands they wore for Rick.

Elaine rose and was standing as they performed their tribute. They all nodded and then started into the game, as Eddie jumped on the ice to fill the line spot for Rick.

After it was over, a tough 3-2 loss, Elaine had asked Jeff if she could thank everyone in The Room.

"That's highly unusual," said Jeff with a soft smile. "Women haven't been allowed in The Room since Major Atom. I'll see what I can do, but you're going to have to do it immediately after the game, within moments of us going in there. Be there and I'll give you a signal."

And that's what was arranged. The boys assented to the visit but not without a few scowls and narrowed eyes. Elaine knocked first and Jeff let her in. She stood just inside the door beside Jeff. Jeff held the door open - it didn't seem appropriate to close it.

It was a tired, sweaty bunch of aging weeknight warriors that faced her. Some were clearly uncomfortable with her there and Pete and John even put down their beers as she spoke.

"Thank you everyone for your calls and particularly your tribute to Rick at the start of the game. It would have meant a lot to him and it did mean a lot to me. Rick loved this team and would have been proud of you all tonight. I think he picked a good bunch of guys to play with. We will all miss him."

Elaine bowed her head, forced a brave smile and left. The door closed.

The room stayed silent.

"Well, we gave it our best tonight. Not sure what went wrong, they just beat us."

"It was bloody Rick's fault," said Jeff with a snarl and then a big grin. "If that bastard would have been here we woulda had the extra legs to hold on in the third."

"Yeah, I can't believe he'd do us in like this. After all we did for him. Bloody Rick killed us."

"He didn't pass once," another voice said. "Ya gotta pass the puck to score."

"I didn't see a single shot from him either," laughed another voice. "Gotta shoot to score."

"He's off the team - sticking it too us like that."

The whole room was laughing hard now.

"Bloody ungrateful of him," said Jeff trying to add to the mirth, but reality got the better of him. "I am going to miss that ungrateful bastard."

His voice broke, "Who wants to share a ride next year?"

The boys left the room in ones and twos.

The cinder blocks were the same. The painted benches, toilet and sink and showers were the same but the room was different. It took on a little more history, a little more legend as one season ended and another rose on the horizon.

"Who's going to the pub?"

-END-

Prig

There was once a man named Prig who lived in an odd little place.

Prig cared entirely about his own house and garden and not a whit about anything else, except as it might compare to his own space.

In point of fact the boundary of his property was the same as the boundary of his interest, save when he spied an innovation he could approbate.

He was an ordinary man, short and thickly built; well educated, according to the manner of his day, and he would have been interesting to some people, though he didn't know any of those people. However to those who knew him he was more of a case study. He was unusual in no particular way - save his particular way. He worked on his house day after day for many years. He cared for his garden, tending it closely.

His neighbours, and they were many, occasionally wondered about the little man and his obsession with his house and garden. Then they thought of other more pressing matters - bills to pay, suppers to prepare, children to get off to school. Of course they were concerned with their own homes and gardens as well, but only in so much as they contemplated the sorry state of their own homes or gardens in passing conversation when talking to other neighbors and were searching for something to say.

Prig knew how they talked but because he couldn't quite figure out how they felt, he paid them little attention. Oh, he gave his neighbors the customary wave as they went to and fro but he never went out of his way to do it. In fact he thought them all a little strange, sad and unfocussed.

"I live here in this garden, so shouldn't it be as I like it?"

He knew working the long hours on his garden, brought him a bountiful harvest. He knew he was right to spend so much time on his labors as he could show off his efforts in ripe tomatoes, fresh lettuce and large carrots and onions. He wondered, at times when he was particularly sore from all his labors or in the quiet of the evening as the cool air began to seep in and displace the hotter, more arid midday air, why the people who lived around him did not do the same thing.

Their lack of interest was dragging the whole neighbourhood down, he thought. The laws of Prig's country were rather black and white; bleak, some said. As is usual with such things, the bleakness of the law was something of a reflection of the citizenry. They had long ago stopped legislating what citizens could not do and started setting all the rules on what they could do.

Prig decided that he had had enough of the sloppy gardens of his neighbours so he marched down to the Department of Civic Regulations and asked to see the Laws on Upkeep and Appearance. Finding that his garden was the only garden that met the criteria of an acceptable garden according to the law, he demanded a judge issue an order on garden bylaw enforcement.

In the defense of the majority, it was said that most people had more pressing concerns than beautification. Most did get a reasonable harvest, especially reflecting upon the small amount of work they put into their properties. Their neglect was merely a matter of balance to them; a reasonable return for a minimum effort.

The quest for balance of return had gone on so long that most failed to appreciate that a well ordered garden was also a productive one. The power of law had a hold on people. Once confronted with evidence that they were not living up to their obligations they quickly reversed their previous approach and jumped back into their garden maintenance with both feet. Now reminded, henceforth all gardens faced an inspection by an Official who was empowered through due process to prosecute any horticultural failings with the full weight of the Law. Penalties were somewhat ambiguous - and likely the main reason that strict adherence had fallen by the wayside.

The townspeople grumbled at first but began to comply after a few spirited and vocal offenders were dragged away to answer for weed violations. These misguided souls claimed that some of the weeds were beautiful in their own way, and besides, they were alive, and surely that counted for something. One even went so far as to prepare a lovely weed salad which he claimed had significant nutritional value.

Officials reserved judgment on the nutritional value citing a lack of desire to eat the weeds which disqualified them as foodstuffs. The apparent beauty of some of the weeds failed to register with those given the power to decide. In the end, crowding out edible plants in areas where edible plants were being cultivated was deemed a violation and subject to the full weight of justice. Beauty was reserved for designated locations, usually near doors and windows.

Prig continued to work on his garden but he found it increasingly difficult to maintain his highest of all standards. After a time all gardens in his neighbourhood were now so productive and so beautiful in the legally designated spots, that his was only slightly better by the inspectors' judgement. Prig himself had to point out the smooth earth and the rich furrowed soil to the inspector before he was granted top marks. It made him uneasy.

He took to sleeping less and considering his options more, sometimes sweating details that would contradict other plans for improvement. He knew that the advantage of good soil was only a product of time, that others would soon have good soil after they had worked their earth for a while. Still, after the laws had been enforced for some time, Prig's was now a lovely country with thick, close cropped grass and quaint cottages nestled in the budding gardens as far as the eye could see.

People chatted to their neighbors now about their work in the garden. They shared ideas but in fact they all had much less time for idle chatter.

What mattered was the next visit by the Inspector only just around the corner and the amount of produce they could extract from their land. Some larger scale farmers had difficulty selling their wares now that the land seemingly overflowed with bounty.

Now, more and more Prig began to look at his garden and find little flaws in the arrangements of plants, and in the plants themselves, as he had included a few plants just because he liked the way they looked and smelled. He had to consider production first.

He started a little rearranging and uprooting but he was never satisfied. Little repair jobs grew larger and took longer.

Toiling one sunny, warm afternoon, considering the line-up of projects he had decided upon, sweating from his brow with drops slashing on the inside of his eyeglasses Prig threw down his hoe in frustration. Sobbing into his hands he gave a sudden start. He would tear everything out of his garden and leave only the bare earth. He was going to begin the garden over again, this time with an eye for value, beauty and satisfaction of the whole.

He marched down to Civic Administration and filled out the proper forms in triplicate. Officials were wary of his plan but his reputation won him the right to try. After all, the neighbors were beginning to talk.

Everything came out. He even contemplated changing his house's footprint around, dismissing the idea only after he realized such a change was not on the Council permit he had painstakingly shepherded through proper channels.

Once cleared, Prig started the project standing surrounded by bare earth, his hands on his hips, staring at the space that had once been his garden. He didn't like the slight slope of the land so he planned an elaborate tiered effect.

He brought in tons of clean soil, rocks for drainage, sand for a good base and landscaping materials that his neighbours had never heard of. In fact he concealed some special soil and mulch so his neighbors wouldn't know what he used. He wanted to keep his secrets close. He started his gargantuan task knowing full well that it would take much time even for a young man. Additional licenses were applied for and granted and heavy moving equipment was brought in. Prig even hired the services of a few stout lads who were plentiful in that country and now had much experience.

There were some rumblings from the local citizenry regarding the legality of horticultural contracting due to the personal statement and individual industriousness that the gardens were supposed to convey. An underground trade in these services had begun with the first enforcement of the Laws. However, Prig's direct action merely legitimized the whole industry to most everyone's satisfaction. Nobody wanted to complain and force an end to the practice lest they would require it themselves.

Prig moved the land about in all different ways, first pushing it this way, and then that. His lads piled it up and then smoothed it down. Prig liked the idea of keeping his garden private so he began to build the tiers up and away from the cottage. He soon realized that the scale of his plans for elaborate tiers would bury his little cottage and his privacy would be complete - even isolating. He liked that idea. But he didn't like the idea that he would not be able to see about. He thought of raising the house, but that required engineering permits and official approval, which might take years or not be granted at all. Above all it would be a difficult task as he knew little about building.

He thought of the wonderful view he would have sitting at the bottom of his garden bowl. He thought of the pleasure he would take in being higher, and being able to see all around him. It would be nice, he thought, to see all around past the troublesome neighbours. He became rather enamoured with the idea but he couldn't figure out a way to raise the house.

Then it hit him. He would keep the garden tiers up and away from his home building them in a wide bowl shape with his home at the center. And he would build a high addition to the cottage so at least part of his cottage would be high enough to see beyond the tiers of plants. He started to build a round tower out of stone at one corner of his home.

Prig realized that he would have all the privacy he wanted. Civic inspectors looked at him very skeptically but did not stop his progress. They only wanted to know how they would gain access to the property to inspect it.

Not wanting to get on the wrong side of the law, nor compromise his grand plan, Prig built a tunnel into the outside of the bowl which provided access to his home at the center. It had a cunningly engineered entrance and exit, making it virtually invisible unless it was right in front of you.

Plenty of room around the cottage was left for smaller gardens of sweet smelling flowers. The amphitheater of the bowl was tiered into various types of gardens with plants and flowers of all descriptions lining the spaces between vegetables. Prig had a small rock garden with fountains and streams near the cottage, powered by a cleverly hidden pump. He had a crop garden, a show garden and even a small maze of shrubbery built with the cottage at the center.

The gardens bowed to classical standards and all were very formal with the exception of the smaller gardens around the cottage. Even the crop gardens were laid out precisely to maximize their growth and their beauty. Even the Civic Inspectors were in awe of how tasteful, lovely and productive Prig's new garden had turned out. The areas very near the cottage had retained the original quaint country feel Prig had so long prized. The tiers soared all around his house so they had the added advantage of blocking the free view of his splendorous efforts to any passersby.

His property was now ringed by a high rock wall to support the high tiers inside. Only the small tunnel with a pilastered entrance allowed anyone inside.

In this way old Mr. Prig got his wish. He removed himself from the general populace and was totally surrounded by his spectacular and beautiful gardens.

After several years without being able to see Prig's masterwork, life in that country pretty much returned to its pre-Prig normality and slowly the strict provisions of the Garden Act once more fell into general obsolescence.

Even today travelers to that faraway land are struck by the austere homes and offices, which are festooned with flower boxes rife with colour. Most of the inhabitants don't know the origins of this custom. Prig's home was sold after he no longer needed it and gradually the hard edges of the landscaping eroded until the little cottage appeared to be the stage of an ancient amphitheatre, with rows for the spectators to watch ritual dramas.

In that country, the production of food stuffs remained high. And Prig's secret garden was all but forgotten.

-END-

The Silence and Sold Sources

Chapter One

Of course he couldn't laugh loud, his editor might hear. Anyway, he had the quiet show of amusement mastered. A broad grin spread across his usually inquisitive face, and only someone who knew him well and was looking for a reaction, would realize he could hardly restrain himself.

He was a couple of inches over six feet but his always rumpled appearance and slightly stooped posture made him look shorter. Fortyish, he still had all his hair and an athletic agility that surprised most people in the rare times he flashed it. Quick witted, he most often made his jokes in little asides to those nearby, fearful that an unsuccessful attempt at humor would single him out. As people got to know him, and felt they knew him well.

He studied the paper that was thrust at him. Fortunately, among the group gathered in closer than normal to his desk, or fellow writers waiting nearby with creased faces, there were no corporate types. He folded the paper up, made eye contact with his closest compatriots and settled into his chair with a shake of his head, the grin unchanged.

"Another mistake," he thought to himself, "Griffith won't like it," even if it was amusing. It wasn't funny however to those whose job it was to insure that each edition of the Daily Times hit the streets without mistakes.

"Griffith is going to start thinking sabotage, what with contract negotiations heating up. Maybe he's right. Some of the union radicals can get a little carried away," he said aloud.

His colleagues had been interested in his reaction so he just shook his head with a smile, "Well, if it's sabotage at least it's only a bit of harmless fun."

He refused to go any further, but he knew what everyone in the newsroom was thinking, as he switched his attention to his desk full of messages.

Bill Lardner was the point man in an office full of them, an office full of reporters. They made a career of being cynical, of doubting everything, but here in the heart of the newsroom they needed a focal point, someone to lead. They looked to him to drum out the tune. They might not all march to it, but they needed a beat to play along with. Today, for the third straight day, those individuals wondered aloud why there had been a screw-up on Page Three.

After the front page of each section, page three had the highest visibility of any page in the paper. If you talked to the news desk, however, they were convinced that it was second in impact only to the front. Of course they were all news junkies, biased to their own beats and strongly of the belief that their contribution was of considerable import and significance each and every day. Some reporters couldn't even muster up even a show of interest in other matters.

Hard news was all over the front page, and always had been on the front page in every newspaper in the known universe. Well, except for some of the weekend editions of Florida papers which ran comics on the front; and that was all you needed to know. That being the exception to the rule and all, it followed that hard news carried the weight of the paper.

None of the three consecutive foul-ups were serious breaches. Not like reporting the wrong person dead or referring to an accused as convicted before his trial had started. No, they were actually amusing. Not knee slappers perhaps, like an unintentional spoonerism where typos make sense in a twisted or comedic way. Yet they were still funny enough to bring a smile. And three in a row was hard to fathom as an accident. What was the old saying, once is happenstance, twice is co-incidence and three times is enemy action. Now that there were three in a row it was becoming obvious the mistakes were not accidental.

Most newspaper mistakes are immediately identifiable as such because they are random typos, or omissions that even the dimmest of readers can instantly figure out. However recent events on page three made things different at the Daily Times.

For three days the Times had been plagued by a series of mistakes that were not obvious. Hence the conspiracy theories by those whose job description included 'maintaining a paranoid attitude regarding all possible subversives.'

Because of the high readership of Page Three it had been decided in the recent redesign of the newspaper that bullets of information on high readership features would be included. Readers, who had identified these high profile features in a survey, would be directed to turn into the paper for the main body of information on each subject. Weather was a new staple of Page Three, as was the photo feature "A Thousand Words" ; an obligatory column of bullet items, essentially headlines and lead sentences for stories inside the paper. Also sports scores, information on upcoming feature stories and special sections as well as commuter news, dominated the third page.

Monday's mistake was in the picture caption. The photo was of the city's mayor, who cultivated a happy, blue collar image. He was with his well-known mutt at a local dog show. The mayor and his dog, happily out of their element had their names transposed in the caption. That was not a mistake that anyone in the editing suite would make.

It was perhaps not the most amusing thing people saw that day, but for a newspaper to make such a conspicuous mistake, people talked about it. When that mistake is compounded by others on consecutive days, people really started to notice.

Letters to the editor had begun to arrive poking fun at the newspaper. People at rival papers began to think it was a publicity stunt. While that was dismissed as ridiculous, people were talking about the 132 year old newspaper rather than talking about what was in it.

"I hate it when everybody laughs at us," Griffith's familiar voice echoed in Lardner's head. It took him a moment to realize Griffith was standing behind him.

"Yeah, chief, it bothers me too. I wonder if they're laughing at us or with us."

"I doubt very much that people would think that we did this on purpose."

"More's the pity," thought Lardner, as Griffith walked away. But he's right, people don't expect too much subtlety from their daily news.

Still, the three mistakes were a bit disturbing. Lardner ran over them in his mind: Tuesday's dropped word in a headline, Wednesday's change in the predicted temperature from 84 degrees to 48 and now today's picture caption. All were simple mistakes, all could have been made at any time, thought Lardner; but three days in a row? All on the same page?

He watched Griffith disappear back through the newsroom doors on his way to the executive wing. When Griffith was gone he turned back to face his desk and the pile of mail and messages. Even in the midst of a mystery, life went on, and there was a paper to put out.

Chapter Two

"I want that paper!"

Christine Wakefield cringed slightly. Her boss was demanding, unreasonable, authoritarian, and arrogant but he was usually right and he paid her well.

"I'll be in Edinburgh tomorrow and back Friday. When I return I want your report. I am going to buy that paper," he stormed. "Is everything prepared for the trip?"

She nodded and he smiled his kindest smile knowing that everything would be in its usual place, tickets, transportation and accommodation.

"Friday," he said with a nod as he disappeared from his office through the door to his private apartment.

They were high above the downtown core, atop an inconspicuous office tower. The tower held numerous law firms, corporate head offices and three floors from the top, a floor for the offices of Apex Corporation, an acquisitions firm specializing in transportation and communications companies.

Apex had thousands of shareholders, the biggest of which was Myriad Holdings which held 35 percent, which in turn was owned 100 per cent by James Noble Harris. His 35 per cent gave Harris effective control, and an additional 16 percent of the Apex stock in the hands of Noble Enterprises' pension fund, gave him absolute control. Noble Enterprises was the family company which he inherited from his English ex-patriot grandfather who had built the successful management and financial company on honest dealings and a shrewd mind for real estate development.

James Noble Harris was his grandfather's pride and joy. When the old man died, that didn't stop him from willing 20 equal shares to various family members. It took James three years to wrest control of the company from his disorganized and uncooperative relations, two more years to re-establish it as an industry leader and all that time to leave behind most of the conservative values which the elder Noble had built his company and reputation.

James figured that his grandfather hadn't given him the company straight away because the old man wanted to give him a short course in business experience to prepare him for the challenges of running it. He always smiled a wry smile when he thought of the old man. He was the only person that Harris looked up to, and he was now long dead.

Consolidating the company after it was split into 20 pieces was just that experience. The experience of acquisition and on-going management, that gaining control foisted upon the young James was the best education he could have gotten. It also made him fiercely defensive about his company and bold in his plans. In 15 years he had doubled the size of his grandfathers' holdings.

Christine saw the door to the private apartment close and heard the echoes trailing off. Yet the sound of the closing door still echoed in her head as she slowly turned and began to collect papers from the desk, shaking her head at the impossibility of her task of buying the Daily Times in such a short time. And yet her mind was already plotting several alternate courses of action so that even while doubting her abilities, she was forming her plan.

Harris had wanted the Daily Times for years, since the first time it printed a series of unflattering articles outlining his real estate ventures in the city. He wanted to be loved or at least highly respected in all circles. He received invitations to every social event of any significance in the city despite the fact that he had never attended. All he wanted was respect for his accomplishments but all the popular press wanted was to root out his mistakes, embellish them and make him seem a fool, despite his success.

What did these people want? He built them nice homes, provided services that they demanded, jobs, and all they ever returned was money and grief. The money at least was part of the deal. At any rate he was off to Scotland for a few days, to visit the estate which his grandfather built late in life.

It was a grand estate and formed the base for all the Noble holdings primarily because that was where the master, James Noble Harris spent much of his time. It formed the lion's share of his original inheritance from his grandfather. Both men loved the place and the younger Harris realized only later that he was given it because he loved it and because he would have to work hard to keep it.

A huge, old manor house surrounded by traditional gardens dominated the landward entrance to the property while an ancient castle, meticulously restored and equipped with all modern conveniences stood on a high promontory overlooking a small North Sea inlet. Between the two structures a helipad and hanger stood, hidden in the woods. The estate was a wonderland, the only real indulgence of a rich man obsessed with little more than riches. However James Noble Harris wanted more than his grandfather, he wanted popular respect borne out of admiration. He wanted a place in history.

He knew his only truly admirable quality was a ruthless head for business, which was not an image to inspire millions. The media could help make his place in history. The Daily Times offered the necessary tools to work his image locally, allowing other media to finish the job. Media moguls had used their power to gain political power, knighthoods and other honors, he could too.

As he prepared to leave, his assistant Christine, realizing the day that he might make good on his rant to purchase the Daily Times had finally come, went to work.

Harris thought out loud incessantly, threatening to buy this television station, that newspaper and this manufacturing plant, usually after it had foisted some imagined indiscretion his way.

She knew him well enough to know that he might not act on his seeming whim immediately, but that he was hatching plans to act at a later date, a date when the company was not aware that they were particularly easy take-over pickings. As soon as he mentioned a mere interest in virtually any company she went to work on adapting the Harris methods for take-over. She constantly jumbled ideas about for a way to gain control.

He was shrewd in those things which he chose to pursue and she was equally shrewd in determining which of his myriad of dictums he was serious about and then how to go about attaining them.

She had learned everything watching him. Since she was a little girl she was fascinated by his machinations of control and the accumulation of wealth. While he had, in recent years, tried to polish his public image he still understood only naked aggression in business practice, and so came more to rely on her more subtle approaches.

Before going to work for him directly she had worked at several of his companies, first in an office, then in a newspaper's advertising department. From there she worked as a radio producer and then as a feature writer for a English language newspaper in Paris. He had called on her in Paris, just showed up at her beat-up flat overlooking Pere Lachaise Cemetery, asked her to dump her date and go for a walk with him along the Seine.

She was used to seeing him this way. The date was of little promise anyway and when James showed up, rendered meaningless. She would be leaving Paris, probably before the week was out. That's the way it always was when he gave her a new assignment. She waited until she returned to the States before finding out that her education was complete and that she would work directly for him. In effect her education had just begun.

She jetted around the world with him working with locals on business dealings. He liked to remain in the background pulling the strings on deals but leaving the social engagements and face-to-face negotiations to her. It was in large part due to her abilities that his plans had been as successful as they usually were. He knew that and acknowledged it. After all he had firsthand experience working with family members in the business.

In an office full of telecommunications equipment she opened a drawer and picked up a small mobile phone, "No I won't tell you my name. Just tell Mr. Griffith that the sabotage on Page Three comes courtesy of his brutal treatment of workers." She hung up.

The cell phone registration was not connected in any way to Noble Enterprises, it's bills were scrupulously paid and maintenance done by a hired hand who had little idea that he was working on the primary tool of business for one of the country's richest men.

Cellular telephones were of little practical use so Harris expressly forbade their use by any of the company workers. He said that he had faith in his staff and that they were capable of working independently and didn't need to be tethered to the office. She, however, knew that a cell phone had its uses.

Another call went out to the rival Post-Courier, similar information channeled to the business editor regarding the strange happenings on Page Three of the Daily Times. She knew it didn't even matter if her insinuation made print, because the information mavens had a word of mouth circulation almost as efficient as their publications. And more influential, much more influential.

All she had to do now was sit back and wait, and watch.

She stood looking over the city, through the deepening evening and polluted gloom. "I wonder what will happen on Page Three in tomorrow's paper?" she said aloud to the empty office.

She stood at the window, with the office lights off, curious and reflective, vaguely running over the episodes of her life, episodes that brought her to this moment in the gloaming.

Chapter Three

Across the city people were thinking of tomorrow. Spring was late in coming, nerves were raw, worn down by the annual war with winter. People were on edge. They had patiently waited through the winter months, even grateful for the chance to hibernate in their own lives for a few months.

There were limits. After the requisite amount of time passed and a few warmish days tantalized the city's denizens they turned surly, looking for a change. The city craved it. Action, as defined by the night crawlers, it had in plenty. Through the long months battling the cold, the city had settled into a pattern of existence where sunset and sunrise were the drumbeats signaling everyone to move on to the next action, or reaction. The city needed a jolt, and one was overdue.

Lardner flipped on his laptop. Years of coming in each day and he still couldn't get over the silence of the newsroom, where nothing but soft clicks permeated the air. Sometimes he still wished that the newsroom echoed with the clattering of manual typewriters. It seemed impossible but a loud steady noise was almost a blanket to distractions in a way that silence couldn't be.

"You could hide with your thoughts inside that god-awful noise," Lardner thought. The crashing keys drowned out distractions, made it easier to bang out a story.

Not that he couldn't handle change, no, he welcomed it when it made sense. The fact was after his first two months writing on a computer he couldn't imagine returning to an electric typewriter much less a manual one. And yes, he remembered manual typewriters. In the dimmest recesses of his employment, his first writing job, the small paper he worked for had resisted the coming technology and manual typewriters held sway.

They held out for several years but eventually change came and came swiftly. Jobs were lost outright when the paper made the technological switch and old employees were untrained for the new ways of doing things.

For Lardner it was the noise he craved. "Maybe they could simulate the noise," he thought, "a recording of an old-fashioned newsroom piped in would do wonders for the soul."

He even went so far as to suggest it at one drunken Christmas office party. The publisher, who despite keeping Griffith as editor, had a sense of humour, and laughed at him. He was a creature of technology. In the publisher's mind technology could solve the world's problems. Lardner was beating on the wrong door.

Lardner knew when he was beaten. He knew it especially when he was drunk. He joined in the laughter as if he'd made a great joke and the publisher, who really wasn't a bad guy, grinned broadly.

"It's that funny bone," he said, "that keeps you laughing." Lardner crinkled his eyes, shook his head, smiled and waited for a decent interval before excusing himself from the circle which had gathered around the publisher. There was only so much he could take.

Even his desk was a throwback. It was his. His alone. Nowadays, the newsroom was a small collection of desks where the writers could work if they chose to come into the office. So much was done on the fly, in cabs, at home and on site, that it was almost unnecessary to ever go to the office. The web ruled the roost.

Lardner was in the office so much that he never gave up his desk. When technological changes and economic considerations conspired to make the office redundant, Lardner was asked to share a desk. He argued. He fought and to offset his bitterness the two writers assigned to the desk with Lardner just made other arrangements. Management won, Lardner won and the two other writers didn't have to face a cranky colleague.

The desk was the centre of Lardner's professional life. It was equipped with his own pencils, reference books, bits of scribbled information covered papers, and a telephone. And there were the chewed pencils and pens. Various styles of pen produced various styles of chew. Too hard a chomp and the taste of ink was pervasive and unpleasant. Still in Lardner's world the chewed pens took the place of gum and were necessary to the thinking process.

Lardner needed the desk as an anchor to his job. "Some people can juggle the various considerations of their lives while working at home," Lardner argued while defending his desk. "I cannot. I need to keep the two things separate. It is difficult enough, in as much as almost everything I do, 24 hours a day makes its way into my columns. I need to separate that from the actual business of writing."

While he liked writing on the computer he wasn't so integrated into the modern that he liked using the web, or accessing the paper's library, or his messages that way. In some ways it was a battle he was destined to lose.

In fact, message delivery was a bit of an ongoing feud with the front desk. The paper had an automated phone system and an electronic mail arrangement but Lardner chose to avoid these over exertions of technology. He figured, if it was important enough he'd find out about it. He was in the office every day, that was as in touch as he wanted to be. His contacts knew enough to insist that important messages be written down and placed on the desk. Even the more sympathetic receptionists knew his peculiarities and respected his insistence on the human touch.

He wrote an everyday column on Page Four, and he'd been doing it long enough, and successfully enough that he pretty much got his way. It helped that he was a reasonable man. He'd pitch in at election time, and he wrote the odd hard news story when his interest was sparked, but the demands of writing an everyday column were enough to put him in the hospital on two occasions.

In for writers' block he'd tell his friends, when they trooped through the hospital to visit him. He knew that chronic expectations lead to tension and tension led to very real physical problems, or had at least twice. However, the expectations were his own and there was no kind of tension that three days of rest, a good book, regular eats and pre-written columns couldn't cure.

Writing an engaging, entertaining, topical column, every single day was a daunting task for most writers. He'd been at it long enough to know that daily columnists had to give themselves a constituency, a broadly defined block of what they were interested in and what their readership wanted. Most times he was compelled to remain inside the parameters that he himself had created. He could, and did, leave his standard format on occasion when something of import needed to be said. Leaving his standard style gave his message some impact.

Usually he wrote about things. Things which caught his attention, things which seemed important but which were merely the day-to-day concerns of the modern city in which he wrote and the readers lived and read. He wrote about things that morphed into ideas. However, he was careful to keep the focus on things as ideas had a way of coming unglued from the everyday and it was to the everyday that he was attached.

He tried to be lighthearted and occasionally was successful, but he found that he was best, and most appreciated by his readers when he was concerned and passionate. Readers constantly communicated to him and to the paper that they enjoyed his point of view, that they wanted to know what he thought and why, because it gave them a platform from which to work out their own opinions and standards. He kept his public opinions to things and consciously avoided the pull to ideas.

Knowing your readers is important for a columnist but deadly if you let them dictate the agenda. It was a battle and it was stressful coming up with a fresh angle every single day. In addition to his concerns he had to be at many of the events he wrote about. Firsthand experience was the lifeblood of his work. Merely commenting on someone else's impressions was the work of a critic.

He knew he ate poorly. Pizza was his weakness and strength. "Where else could you so quickly and easily grab the portable delights of all four major food groups," was his defence of pizza to his doctor, who admitted to a similar weakness for the stuff. Still pizza was eaten on the run and Lardner knew, that on the run, was bad.

The poor diet wasn't the main reason for his hospitalizations. It was his belief that he couldn't miss a day, not of work, but of existence in print. He lived for his column, his daily comment on the absurd, the homely, the melancholy, the comic and the tragic. If his column was lighthearted, it was only as he was lighthearted and that usually meant some underlying message which meant that it was underlined with passion. It was the only way he knew to be respected and above all to be read.

He used to wonder about the beat writers, who almost to a person, loved the world in which they travelled. So serious were they in getting the facts, back grounding the story and presenting tortuously slow moving events with a daily dose of immediacy, that they didn't realize that almost nobody read their stuff. Perhaps they didn't care. Somebody had to have a handle on the daily doings of politicians, sports teams, local and international institutions and the like because they all manage to be important to someone at one time or another. Those people needed a watch dog and it fell to the news beat writers many of whom probably grew up as classroom tattletales.

Lardner took care of what interested him. Being interested in everything helped. He didn't want to know all the shades of gray on a given subject, he merely wanted to understand why there was gray and where it started and where it ended.

Chapter Four

Griffith sat in his office and watched the clock while pretending to finish a few small tasks. He reviewed his private phone number list. He tapped his daily calendar - he had a meeting soon with the publisher. The publisher, though jovial with clients and those of both higher and lower social standing than himself, was competitive, particular and demanding with his immediate subordinates. Their relationship was one that Griffith knew he had no hand in shaping. At one minute prior to the prescribed meeting time, he rose and began the short walk down the hall.

He actually feared his boss, though that was probably standard for most of the North American population. Your boss, your mother and your wife are the only three people who exercise any real control over a North American male's life. Only the boss doesn't have to reciprocate the control. Some poor saps have those three people embodied in two or even one person. Pity the poor guy whose wife or mother runs the family business.

Griffith feared his boss for two reasons. First he was demanding and seemed ready and willing to exercise his option to discharge Griffith from his duties, and second, because his boss didn't seem to really understand the newspaper business and relied on Griffith for more than he wanted to.

"Good morning Frank," he boomed, knowing that he was on time and thus in control of this particular moment. As usual it was a short lived control.

Frank Anthony was the corporation's idea of a publisher. He had worked his way up the corporate ladder. He started as a comptroller for a small manufacturing company. When the founder and owner decided to give his three sons their inheritance he split the company four ways and sold a share to Anthony who he figured would insure that the company remained in business, and would guarantee his sons an income.

The company was in turn bought by a large corporation, which needed the plant's capacity quickly to complete a lucrative deal with a third company. The terms were particularly good for everybody's purposes. The sons made a killing, Anthony walked with a tidy profit and the respect of several corporate bigwigs. He then played politics a little, and made his reputation volunteering to re-organize poorly run segments of the company, which could be easily turned around by applying a little sound business sense. The corporate guys loved him.

Six months later the corporation purchased the Daily Times in an effort to broaden its holdings and influence. Knowing everything about big business but nothing about newspapers they put their most adaptable man on the job. Anthony had spent most of his time arranging for management to hate and fear him, while attempting to curry favour with the hourly and salaried workers, especially those in the newsroom. He figured that opinions flowed to the public from there so they probably filtered through the rest of the enterprise from that same source.

"Griffith," he barked with his hand over the phone's mouthpiece, "I'll be with you in a moment." He roughly motioned him to sit. With Griffith, Frank Anthony knew he didn't have to feign his irritation. He put the phone back to his lips.

"Oh no, as I said, random chance provides the possibility of three consecutive occurrences, maybe even four or more, I don't think anyone would consciously do harm to the institution that employs them," Anthony said soothingly into the phone. "I don't think that any of the staff are as mad as all that," he forced a laugh, "We just have some minor differences in opinion. Our major labor battles were fought a long time ago. And it wasn't the stone age, there's no need to update our premises. Is there anything else? Fine, goodbye."

He replaced the phone with a slow precision. Griffith wasn't about to make any presumptions. He waited for Anthony to speak.

Anthony took a deep breath, and plunged in. "That was the Post-Dispatch. I've just been on the phone with virtually every media organization in the state. Seems they think our Page Three problems are union sabotage."

"I wonder if they heard it through the union," Griffith said. "All those guys are hooked up through the same union and they all talk."

"I'm aware of that Griffith, what I want, is to be aware of all of their plans. I was thinking about this angle before the inquires began to pour in, now I'm almost certain. Griffith, find out everything you can. This is important, call in your favors, and dig. You were a reporter once, I'm sure you can still remember the methods of getting information. I want a report on my desk by Friday afternoon. While you're at it, post yourself in composing and watch the production of Page Three, perhaps we can nip this in the bud at least for tomorrow. That will be all," he turned towards the phone.

Chapter Five

A button was nudged with a practiced hand. Only a desk light illuminated the room. The computer screen came to life. A sandwich and glass was set down beside it.

The keys were hit in a practiced sequence and access gained to messages, bulletin boards and finally games. He played a couple of games each day before going on to the day's task. First it was just a way to familiarize himself with the keyboard, then it became a ritual, a few games chosen to keen his mind and increase his dexterity.

There is no denying it computer games are fun. You have an infinitely patient opponent and one who doesn't taunt you when you make a mistake or try some tremendously unorthodox method to win. Unless of course, you program your opponent that way. Conversely there is no one with whom to discuss strategy and to celebrate a victory or achievement. Trying to explain your success in a difficult computer game to an outsider was more frustrating than anything should be.

His keyboard had coffee stains on it, ends of his long thin hairs reached out from under the buttons. In moments of deep thought he would try to squeeze the end of one with his long fat fingers, pull it free and dispatch it to the floor.

The rest of the room was piled with books and boxes of books. A few old art posters hung, mostly at weird angles due to loosened tape. They played with the strange shadows coming obtusely from the single light source in the corner of the room.

There was an old dusty stereo in the corner with various technological innovations attached to it. A small flash memory key sat on top of a small pile of CDs, which jumbled beside a similar pile of cassette tapes on a shelf above a box full of ancient vinyl albums. Music squeaked out of the speakers. A continuous flow of music was programmed to play rock classics on Monday, Wednesday and Friday; old favorites on Tuesdays and big band music on Thursdays. Saturdays and Sundays were left unprogrammed because he usually wasn't in the apartment.

His fingers jitterbugged around the keyboard. Benny Goodman swung from the speakers in keeping with the good mood of the room's lone occupant. For a fleeting moment he realized that taking typing in high school was the smartest thing he'd ever done, until now anyway. Like any maestro he'd developed a style of his own, a six fingered cross over, three fingers from each hand, with his eyes darting from screen to keyboard in a syncopated rhythm much like an accomplished driver during a particularly busy rush hour.

"I wonder if they still call it typing in high school," he said to the shadows.

Chapter Six

Contract negotiations between the newspaper and its various unions followed the same strained path as most labor-management scuffles.

Newspapers provided a different dynamic than most. Traditionally poor paying, large operations had over the years given in to a reasonably well educated work force due primarily to the huge profits the newspaper industry generated.

So while the unions patted themselves on the back for enlightening their employers the employers patted themselves on the back for being in a business with two streams of revenue. Not only do they charge advertisers for the right to place information in the newspaper but they add some news and entertainment, comment and information and turn around and sell the whole mess. Not a bad scam.

However the business was changing as more people got their news fix from the web. The shift to digital had not been smooth for the industry.

Negotiations had produced hard feelings and vandalism in the past but most newspaper workers realized that vandalizing the very means of your livelihood was not a smart long term policy.

"Think any of the hard-core union types might have done it?," Lardner was asked.

"It's too early. Hell, they haven't even set a strike date. Sneak attacks on the paper aren't usually done until a strike is imminent. Plus, nobody'd do anything that would appear in print."

"Yeah . . . but three days in a row? Maybe the radicals have a new strategy. I've heard you saying that they mostly just vandalize stuff for fun, anyways."

"Well Carl, I don't know if I used the word 'fun' but I know what you mean. However, that's the attitude of the computer geeks not the guys who work here. What about you guys in composing, you been looking for it?"

"We will be now. I mean, shit happens right? We make mistakes, everybody does. A few times a year something like this happens. Most of the time the mistakes are obvious mistakes, dropped letters, misspellings, you know? But three days in a row, when the mistakes aren't immediately obvious and, at least to the mayor, downright malicious. Oh, he was mad, I heard."

"Yeah, he was mad," said Lardner. "You would be too if you were identified as Trixie in the paper, especially after that office hiring scandal last year. Griffith had to deal with him and his mood is usually no ray of sunshine, but this morning . . . I'm just glad I wasn't here. At least that's what they're saying upstairs. You might know better, Carl, I imagine you guys got an earful."

Carl nodded knowingly, winced comically and started down the stairs with a smile while Lardner hit the elevator button.

"Well, he named the dog didn't he?" said Carl as he walked away. "Maybe he should have called it Champ or Fido."

Lardner caught the elevator to his very own desk. He toyed with writing about the mistakes, considering mostly the mood Griffith would be in after he pointed them out to the great unwashed, most of whom probably didn't notice them in the first place, and he decided to let it go.

Lardner knew he had a strong voice but he was also conscious of the dangers of ridiculing one's employers. Still, he'd done it before. Usually a little flattery off the top was enough to defuse any bad feelings, and if they didn't notice that, a little criticism made them appear broadminded in the public's perception. At least that's what he told them.

Chapter Seven

"This is great. I don't know who's doing it but it's great," trumpeted Paul Desroches to anyone who would listen. He held a copy of the Daily Times folded open to Page Three and waved it around. Various people smiled at him, some scowled and others attempted to ignore him. The latter had the hardest time, because people had been ignoring Paul Desroches for years, and Paul Desroches wouldn't stand for it.

He was an oily little man, short of stature and short on smarts, someone who took great pleasure in reducing anyone he could into a fool, because he had played that part so many times himself. As high school teetered on, he became involved with the student newspaper. The long time clique didn't like him so they made him the photographer, which kept him in the dark room most of the time and away from the rest of the ink stained crowd. After he realized what had happened he began taking to his job with relish trying to capture damning photos of anyone who possessed either popularity or authority.

A photograph of a young male teacher leaving the school with two senior female students gained him a reputation and got the teacher fired. After that many people decided that for their own good, Paul Desroches wasn't such a bad guy after all. The power of the press sent Desroches in the direction of journalism studies after high school. And he landed a job after graduation with a small town weekly, where he began the process of making contacts within the industry.

He decided to run for a union position for his local at a small town weekly. He prepared for the competitive election and finding no opposition went on to an illustrious career, rising through the local ranks to land a job with the union office. At the beginning he loved the narrow looks of contempt which small time publishers used to hide their fear of him. As his position of authority grew he continued to enjoy the same reaction from big time publishers, as well as their obvious attempts to intimidate him.

One of his cohorts hung up the phone. "Yeah, it's great, but I was just talking to some people down there and they don't know who's doing it. They really don't know."

"More's the better," said Desroches. "I like our members taking the initiative, especially with contract talks starting tomorrow. The loose cannon stuff gives us a little edge, even if it's only psychological."

"A loose cannon is a scary thing, it can deliver the knock-out blow but sometimes it blows up in your face. If I was you, I'd try to find out who's behind it. That keeps you in control."

Desroches nodded, he didn't get this far by not taking advice and being able to read people. He needed to know but not until after the initial bargaining session. He wanted to have his exhibitions of ignorance untainted by deceit when management first brought the subject up, which they undoubtedly would do in tomorrow's opening session. Just like a bunch of management guys to set the initial meetings for a

Thursday and Friday.

He went to his desk and flipped open his notes. Job security was the number one issue of the talks according to the membership. Money, benefits and other issues had been settled before Desroches arrived to play point man to the Times' unions. All he had to do was act as a mediator and play the game to get his salary.

He knew, as did the Times' team, that a quick settlement was not in the best interests of either group of negotiators. A major part of their jobs was taking care of the always acrimonious labour negotiations. Remove that from their job description by being reasonable and their jobs would go up in smoke. So by mutual unspoken agreement acrimony reigned. Anyway, it was fun to trade insults with a bunch of pompous underworked management types who hadn't made a decision of any true impact for years.

So Desroches prepared to ask the management team for everything imaginable. They would have things to argue about, he would give a little and the management team might even see fit to grant the union some small concession at the end to avoid a strike which everyone knew was in nobody's best interest. During a strike the company would cease to make its outrageous profits, causing shareholders and management untold grief; the unionized workers would cease to be paid, hurting their families; and, the negotiation teams would have to continue under adverse conditions with all the preconceptions thrown out, thus causing them to miss their summer holidays. In all, not very pleasant.

That the public would lose as news sources shrunk, wasn't a consideration, but the fact that regular readers would go elsewhere and might not return was.

Desroches didn't doubt for a minute that his counterparts were engaged in the same preparations across town. The only thing he didn't completely understand was that they had previously been given the bottom line in a report by the corporation's accounting firm. They could dance as long as they wanted but they paid the band. After the music stopped, the union would have to decide if they wanted to stay at the ball.

Chapter Eight

The downtown streets were quiet when Lardner wandered slowly down the front stairway of the ancient newspaper building. Tomorrow's column had gone to press and Lardner, true to form, stayed and roughed out the next day's effort.

The building had undergone numerous renovations since it was built as a waterfront warehouse more than a hundred years before. The newspaper offices had been in the building since before anyone could remember though the printing facilities and distribution had moved out in stages years ago. The downtown location was essential for the editorial and administrative offices.

As the paper grew it had changed offices several times settling on this warehouse early in the century. Renovations and the moving of departments created the extra space needed when required by the growing enterprise. The building had a blue collar look to it which probably kept the newspaper's executives from getting too corporate in their approach. It was hard to project an air of sophistication when your office building looked like something out of 'On The Waterfront'.

Generations of newspaper editors had played on this image and presented the newspaper as the only one willing and able to tell the whole truth because there were no pretenses, no shareholders to satisfy and no Jones's to keep up to.

For years it had worked and the paper was consistently the most read in the city. People and employees had wondered what would become of their paper once the corporate ownership came in. Until the recent redesign little had changed. Griffith was sure that he kept his job only because of the corporation's interest in maintaining at least the appearance of remaining unchanged after the takeover. It was carefully explained to him by Frank Anthony that the study which resulted in the changes was initiated prior to the buyout and in any event would have occurred whether or not the sale had taken place.

Like other large corporations the one that purchased The Daily Times wanted to broaden its business base. At the same time it needed a conduit to the public so a newspaper or radio station seemed the logical choice. The Daily Times had credibility, history and a cheap price due to some business failures, which included a state-wide edition, and lagging technology. The family that had owned the paper for years sold, happy to be rid of a dowager queen of what they saw as a fading industry. They turned their money around and invested deeply in a computer network for information, which had been begun under the auspices of the newspaper but was not sold along with it.

Lardner exited the building. He always paused on the top of the wide stone steps after passing through the doors, just to look out at the streetscape and do a quick visual check of the city he had lived in all his life. He was one of those men that usually walked with a slow, steady gait, head down, as if considering a great question. Actually he was just trying to avoid stepping in some unpleasantness.

More often than not the question related to mild considerations on his evening, his evening meal or his evening place of rest. He liked to simply think, usually about nothing in particular, just whatever crossed his path or his mind. In fact, sometimes, while seeming to be in deep thought, he actually blanked his mind and thought of nothing at all, letting his walking be controlled by the same involuntary drive as his breathing and blinking. Putting his head down he found was the only way not to be constantly bombarded by the demands of modern life.

Sometimes it was loneliness, Lardner had enough of that, but ideas kept him busy, even if he didn't seem to do anything. It was that insular attitude that drove his women friends crazy. Rarely did he like to talk about those things that seemed to so absorb him, because in talking about them he found himself merely thinking out loud, with the other side of the conversation working like a little devil to change the subject or move it into directions and realms which he did not want to travel.

He thought of companionship, the women he attracted wanted to share his thoughts. Lardner was on his way to Laura's place. He walked. Laura lived a long walk from his desk and sometimes he thought, that was why he continued to see her.

Laura hinted about making the relationship permanent, but he was wary. It wasn't that he didn't like her, she was entirely serviceable as a companion, lover, mate; he just wasn't sure that he wanted the domestic thing. He liked the idea of not being too involved, of not having to care particularly. He had cared once and its result was something he was determined to avoid. Of course he considered what he would do if she ever gave him an ultimatum, and he knew he'd most likely capitulate, mostly because he could see no good reason to fight. Besides, if it made her happy then, why fight it. He considered himself lucky that she seemed too timid of breaking their arrangement to force the issue. They had lived this way for nine years.

Laura was expecting him. After nine years she knew that if he wanted to talk, he would, sometimes so passionately that she couldn't shut him up. Even if a subject had been exhausted sometimes he would continue on saying things over and over, hoping that keeping it in the forefront, turning the subject over and over, would force new thoughts and new ideas on the matter to emerge.

The table was set for dinner. Her kitchen was bright and large. Bread boards hung on every square foot of wall space not devoted to cupboards. The room was almost the same size as the living room, a perfect arrangement because she did most of her living there.

She was a photographer, mostly weddings, portraits and studio work but occasionally she took a freelance assignment for the paper. She was in demand and well regarded in the industry though she didn't seem to know it. Her work was technical and of high quality though often uninspired. Flare was not her big thing and that suited him just fine. Too many wedding photographers searched for flare by putting their subjects into silly situations - covering their promised photographic output with pictures that produced quizzical looks from friends and blunt comments from family.

The kitchen had a small pantry room opposite the stove which she had converted into a dark room. She used it less and less for photo work as everything was moving to digital. In fact she had started to store some canned goods there. It worked, as she could tend her dinner recipes as well as her developing fluid at the same time.

When Lardner described her work as postcard perfect, she would smile, either not detecting, or refusing to react to the velvet jibe. Still, the perfect postcard was a serious improvement on the 'art' shots to which so many of her colleagues were addicted.

He wound his way through the evening streets nearing the flat with every step. Rush hour had long ago passed, causing him to wonder briefly why that part of the day was referred to as "rush hour" inasmuch as it usually took several hours to clear the city streets of commuters.

He approached her apartment, on the upper floor of a large, old house just north of the city center. Though he practically lived there he still liked to knock, to maintain the formality of their two living places. They had once talked of the silliness of having two residences but he had won when he described his almost pathetically small downtown condo as a den/office that just wasn't attached to her place, their main residence. It helped that shortly after their discussion he caught a particularly bad strain of flu just prior to one of Laura's big freelance jobs and was able to hole up at his place and not infect her. That quieted the discussion.

"In here Bill," she called when he knocked.

He pushed the door open. "How do you know it isn't some crazy person come to do evil deeds, or at least ask for your mortal soul?"

"The Jehovah's Witnesses were already here this month," she said brightly. "Besides you said you'd be here at eight and," she glanced at the clock, "it's eight."

"I could have been late, I had something to pick up in the den."

"But you aren't late," she said before changing her tone, "but if the den were just down the hall instead of across town . . ." she trailed off, her point made.

"You mean apartment 2B is coming open?" he grinned.

She let it go, changing the subject before it became too thick.

"How'd it go today," she said, turning back to the stove and mouthing the words of his standard reply while grinning to herself that she'd really miss it if he didn't say . . .

"Same old dull routine."

She laughed to herself. The same old dull routine, every time she asked. Same old dull routine even when he'd talk about it for hours unable to shift his mind out of the subject. Same old dull routine when something captured his imagination enough to inspire several columns.

"Well I saw the paper today." As a rule they never spoke about his column. "Mistake number three on Page Three. How'd they all take it?"

"About how you'd expect. Griffith just about blew a gasket, the newsroom thought it was hilarious, composing thinks they're all about to be fired and nobody outside the newspaper business saw it, except you."

"I am in the newspaper business, at least I was today," she said. "Didn't you see the front of the leisure section?"

"Yes, I did," he said, suddenly reminded. "I was going to say I thought that was one of your best shots for the paper. You're really getting the hang of giving those shots a newsy feel."

She smiled. As she rose and turned away to tend to the stove she couldn't keep her grin tight and it spread rapidly across her face. He rarely was so enthusiastic about her pictures.

"It must have been good," she thought.

"Did you really like it? I tried to get several elements into the shot other than the models. We stood around for more than an hour to get the crowds in the background just right."

They ate dinner, spoke about an upcoming wedding shoot, a little longer than Lardner felt comfortable with, went for late walk and retired. She drifted off wondering how fast she should push him into giving up his apartment and he slept thinking about how nice it was to have options.

Chapter Nine

Most people sleep at night. Unless you are one of the few who don't, the statement sounds vaguely absurd. At night an army of people work to maintain the places we live and work. They paint and clean our streets, they stock shelves, they deliver packages, they fix faulty wires, they do a myriad of chores and provide the modern means to maintain our fast-paced society. If enough people are willing to pay for it anything can be prepared overnight, ready for consumption by the masses the next morning, including the news.

With reportage of events able to take place as it happens, news has become a behemoth of up to the minute information. A deluge of detail pertaining to right . . . this . . . instant. The major sources of news: print, radio and television; have developed their own style of reportage and their own strengths. They were being challenged by the web and an army of information sources - the wired public.

Radio can flash information the quickest. However radio and all media are limited by connectivity. If you are not connected, even the most immediate source of information is a million miles away. The ubiquity of cell phones was migrating immediacy to those who carried them. For decades the most important events were first heard about through listening to the radio. Radios were on in many places all the time so a flash newscast could get news out quickly. Television brought an incredible detail, pictures of events, to the eye of every viewer making them both a witness to, and a participant in history. Newspapers, because their speed could not compete with the other two mediums, and fell into an analytical role, a provider of background and related information. Newspapers give events a context - a shape.

Because of the time lag newspapers have gone to extreme lengths to get the whole story, details, spellings, measurements that the other mediums merely gloss over or assume you know. These details, and the incredible consistency of the best newspapers, give weight to what they say. People believe.

Three big, obvious mistakes on three consecutive days. Newspaper people all over the city smelled something - something planned.

In a small room, high above the streets of the city a light was still on. The deed had been done, and one man thought not of three consecutive days of mistakes, but four.

He usually sat at his computer terminal, playing games, accessing web pages, trying to access code and just doing this and that. Tonight, as well as the last three nights, he sat at the screen and typed in the code word, EDGE, which stood for "editor - Griffith - evening" a code which a little logic, luck and larceny had provided.

Subscribing to the newspaper's computer edition was easy since they had been selling it for three years. Hacking through the system, he gained quick access to the internal memo files. After stumbling on a stray memo to a new employee on computer coding formats it was easy to experiment with the editor's name to arrive at the appropriate code.

Three days ago he changed a caption around. He didn't want to stay accessed into the system for long, in case there was a tracking mechanism. Two nights ago he got bolder, making a change in the weather forecast. Then last night he did it again, this time staying on-line long enough to make a sophomoric joke by switching the mayor's name with his dog's.

Word on the street had it that several businesses, including golf courses and automobile dealers, suffered particularly poor days because of the bad weather prediction.

The beginnings of an idea were intruding on the more noble parts of his mind. Oh, the havoc he could create. Today he would enter a small news item, this time on page one, but this time designed to make things happen. He held the power of news and while nefarious plots had crossed his mind he dismissed the more criminal uses of his abilities. Okay, he had simply put them on a shelf, he just wasn't predisposed to the criminal life.

He erased a front page story on money allocations to city street repairs, and in, with the push of a button, his button, jumped havoc.

By Nicholas Rodgers

City Hall Reporter

Mayor Bob Branch was ruled in contempt of court last night and arrested after refusing a court order to reveal information concerning a terrorist threat to the city.

The mayor was handcuffed and taken by a police cruiser to the municipal jail where he spent the night. He was to appear in court early this morning.

Police said that the court ordered the Mayor in contempt when he refused to reveal specific information regarding a terrorist threat to the city's subways and water system. The original request for information came from the state police department working with members of the Federal Bureau of Investigation (FBI).

Court records revealed that the FBI has been attempting to get information from the mayor for eight days. Special investigator William Defries said that the Bureau considered the case too important due to the widespread nature of the threat.

The mayor's office issued a statement in which the mayor defended his actions.

"I have sworn an oath to protect this city and further the goals of its citizens and in that I have not wavered. The threat the city faces is real and serious and I felt it was better left to the quiet investigations of city police. I felt that the potential for panic was a worse threat than the likelihood of a real attack by terrorists. Now that events are public I will make a full disclosure and co-operate fully with the FBI."

City officials have now issued a warning to residents that the threats are real and extreme caution should be exercised when using public transit and municipal water supplies. These are being constantly monitored but both systems are so widespread that caution is advised."

He rubbed his hands together, took a deep breath, and pushed 'Send'.

Chapter Ten

"I'll take a six pack, no, make it a case of bottled water," said the man, who tried to appear calm. The clerk rang it in, collected the money and wondered as she watched him haul it away. Strange things happened in the early morning. She was at the end of her shift, and one of the stockers had come in, a few minutes before, to fill the shelves before going to school.

"Any idea what that was about, Manny?" The boy shook his head.

She watched through a window as he left the store, and a man stopped him and started yelling something. As he began loading it into a station wagon, he was forced to push the man away, before gesturing toward the store. The second man broke for the store at a dead run.

The clerk got scared. "Why is there a run on water?" she wondered.

A quick check into the storage room through a door behind the counter eased her mind. A stack of large water bottles were piled in the back corner. She braced as the store door was opened.

"How much water do you have," the man asked, frantic and out of breath. She pointed to the water display which held another dozen or so bottles. "I'll take them all," he said.

"Sure, what's the problem."

"Haven't you read the paper? Terrorists have threatened the water supply. It's getting crazy out there."

Chapter Eleven

The front page, and it's little change, appeared on the street. The story appeared on the bottom half of the page under a large central picture, referring to a city event. Thus was not visible to the bundlers, truck deliverers, carriers, or most merchants.

Early morning radio broadcasts, accustomed to using the morning papers as their sources, carried the news, despite being unable to verify its accuracy but afraid of being upstaged by their rivals.

Even prior to 7 a.m. people were asking questions, wondering if it were true and rumors began circulating the city. Most people heard the news from someone else as it spread quickly. Media outlets bulleted their reports as unconfirmed.

Officials were caught in a trap. Denials were issued from city hall, from the governor and from FBI sources. But denials looked like a cover up and ordering the paper off the streets would only fuel the fire.

As the morning wore on the truth was sorted out and statements issued. The Daily Times even went so far as to buy commercial time on radio and television stations to set the record straight and condemn the sabotage of their front page.

The damage was done. The reputation of the newspaper was seriously called into question, the newspapers' unions were privately being blamed even by their members and the city was in an uproar.

Store shelves had been stripped of essentials, food, water, generators and medicines. People avoided public transit and days later ridership levels were still significantly lower than usual. Even with the denials, sales of essential items were brisk.

Chapter Twelve

"Well, Mister Editor, I suggest you determine where the breach in security came and then fix it."

Griffith hated police. Ever since he edited a small town newspaper, years ago, which did a major expose on the local constabulary, he had hated the police.

He and his staff had been harassed with tickets, safety checks, and all sorts of legal wrangling. He had been idealistic and stuck to his guns but the experience mitigated his interest in rocking the boat. It wasn't fun to have people in authority hate you. After that story he wasn't so idealistic.

Griffith particularly hated police in business suits, they were a little ominous that way, almost like meeting a priest without his collar on, it sort of froze your soul. This particular policeman was in a business suit, his fleshy neck bulging over a tightly bound collar. He was not happy.

"Unless we get full co-operation from The Times things are going to get very uncomfortable, Mr. Griffith.

He didn't like the media. They were always sticking their nose into places where they weren't welcome. They made his job tougher, they aggravated people already under duress and they thought they ran the world.

"Detective, I assure you, we have been conducting an internal investigation and I have no reason to hide anything, nor do I intend to. I will provide a copy of the report when it is ready."

"No!," the detective slammed his fist on the desk. "Wake up Griffith, there is a list of charges against you, the publisher and the reporter a mile long. We are in charge of the investigation. We will need a number of offices here in this building to set up a command post. We want to interview every employee. You can co-operate or we can make this whole thing much more unpleasant than it is already going to be."

Griffith knew when he was beaten. "Would you object if we ran a parallel investigation?"

"If you get in the way of police business I will have you and half your staff charged with obstructing justice," he stalked out, leaving several subordinates behind to begin the investigation.

Chapter Thirteen

"I don't know who did it."

"Okay, okay; who might have done it, who are we looking for?"

"If you mean, let's begin the investigation by determining means and motive, the police are doing just that."

Frank Anthony hovered over Griffith, stalking around the small cluttered meeting room, to conceal his frantic edge. Initially Griffith had been too frightened by the police detective to enjoy Anthony's collapse into fear, but with his outward calm shed and Anthony's gone forever, Griffith saw he had finally established some control.

"Yeah, but you secured the right to conduct our own investigation, let's use that."

"Let's use that, how? Remember Frank, we're the innocents here, and the cops for all their bluster know that." Anthony didn't acknowledge the use of his first name, he was too wound up.

"Well, what do we know?"

"We know nothing, I've put my assistant on the case of finding out what the police know or think they know, he's hanging around with them explaining procedures, locating files and people to be interviewed. He knows what they're doing and what they find almost as soon as they do."

"The cops are speculating that the unions may have done it, that a disgruntled employee is behind it or that someone is playing a practical joke."

"I thought they were professionals," Anthony barked, "they haven't thought of anything we couldn't have."

"Actually, the running theory is that the first few mistakes that we had were practice sessions for the mayor's story. Some cops think the story is a terror groups' attempt to warn the authorities of their plans. Other cops say they may not need to actually do anything, that the mere suggestion is terror enough."

"And you say that they must have confederates in the composing room? What about the printing plant? It's those damn union shitheads, I know it. You can smell their shit miles away," Anthony yelled.

"No, I didn't say that. In fact the cops believe that someone has penetrated our computer. They don't know if it's an inside job or not, but they figure that the changes have been done electronically. If it were done in composing or at the printing plant there are either too many people in on the conspiracy or too few and they would be caught easily."

"Well change the codes or something," Anthony found himself wishing he knew more about the production process.

"If it's an inside job that won't help and we couldn't change all the codes quickly without hampering our ability to publish a newspaper. Something like that would take weeks," Griffith explained.

"And there is no back-up system because our system has evolved with the succeeding generations of computers. Our system is integrated but a long way from consistent. We have virtually every piece of computerized office equipment invented since the mid-1980s. The life of each machine is lengthy but the practical applications change every few months. We've been updating our equipment twice, three times a year, for 15 years. All the access codes are a hodgepodge of built-in operations and selected security codes. Our own systems are not on the web, they are run on an internal server not connected to the public internet. We only accept computer information in page production from our own sources so we never thought it necessary to maintain and pay for a high security net. Hell, I can still remember when we didn't have computers at The Times."

"Well, is there any point in beginning the process?"

"Yeah, we have our computer department working on it but they have to deal with the cops, who are poking around, manage their own investigation of their department and still do the work required to put out a paper every day. If they change codes they might destroy evidence of the computer hack. It's going to be slow. Real slow. It'll take them days just to get a listing of all those who have access, who need access and marry that to when and how they need access to the systems. If it's an inside job, all that effort will be for naught."

"What about protection for now? I guess we'll have to have guards watching the paper as it comes off the press to make sure it hasn't been altered," Anthony answered his own question.

"What about our reputation? What about the guy in the street?"

Griffith thought for a moment. "Well reports I'm getting are sketchy, but I think we are being perceived as victims. Right now we're alright. I think, if it goes on much longer, though, we'll have a problem with credibility. What good is a newspaper when you can't trust its news?"

We will have to report on this problem in our own newspapers and we'll need a special letter from the publisher as well. I'll have something on your desk shortly for publication in tomorrow's paper.

Chapter Fourteen

By the time Lardner reached the office the real panic had subsided. People were nervous, people were unsure who or what to trust but they were no longer running traffic lights in search of water, no longer acting as if all social structure had broken down.

"We're a remarkably resilient lot," thought Lardner as he walked to the newspaper offices. Fear had only gripped people for a few hours at most and then the majority reacted by taking stock of the situation and listening to official reports for news.

Black humor, always present in such circumstances, had arrived in the city and set the population thinking. If it was a terrorist threat, why wouldn't the terrorists have just used the newspaper as a carrier for their fear tactics? It probably would have worked better. If it was a disgruntled employee why would he go to such lengths as the front page story, especially after the industry buzz was that quality at the paper was falling, due to the three consecutive small mistakes. The union theory held the most credence because they could effect and hold a wide conspiracy, they would prefer the minor incidents as not damaging to the paper's reputation. But the big story didn't fit with their motives. It had to be terrorists, and the speculation went full circle.

Lardner couldn't help but be secretly pleased that the usually smug news writers were going to be sweating. Their precious credibility was being called into question. When all you have to deal with are the facts and those precious nuggets desert you: well, you might as well start calling what you write fiction.

As he stepped up each of the stone steps to the newspaper's front door, Lardner could feel the weight of eyes watching him. He slowed his pace and raised his head to get a look at whatever was so ominous. Behind the usual hubbub and stream of people there was a pair of security guards and they were chatting informally with a pudgy, small man, dressed in a wrinkled windbreaker and jeans. He passed through the doors and saw the security set-up in the building with metal detectors in the space leading to the stairs and elevators and a couple of extra guards.

"Mr. Lardner! Mr. Lardner! Over here! " Ernie, the newspaper's ancient security guard, stood in the circle of the reception desk. Lardner walked to the desk. "Guess you heard.''

"Yeah, what's going on here."

"The police are all over the place. Mr. Griffith has given them a couple of meeting rooms upstairs and he hired a couple of new people for security," he stood a little straighter, "and I'm supposed to keep them busy. Thing I can't figure is, if they, the terrorists I mean, are fooling with the computers then why do I need more people? I'm not really expecting a full frontal assault on our office building. I can't see what's going on in the computer room let alone what's happening across the wires. I do know that the police are talking to just about everybody."

Lardner smiled. "Ernie, I don't know that anybody knows anything more than you."

"Meaning that I'm in the know or meaning that nobody knows nothing?" Ernie shook his head and smiled. "Cause I know nothing, just rumors. Mind you people have been speculating."

"You don't say."

Lardner started up to his desk, running into small clusters of uniformed police three times on his trek.

"Bill, the police would like to have a word with you," Griffith said almost apologetically. "No big deal. When you get a chance. Just don't wait too long. They're talking to everybody with computer access."

Lardner went to his desk. He figured he'd find out more from the police questions than they'd find from his answers. He started in on the day's correspondence and thought it might be interesting being the interviewee for a change. In fact, it might make a good column.

He sawed letter after letter open by sticking the writing tip of his heartily chewed pen in the edge of the unsealed flap, working a small opening and then bringing the strength of the pen against the inside of the envelope. He hoped the detective would come to talk to him soon because he hated to get into a column and have his train of thought interrupted.

Letters were few and far between these days, except for the formal announcements of various events and letters from old people who hadn't made the transition to computers. Somehow things in letters seemed to hold a bit more import than those transmitted by email. It likely came down to the extra effort required to send an old fashioned letter.

He grabbed at a strange looking letter and started to saw it open when his desk intercom beeped. "Lardner here," he said while absentmindedly pulling the contents of the letter out.

"Detective Ed Marginot wants to speak to you now, Mr. Lardner," the woman's voice said from the front desk. "He's on the executive level in the small boardroom, suite # 5."

"Ok, on my way."

Lardner glanced at the letter as he was about to put it back into the envelope. Black splotches and glue patches caught his eye and he opened it. Each word had been cut out from magazines and newspapers and glued into place. He put it away. "Better to read it after my talk with the police," he thought. "I can always tell them about it later."

He walked away from his desk with his mind racing. He was no detective. Why send the letter to him. It must have been because of his high profile. He had nothing to gain from keeping it a secret so he turned around retrieved the letter and made his way up to Suite 5.

On the way he gave it a quick look.

"Hello, Mr. Lardner," said the well dressed, even dapper detective when the columnist stuck his head in the door. "I hope we aren't interrupting you, it shouldn't take long." The detective stuck out his hand in greeting. Lardner, shook it and then held up the letter.

"I received this in my morning mail, in fact, I just opened it as I received word that you wanted to see me. I figured you'd want to see it."

Marginot's eyes widened for the briefest of moments. "I certainly would." He took the letter, scanned it quickly and then read it aloud.

"Big business is at my mercy. I control The Daily Times. It is my voice. You can't stop me. I want five million dollars deposited to the bank on the corner of Broadway and 10th Avenue in the name of Fred Freehan. You have until Monday noon or I will strike. Republican convention."

Lardner had read it on the way up in the elevator. Not to have read it would have seemed unnatural. "Yeah, I don't know why it was sent to me rather than anybody else."

Marginot motioned him to a chair, "Well, this will at least make my questions a little more interesting." After a half an hour of questions regarding his contacts, union connections and understanding of anyone who might be upset with the newspaper, Marginot dismissed him. "We will probably want to see you again tomorrow. If possible keep trying to remember anything that might be significant. And let's keep this letter quiet for now. Thanks."

Lardner left and thought little more of the interview. He had a column to finish and a dinner date with Laura at a little restaurant they frequented on the east side.

At the end of the day, column filed, and tomorrows sketched out, Lardner made his way out of the newspaper building. He stopped on the top step as was his custom, this time a little apprehensively due to the letter. Might someone be watching. He scanned a little more carefully than usual. As he put his head down and turned left at street level his brain realized that Laura was standing across the street. He resisted the urge to look up, turned toward the street, looked down its length for traffic and scrambled across. He glanced up as he hit the curb and looked, exactly according to his calculations into Laura's face. "Hi," he smiled. "Spying or waiting for me?"

She smiled, "A little bit of both actually." She patted a camera. "I had a picture assignment close-by so I figured I'd kill several birds with one flash. I knew I'd be late because I have to drop the film, so I thought I'd meet you and you could accompany me rather than waiting in some dingy dive on the east side."

"I thought that was your favorite restaurant?"

"It used to be. I guess it was fun to be a little daring a few years ago, but the last few times we've been there I've been accosted once, afraid for my life twice and scared for my wallet every time. And I don't mean just because their health standards have gone down while the price has gone up," it's actually just not the same, or maybe I'm not."

"Well we can go somewhere else," he shrugged.

She smiled, this is what she'd wanted all along. "I know this great place over on Seventh Avenue, just the other side of the university," she waved westward, "It's nice Hungarian food, you know goulash, potatoes, veal cutlets and," she threw in the coup de grace, "it's simply the best value for money I know."

He looked at her skeptically, boy did she know how to push his buttons. "Well, what are we waiting for," he gave in.

Chapter Fifteen

There was a knock at the door.

He continued to tap away at his keyboard but slower and quieter than before the knock. He hated to be caught off-guard. The apartment building was cheap but it had all the required security that an inner city building needed. It was possible but unlikely that anyone could get past the doorman but salesmen did it all the time. They'd get a delivery in the building and use their access to do a little door-to-door before someone was upset enough to call the doorman.

The knock came again. Just a salesman. He cocked his ear, waiting for the inevitable knock across the hall. He heard nothing and was just about to go back to his keyboard when he heard a curious but unmistakable sound of someone picking his lock. He rose from his office room, strode toward the door, alternately afraid, angry, and curious. He moved quietly through the hallway, thinking that it couldn't be a robbery, his car was in its spot which signified his presence. He didn't owe anyone money, he didn't have a lot of business or social contacts. He reached the door and moved his head toward the eyehole.

He stared into the barrel of a gun pointed right into his right eye only two inches away through the glass. He flung himself back around the corner of the wall. It was a robbery.

"Your shadow gave you away Mr. Ash," said a smooth voice muffled by the door. I want to speak with you. Certainly you know I'm serious and I can simply wait until you leave."

The lock on the door clicked and the door swung slowly open. When Clifton Ash was fully revealed the smiling man said, "Now that's better. I figured you were a reasonable man. I think we can have a productive conversation. We might even become friends." Ash moved aside to allow him into the small apartment.

"I'll get right to it Mr. Ash," the dapper man said. "My associates and I have been carefully monitoring the web for IP addresses linked to The Daily Times." Ash started hard. He was caught so easily. He thought he'd covered all his bases, the payoff, the third party IP link, he'd bought after a few inquiries from a mom and pop computer supply store in mid-town. Damn he knew that the IP link was his downfall.

"I assume that you will make this conversation easy?" Ash nodded.

"See Mr. Ash, I knew we'd be friends. My associates want to begin a partnership, one that can be mutually profitable."

Ash's mind was going a mile a minute. This guy didn't sound like any cop he'd run into before.

"I'm afraid I didn't get your name."

"I'm Jerry Morelli. My uncle Anastio wanted me to meet you. He sells off grid wi-fi access through a small computer parts store and decided to keep track of web traffic to the newspaper. You never know what you'll find. Information is power Mr. Ash, though I suppose you are more aware of that than most. In any event he found that you had connected to the paper's servers quite late on four consecutive nights, and the next day something funny happened to Page Three."

"What is your organization and what do you want."

"Now Mr. Ash, I thought I made that clear. I work for Anastio Morelli and he likes information."

"I just don't want to get into anything illegal," stuttered Ash. Morelli laughed gently.

"It's a little late for moralizing now Mr. Ash. If you like I can let the police know about you. However, I think you should meet my uncle tomorrow. He's always in a good mood on Fridays. He'll be at the Trocadero restaurant on Columbus Avenue tomorrow at 2 p.m. You should meet me in front of the building at 1 p.m. and we'll get some lunch before he arrives." He rose off the couch. Thanks for your time, Mr. Ash and I'll be waiting for you tomorrow. Don't disappoint me. He grinned, "I know where you live."

The door closed and Ash stood quaking. "The mob," he thought. How could he have let things get so out of hand? It all started just for the challenge, for a laugh. He paced the room. He picked up the phone a dozen times to phone the police but he couldn't, he was in too deep. He went to the refrigerator. His nerves were shot so he reached for the ice cream.

"Things could be worse," he said out loud, digging a spoon deep into the cold chocolate mass. "I could be outta ice cream."

He wasn't in jail, nor in any danger of going there, or the mob wouldn't be interested in him. He could play along and see what they wanted. He could always run away if he was desperate. Hey if they could do his dirty work for a piece of the action maybe this could all work out. After all, what would they want? Probably get him to fix race results or something.

Chapter Sixteen

What a meeting thought Paul Desroches as he dropped into an easy chair in his hotel room. He reached for the television remote and cursed that it was screwed to the table top.

"Crap, if the union would only spring for a bit nicer place, one where the hoteliers weren't afraid their customers would steal everything not nailed down," he thought. He needed to relax. He didn't need an ordeal to merely turn on the boob tube. A little mindless television always helped him to crystallize events of the day.

He flipped on a news channel and returned heavily to his seat. He couldn't fix himself a drink. He was scheduled to meet again with his management counterpart in three hours for an evening session that threatened to extend deep into the night. He didn't expect anything like this to be happening so early in negotiations, hell they had months to nail down the contract, but the management guys wanted action to quell any possible connection to the sabotage problems.

There was a knock at the door. Desroches grimaced and slowly eased his stiff joints into the upright position, took time to stretch the muscles, and then answered the door. He was not surprised to see Jeb Cross a member of the union negotiating team, who had mentioned meeting for dinner as the negotiating session had broken up.

"Come on in Jeb. If I'd a-known you wanted to go right away I would have showered by now."

"I just wanted to find out when and where you wanted to eat." Cross noticed Desroches stiff jointed walk as he made his way back to the chair. "If you want to call me when you're ready to go that's fine."

Desroches nodded.

"Hey, what did you think of Masterson? What an asshole."

"He's not so bad," said Desroches. "I've dealt with him before. He's supposed to laugh at everything we ask for, anything else is a sign of real weakness. And he knows we'd exploit that. He's taking orders from the corporate boys."

"But what about all that bullshit about the sabotage being our fault? And him claiming that they know that one of our guys is behind it?"

"Just that. Bullshit. They don't know anything more than we know and we know nothing. It's just a tactic to see if we'd show weakness. They're just trolling for an opening. Hey, you were good on that, telling them that our names went on the product and that we had more than just money to lose. I give you a point for that one."

"Thanks. It just gets me so mad, all this acrimonious bullshit. Lies back from anything we tell them. You can't even try to make a valid point because that assumes premises and premises assume facts. Give them facts and they'll twist it into some advantage."

"Hey, just relax. You can't get yourself all worked up," said Desroches. "We have a long time in front of us, including tonight. How about I come and get you for dinner in an hour and a half?"

Cross nodded and left.

Desroches was alone trying to get up the courage to make his way to the shower. It had been a pretty grueling day. Masterson was an asshole and he was tough about that sabotage thing, Desroches thought. He didn't want to worry Cross but he realized that the management was playing hardball, all the signs pointed that way. It's still wait and see time

Desroches thought, he's really just a puppet, I wonder what the corporation's real intents are.

Desroches never before even considered the possibility that the sabotage was union related - a rogue union member with a grudge . . .humm.

"Might be time to do a little fishing," said Desroches out loud as he picked up the phone.

Chapter Seventeen

This was the biggest pain in his newspaper career, thought Griffith as he walked down the hall to Frank Anthony's office. But he knew that big events often heralded major changes. One of which was his new relationship with his publisher.

He pushed his way into Anthony's office. "Hi Frank, how goes the battle?"

Anthony looked up from his hands, gave his eyes a quick rub with his left thumb and forefinger, and motioned Griffith to a chair. "It's been hell, I gotta tell you. Masterson just called, the first session of negotiations is over. He's convinced the union knows nothing about the sabotage. However he doesn't dismiss the possibility that a union guy is doing it without union knowledge. Head office is all over us to get this thing cleaned up and out of the way. They are worried about the reputation of their investment. I can't say as I blame them. Our corporate stock price has taken a beating today. The cops are still here, in fact they are maintaining a 24 hour presence until further notice and my wife is pissed off at me because I'm not likely to be home until late tonight and it's her birthday."

"My report?"

"Thorough, very thorough. I must say I was a little rough on you to get it done, but you managed admirably. In fact if you've got that capacity for work in you, I should assign you some extra duties," he waited, straight faced for a second then snorted a laugh.

For a fleeting moment, Griffith thought, he treated me like one of the more junior employees he's always trying to court.

"Tomorrow's paper is on the press and it is being watched around the clock. I have extra people on tonight and we will be paying overtime to the composers but everything will go smoothly tonight, nothing to worry about there. Each guy has one page to keep an eye on. The police and our own computer department are monitoring access to our internal system and we're ready."

"Good. Frankly, I figure nothing's going to happen anyway. Whoever is doing it knows our system and they will know that they had better lay low. And we can't maintain a 24/7 monitor of the system forever, it costs a fortune. Actually the police have begun an investigation into IP addresses that access the system from outside. They say they can find out if that was the breech but likely will not be able to trace back to a perpetrator. Only a future event will provide enough real time info to trace. If nothing happens then they say they'll try a different approach."

"What about the note to Lardner?"

"Well, we aren't going to do anything immediately. We'll wait until early next week and see if our madman tries anything. It was determined that the note was hand delivered so I have security looking through the tapes of front desk surveillance to see if they can determine who dropped it off. It's a bit of a shot in the dark with all those people there. Also, police aren't even sure if the note is real or just concocted by somebody trying to cash in."

Chapter Eighteen

Chris Wakefield snapped the lid of her briefcase, closed and spun the lock. She started out of her office and by force of habit slowed just before reaching the door and looked back at the tidy desk to see if she forgot anything important. She had arranged everything necessary well in advance of this meeting even though it was hastily called.

She had made a routine call to Systems Corporation head office to enquire about some properties that Apex Corporation was interested in purchasing. During the course of a conversation with a vice-president whom she knew from several conferences they had attended together, she found out that the Systems board of directors had had sharp words at their weekly meeting over the health of their investment in The Daily Times. Some wanted to dump the holding as soon as possible and eat the minimal loss of stock value while others wanted to weather the storm and hang on through the rough times with a mind to not even selling at all.

"The old guard says that the newspaper business is out of our realm and that it is too unpredictable in its profitability to make it a worthy investment," said her source. "You know, the old arguments on both sides. The younger guys engineered the takeover and showed their boardroom strength by pulling it off. They don't want to give that up."

Wakefield could see a potential weakness that she could exploit. She had to be careful. If she seemed too anxious to purchase the pro-newspaper segment would use that to solidify their reasons to keep it. If she didn't push at all the anti-forces might stop pushing because of the lack of a qualified buyer.

She laid her trap. Her fingers danced across the lap top computer. She preferred processing figures, asset information, and other concerns and she realized that she could offer Systems Corporation $1.3 million dollars more for the Daily Times than they had paid for it six months before. It was no secret they had paid the family owners $48.7 million, mostly in cash, while the family held on to several million dollars in shares. She realized that if she offered them over $50 million that they would probably jump, just because it could be justified as a good business decision. She also realized that they would probably not concern themselves with the four million dollars in new equipment and employee buyouts they already spent money on. Sure somebody would mention it, but in all it would be forgotten in talk about the purchase price and the selling price. The real trick was to get them to bite for $40 million. Her stock in trade.

She did not smile as she exited the building. She would stroll across downtown to the meeting she had arranged with Systems Corporation accountants, including her connection. She knew that he stood little chance of advancement in the present corporate structure, but if he sided with the old guard and they were able to convince the other board members to sell, then his stock would rise and he might even be appointed the next CEO with support from both sides. He knew it too and agreed to cut some red tape and get her talking to the right people.

This was the toughest time in the delicate negotiating. You had to convince the other company or certain people within that company that you were in the negotiation as a white knight, someone who they could count on, who's ulterior motives were not to take advantage. She did not hesitate to use James Noble Harris' well known eccentricities to help her along.

She entered the office of the executive vice-president - an appointed position from Systems Corporation, which they had handed to the oldest family member who did not own stock of the original ownership family.

Ty Carrington was middle aged and had lived the newspaper business for his entire life. He was formerly the editorial page editor having worked his way up from reporter to page editor to section editor. When the deal was done to sell the company to Systems Corporation on the death of his grandfather, who had inherited the old newspaper from his grandfather, all his senior relations had a piece of the deal, having been named in the will or having been significant shareholders. Ty was the next generation and had outlasted many of his cousins in the business, mostly because he liked it and enjoyed the work. He wanted the paper back in family hands - preferably his hands.

"Mr. Carrington, a pleasure to meet you," said Christine Wakefield. "As you likely know I am here on behalf of James Harris who is willing to put some money into a deal to help you repurchase the newspaper."

"Ms Wakefield, I'm not even sure there is a consensus among the family to make such a thing happen."

"Does there need to be a consensus?"

"It is true that two of my cousins, Edward and Nicholas Carrington, have a desire to restore The Daily Times to family control, they see it as a cornerstone of our heritage. However, they represent a wish, and are willing to commit only a small amount of capital. I've heard the figure $10 million tossed around. Additionally there is a battle regarding ownership at Systems Corporation. Some strongly favour ownership of media properties and others strongly oppose such investments."

"Mr. Harris has a soft spot for newspapers and is interested in adding The Daily Times to his media group which includes major papers in most important cities around the world."

"I am well aware of his stable of papers, Ms. Wakefield."

"What you might not know is, that had Mr. Harris been aware that The Daily Times was up for sale, he would have become involved in that transaction. And what I will tell you now is that Mr. Harris is prepared to purchase one of the smaller dailies in this market and rebrand it, or even start another paper from scratch if he is unable to make a deal to repatriate the Daily Times to the Carrington family."

Ty Carrington, looked momentarily into the middle distance trying to see the future and where he might be situated on its web as it was stitched together.

"I cannot deny personally I would like to see the Daily Times out from underneath the control of Systems Corporation and into the hands of a media friendly company. However, Ms. Wakefield how much local control does Mr. Harris wield?"

She sighed inwardly. The first hurdle had been overcome - Mr. Harris' interest had not been dismissed outright - now she had to put together the deal, and get Systems Corp to sell.

"Mr. Harris always takes an active interest in his companies however, he rarely interjects into their day to day operation. Once the direction has been determined he lets the people he hired do their jobs."

She arranged for Mr. Carrington to invite his cousins to a meeting to firm up a formal proposal to purchase the newspaper. She also arranged to have an additional meeting with two board members of Systems Corporation who were known to favour a sale.

She checked in with James to see if he was on-side with his plans for the sale and filled him in on her progress.

"The Carrington's are interested and will commit around $15 million to the purchase but only if the new company is called The Carrington Media Group."

"Done."

Ty Carrington very much wants to be the new publisher and frankly I think he's perfect. He's more interested in the newspaper than his family, but the family agenda works for him and being named publisher would cement him as our man."

"Done."

"Systems Corporation is very divided on this proposal - half the board thinks media properties are a good thing, and the other half, while skeptical of media profitability, are absolutely convinced you are playing hardball and they can sell the Daily Times for a solid profit."

"But that's not going to happen. When will they find out?"

"I'm speaking at their board meeting in an hour."

As Christine Wakefield made her way from her hotel to the Systems Corporation offices she wondered what the best approach was in dealing with the board. Usually, the attitudes of board members pointed out the proper direction to take.

"Good afternoon gentlemen, as you know I am here on behalf of The Carrington Media Group interested in purchasing The Daily Times."

"Right, we know you represent James Harris - how much are you offering? We paid $48 million for the company and its office building and need a significant return on our investment to get board approval," said one of the senior board members.

"It is true that Mr. Harris is on the board of Carrington Media, but that company is here to make an offer," she said buying time to consider her approach.

"A look at your balance sheet shows a notable loss these last two operating years and given that it is your only media holding, I'm going to suggest it will continue to lose money for you as it is a business that Systems Corporation is not entirely comfortable with."

"Ms. Wakefield, how much? We are not a sentimentally tied to the Daily Times as your proposed purchaser group appears to be."

It's strictly business with most of these guys, she thought.

"It is a depreciating property especially given today's news," she said.

The board members were taken aback.

"What news?"

"The Carrington Media Group is prepared to offer $28.7 million for the Daily Times and all its encumbrances including the office building at 200 Queen Street."

"All its encumbrances? They are worth at least $50 million, at least. Don't forget the printing plant on Old London Road."

"I was unaware that the Daily Times owned that printing facility. It was recently modernized I believe."

"Of course any sale must include the printing plant, otherwise how would you print the paper. There is no other facility like it for several hundred miles. Nothing large enough to print on the scale necessary."

"Your offer is ridiculous, Ms. Wakefield. You are wasting our time," said another Board member. "We are not interested in Mr. Harris or Carrington Media Group."

"Ah, but you should be, because Carrington Media is interested in you," she let that sink in for a moment. "So interested in fact, that Carrington Media Group recently purchased $10.2 million in the stock of Systems Printing Company to control a recently modernized printing plant on Old London Road."

The Board stopped in stone silence.

"Now Carrington Media can use it to print their new daily paper, or you can make a deal to sell them the slightly less valuable one you already have."

The silence began to become embarrassing.

"Then I'll leave you to it. I will say however that Mr. Harris hates to be kept waiting. In fact the longer he waits the more likely he will be to reduce his offered price should you reject the generous terms he has proposed."

The deal was hammered out in hours. When the Systems Corporation board negotiators stiffened their resolve on the price of $28.7 million, Christine agreed and lowered her offer to $27.5 million.

"But, but, you can't lower the offer. We are negotiating," blustered one of the lawyers for Systems Corporation.

"Yes, we are, any you know I've had second thought, I'm in for $27.2 million."

"But the property alone is worth that."

"No sir, the property alone is worth nothing without the presses, now my offer is $26.5."

He asked for some time to think on the proposal. She granted him a few minutes of privacy.

"Okay, $26.5 but we have to structure the deal so we don't look like we are selling at a loss. We want to announced we sold for $55 million for the whole thing. You've already spent $10.2 for the printing plant, so that leaves $44.8 million outstanding. If you give us $44.8 million and we will give you $20 million in stock shares and options. It's a win - win."

The terms had changed so she pressed home her advantage insisting on

$21.5 million in stock and options.

She knew that after the deal was done she would make several large orders for electronic components that Systems Corporation manufactured, hoping to drive up the stock price. She would then sell for an enhanced profit and cancel any unnecessary parts orders.

Chapter Nineteen

Ash did what he was told. First he checked out the Trocadero and Jerry Morelli on line. There was a strange void in his searches. Jerry was nowhere to be found, although a middle aged man being somewhat invisible on the web was not unusual, however the fact that a mid-town restaurant was not mentioned except on restaurant sites was a bit unusual.

Ash decided to approach the Trocadero from across the street, where he could scope it out a bit.

He made a couple of passes and then figured he'd better show up in front where he wouldn't linger. He was 20 feet from the restaurant when he took a casual look around before scanning back to the street in front of him, where Jerry Morelli now stood smoking one of those small flavored cigars.

"Hello Mr. Ash. Walk with me." But instead of turning to enter the restaurant Morelli started walking further up the street.

"Very nice the way you circled in to meet me. I must say I hadn't been expecting that."

"Ugh, I just wanted to make sure I found the place. It's easier to see signs from across the road."

"We are just going to go around this corner." Once clear, Morelli gave Ash a shove and implored him to follow at a run. Within 20 yards he darted into a black town car whose door opened from the inside in perfect timing with his movements. Ash followed a few steps behind.

The car slid slowly down the street and turned into traffic. Morelli took a few moments to compose himself. Ash was agitated.

"Mr. Ash, we are going a short distance to see Uncle Anastio, just as I promised."

The car slid through traffic, crossed the Brooklyn Bridge and made a series of turns through the southern section of Brooklyn eventually turning into the underground parking of a high rise condo building.

"Come with me, Mr. Ash. My uncle is upstairs."

"Look. I don't want any trouble. I'm not interested in your organization."

"Mr. Ash, you might not be interested now, but I believe once you hear our proposal you will at least consider it. What harm is there in listening to a business proposition?"

Ash shrugged his shoulders, he felt compelled to follow, and he was a bit soothed by the suggestion of choice on his part.

The pair took an elevator up. Morelli inserted a key in the elevator's control panel which lighted up two blanked out buttons at the top of the panel. He pushed one and the light went out. They started to rise with the overhead floor indicator showing nothing past 15 floors.

The door opened and they entered a glassed-in chamber about 12-12 with another door at the far end. Beyond the chamber the space looked like a hotel lobby, with large potted plants, marble floors, statuary and furniture lined up in several groups.

Morelli started to turn around slowly, and asked Ash to do the same. He complied.

A light flickered and the glass door at the end of the chamber slid open.

Ash looked around. The room was similar to the one he had seen through the glass of the chamber but it was not the same. The glass had projected an illusion. A grand piano appeared where he had not seen one. The space seemed more like a pub or grand library, with some musical touches.

Morelli motioned him to sofa in the corner which faced a panoramic view of Manhattan and the outer harbor. The window was 15 feet wide on both sides of the corner of the building . Baffles in the ceiling cut the light they allowed to the rest of the room. However as he passed the baffles and approached the window he saw the whole scene open up.

He still stood there taking in the view when he was aware of another person in the room.

"A lovely view. I very much enjoy watching people's first reaction when they experience it," said a gravelly voice.

"It's striking. As if the whole world was laid out at your feet," said Ash who was so taken with the view he did not turn around.

"Mr. Ash, I am Anastio Morelli, Jerry's uncle. I have a business proposal that I believe you will find most compelling."

"Well, I'd say 'Shoot' but somehow that seems to be a poor choice of words."

Anastio smiled, a grin which pulled is lips tight to his face.

"Mr. Ash, I understand you've been having some fun with the Daily Times?"

"Yes, just a bit of harmless fun."

"Harmless until the other day. I very much wish you hadn't done that."

"Well it's done now."

"Yes, unfortunately. It is too bad that Jerry wasn't able to locate you a day or two earlier."

"What do you want from me," said a clearly agitated Ash.

"Please sit down. Jerry get him a drink. What will you have Mr. Ash. I prefer a nip of ouzo at this time of the day. It keeps me alert."

"I'm guessing I should be alert, so ouzo it is, but just a touch, I don't usually drink at this time of the day."

Both drinks were served and Ash sat in the sofa with the view straight ahead of him while Anastio, sat on a nearby high back chair, half facing Ash and half facing the view.

"Mr. Ash you are a computer expert, and my organization needs the services of such a person. We are willing to pay quite handsomely - an annual salary, additional cash in lieu of a standard benefit program and significant holiday time."

"Mr. Morelli, I already have all of that. I am not interested in having to look over my shoulder all the time."

"Mr. Ash, I'm afraid that with your recent actions, you will be looking over your shoulder for several months to come, at least. I propose you come work for me. I have several projects I need done to get my organization up to speed with the technological times."

"I don't want trouble."

"To be frank Mr. Ash you have trouble. Law enforcement is very interested in finding you. I have ways of making you disappear - so you need not worry about law enforcement."

"Are you threatening me?"

"Oh no, Mr. Ash, I want your help and I'd like you to be able to operate outside of the normal bounds of public view."

"You mean the black web?"

Morelli started, "There is such a thing?"

"Absolutely. I have . . . . I have . . . heard of it."

"What goes on there?"

"Well, I understand a lot of clandestine things, arms sales, shadowy financial deals, drugs, and other less savory stuff."

"I have an interest in this hidden web."

"I am not entirely sure how to access it."

"But with the proper equipment, time and a sufficiently incognito presence on the web you could find it?"

"Yeah."

"Will you help me out, Mr. Ash?"

"Well, can I think about it?"

"Actually Mr. Ash I believe you already have. Frankly you are in too deep too refuse, and why would you, the money I offer is very good, and my organization will provide you with whatever you require. After several projects are completed we can talk about your desire to continue working for us."

Chapter Twenty

"We cannot find anything though our computer guys have identified the unauthorized entries into the system, that produced the changes on the page," said Detective Marginot. "The trail there goes dead. We have been able to ascertain the rough area in which the access occurred, but need additional accesses to try to nail it down. The intruder to the system is no amateur."

"Where is this occurring from?"

"Manhattan," said Maginot. "Well, most likely Manhattan, but it's hard to be sure. We traced the incursions to an IP address in Jersey, which in turn was hacked from a public internet cafe near the Battery. That access could have been from almost anywhere."

"Have you been able to rule out union activity, or some kind of inside job?" asked Griffith.

"Not yet. We will access your personnel files to look for anything that might help, such as the level of skill of your own IT guys, recent firings, stuff like that."

"I understand you already have investigators looking at the files."

"We can't always wait for niceties, Mr. Griffith. I didn't expect any resistance as you want to get to the bottom of this as much as we do. And you've been co-operative so far."

"It would be nice to at least inform us, so our people are not surprised."

"Mr. Griffith, surprise is one of our chief investigative tools."

Griffith was unsure, but did not believe they were harboring some vast computer genius with a grudge. He had considered the IT department and it was filled with regular guys whose biggest fault was they kept trying to add additional functionality into the newspaper's systems, creating functions that were of limited value to the business but which required huge amounts of programming time to achieve.

The bane of business systems everywhere was not malicious code it was nerdy programmers who were more interested in laurels from their peers than they were in the needs of their employers. Basic systems were easy and boring. Doing something novel or doing the mundane in a novel way was what drove most computer programmers. Possibly one of these approaches had opened a door that nobody had known about.

"Let me know if you find anything or if we can be of any assistance Detective."

"Right off the top. Is there anyone you can think of who would do this?"

Griffith shook his head but he decided to ask all the department heads. Sometimes there was a gem among employees. And there was always a rogue unionist.

"The union appears clean as well," said Maginot. "They have offered their assistance and we are looking at their files too."

Negotiations had largely stalled due to the investigation and uncertainty but the system incursions had halted. Griffith had put his editors on notice to carefully comb through the paper after publication to note anything that had changed, even down to the smallest dot. They had found nothing for days and there had been not a peep from the anal-retentive public , not even the grammar-nazis who hounded the paper on a regular basis.

"We will keep the file open Mr. Griffith but unless we come up with something to keep the investigation moving ahead we will be removing resources from it by the end of the week."

The Daily Times had printed front page retractions, explanations and opinion pieces on information technology vandalism, in an effort to put the story behind them.

Their circulation, which had slowed considerably, mostly from a huge drop in single copy sales, began to recover, and actually grew with the news that the paper had been returned to the Carrington family. To most readers it was comforting that the Carrington family was back in charge of their daily read. The Carrington involvement drowned out any noise regarding the participation of James Nobel Harris.

Christine Wakefield had already sold short some of the stock Harris would receive as part of the deal to buy the paper. Apex Corp held the ownership. Harris had cashed the shares he received as part of the deal gaining him a solid 10 per cent return on his investment, over the course of a few weeks.

Griffith took the news well. He felt even better about it when he was offered the post of publisher, overseeing the entire operation of the Daily Times. Frank Anthony was gone, deposed in the sale and presumably involved in managing another of Systems Corporation's companies. Hopefully he had some background he could bring to his new job, thought Griffith.

Asked for his opinion of who he might hire to replace himself he had provided Ms. Wakefield with a list of candidates for Mr. Harris to peruse. She had returned it with a few additions, including Troy Carrington - the obvious choice in hindsight.

Griffith circled Carrington's name, after all he had been in charge of the editorial page, prior to the sale to System's Corp. He added a note of support.

He received a memo from Christine Wakefield saying that Carrington would report to his new position in two days time.

That solved, Griffith left his office to make a tour of the building. He wanted everyone in all departments to know that he was thinking of their situations. His presence is what counted. He made a show of meeting with department heads on their turf and hung around each department long enough to make small talk with everyone there. Frank Anthony had left a mark even if it was a soft spot for long term employees. Griffith was keen to maintain that rapport.

A month had now passed and there had been no more mistakes in the newspaper. The issue was fading.

Chapter Twenty - One

Ash surveyed his new rig. He had four screens, huge, state of the art. It was possible on each of the screens to have multiple windows open and accessible. He had three hard drives, and several portable drives. He was hooked up wirelessly or if he chose he could access the web through cable or telephone. Once connected he could route his access to the web in a hundred ways. He was exploring ways to connect that could not be traced and ways to infiltrate company systems, the deeper web matrix and the black web.

So far Anastio had provided him with anything he asked. He had brushed off progress reports that Ash had tried to give him. Not that Ash actually spoke to him, everything was done through intermediaries - usually Jerry, but he could feel the presence of a large group of people who worked for Anastio and did what he asked very quickly.

"Tell Anastio that I've managed to hack into several companies but I am still investigating ways to do so without detection - that's the real trick."

Ash had asked for cell phones that could not be traced. Jerry had provided him with two small phones and said they were untraceable but would only work on the system for 48 hours after first use.

"I'm told the system recognizes they are unauthorized and strips them from the system 24 hours after it recognizes them and cannot authenticate their validity."

"Well we will have to work with it. I might be needing new ones every 48 hours, as I investigate the web. What I'm doing is using the phones to gain wireless access to the web - then going about my business without being traced," said Ash. "I'm also monitoring the system as it identifies and ultimately kills my access point. It appears to retain the information for some time. The weak spot is any indication that we are buying cell phones at a regular two day interval."

"I will let Uncle Anastio know. I believe it is not a problem."

Jerry knew that the phones were being nicked from shipments coming in from China. They were copped before they could be tagged and formatted for sale in North America. Of course the Chinese may have infiltrated the software. He mentioned the possibility of Chinese involvement to Ash - who stiffened noticeably.

"I had better have a look in the operating system and in the chip configuration to see if there is any nasty software there."

Investigations did find some deep Chinese code - code that could shut down the device, that could use the device as a microphone and that could track the device. Ash erased the code but it returned when he reset the device. So he erased a subset of code that he could not identify nor which appeared to have any use in the basic operations of the device. The malicious code did not reappear when he reset the device.

Ash had been exploring the black web and more than once found himself so deep that he had trouble remembering how much actual time had passed. One day he was concentrating on his screen for so long and so deeply that when he pulled back from his desk to stretch his neck, he realized there were no other lights on in his space, that it had gotten dark without him noticing. He glanced at a clock and realized he had spent 14 hours alone with his keyboard and his curiosity.

The dark web was layered onto, or underneath the more public web. It was unsurfable, as sites usually had no connections to other sites. The chief advantage of the public web was its interconnectedness, where one thing and idea led to another. The dark web had very little connectedness.

"Anastio wants you to source several specific firearms, and make suitable arrangements to complete the transaction and delivery, preferably in another city," said Jerry handing Ash a short list of guns.

"Uh, okay, I guess," said Ash looking at the list. "What city?"

"It doesn't matter, just not this one. Preferably someplace quiet, and easily accessible."

Ash set to work, first accessing the dark web and going to an arms dealer he had scoped out. He made his first inquiry.

"Yes, we have such things," came back the reply. "How many? Quantity affects price. Where are they to be delivered? Location affects price. Payment method? Payment method affects price. Ammunition? We can quote price given your needs. Advise."

Ash waited a few days until he saw Jerry again.

"Have you arranged for the purchases we discussed?"

Uh, no, not yet," he added quickly. "They want to know how many and do we require ammunition."

Jerry looked at him severely and then softened, "Ammunition, hmm. Better get a few cases for each piece and enquire about time frames for this delivery and future deliveries of ammo."

Ash nodded. He took a sip of his coffee. "Do you want me to see if I can find an additional supplier? "We might get a better price."

"Get a price first and we will see if Anastio wants additional options."

So Ash went back to his computer and messaged the weapons' dealers' site.

"Would like to establish relationship - want only one of each - several cases of ammo for each piece - will pay US cash - delivery Nashua, New Hampshire."

The reply came back within a day. "Okay, willing to go slow, however in future we only deal in quantity - smallest order, one delivery van full of product. Large orders can require some lead time. One of each piece, three cases of ammo per - cash - delivery New Hampshire - details to be verified - "$61,500".

After Jerry had seen the note he okayed it and Ash contacted his connection and exchanged delivery instructions which they had to alter due to requirements from the seller. They agreed on a drive through storage locker in the industrial part of Nashua.

"A few weeks later Jerry came to Ash. "Anastio is very pleased with your work." He handed Ash a large manila envelope. "A token of his esteem. He would also like you to make a slight change to the Daily Times in two days for their Thursday edition. Details are also in the envelope. I will be by on Wednesday evening to see if you were able to complete the task."

Ash was a bit concerned. He could only imagine what havoc Anastio had in mind with the newspaper. After Jerry left he tore open the envelope. In it he found a card from Anastio asking him to scope out two other arms dealers and detailing the terms of their proposed transactions. He also found three bundles of $100s as his reward. There was a note thanking him and the details of the hack of the Daily Times. Ash was shaking as he pulled out the third bundle of $100s. He went back to his net investigations, moving through pages and code very slowly as he was thinking very hard about his new assignment.

Chapter Twenty-two

Lardner surveyed his desk. Somebody had sat here and moved things around. As a senior columnist nobody would sit at his desk and actually use anything on it - they might sit there and access their own portable laptop but only when there was no other desk available and the need was urgent.

He knew it had been the previous night when all hell had broken loose along the waterfront docks and in a few uptown restaurants. Reporters and editors had been working through the night when the scope of the mob war had become apparent.

"The old man died an hour ago," said a junior reporter as he passed Lardner's desk. "That's 42 dead almost all from one family syndicate, according to the cops."

Valery Kostinov was the oldest member of a Russian crime family which spent most of its time turning drug money into legitimate business investments. They owned a large number of service stations across several states, using recent immigrants as ownership fronts. They operated the stations and gave the family a healthy cut of the profits. They were beholden to the family to operate the stations for five years after their arrival had been arranged.

Now Kostinov was dead. Killed by a rocket propelled grenade in a small Soho bistro, which now, no longer existed. The bodies of 22 others had been found in the bistro, many connected to the crime family but some of whom were just in the wrong place at the wrong time.

It had obviously been a co-ordinated attack. Two other restaurants met with the same fate - curiously two of Kostinov's sons were at those locations. There also appeared to be significant collateral damage.

Usually turf wars were confined to a number of fairly isolated incidents - police were obliged to restore public safety and frowned on the turf wars going public. With the death toll in this massacre they had to put out all their resources to end the threat. However, they couldn't find anyone responsible and the syndicates with the most to gain also appeared to be unattached to the violence.

That violence included additional attacks at the same time on five warehouse locations near the docks and an additional warehouse and promenade shooting in Boston.

In all the Kostinov family was largely wiped out though the string of filling stations remained intact with their operators waiting in fear of the other shoe dropping. Now 42 had died and there were several dozen more in hospitals in two cities.

"Somebody wanted Kostinov gone and were willing to lay it all on the line to achieve that," said Lardner as his new executive editor Tom Carrington reached his desk. "The breadth of the attacks and use of some heavy artillery is unprecedented."

"Aye, it is," said Carrington. "I have additional problems. There was a breach in our system and a small change was made to our copy for three days leading up to the attacks. The cops think the changes and the attacks are tied together. They have not dismissed some rogue element in our union from being involved."

"Holy crap. Our union? Some of those guys are a bit out there, but nobody I know would do anything even remotely like this."

"I need you to scope out our union and do a piece on their violent past and any connections they might have to organized crime."

"Smashing signs down on a few windshields eight years ago is hardly the type of violence that leads to rocket launchers. As to the connections to organized crime, I'm going to guess the connections are all one way, the syndicates trying to influence the unions and the unions being unaware of the manipulation, or at least trying to keep it at arm's length."

"Well, that's a good place to start. Let me know in a few days if there is any smoke or fire - could end up as one, or several pieces for you."

Lardner sat down. He had some contacts in the newspaper and printers unions. He also had contacts in other unions around town as he had shown sympathy for their working conditions. He got on the phone and had a long talk with the union guy Desroches.

"Well I wouldn't put it past our guys to get a little creative but, off the record, they would never do anything other than damage machinery," said Desroches. "It simply wouldn't occur to them to do anything that would endanger lives, especially innocent lives."

"So you can see them setting up some damage to our plant or offices and having collateral damage unintentionally take someone out?"

"Like I said, and I'm trusting you off the record, we have a few hotheads who might go a bit far, and sure something crazy might end up as an injury but it would be unintentional, like the wrong place at the wrong time - nothing like these co-ordinated attacks."

"I think you are probably right," said Lardner. "So you know I'm supposed to check out the union, including potential links to organized crime. "

"Whooo," whistled Desroches. "Working with the cops now are you?"

"Not me, more like Carrington. He's scared. The cops are crawling around the newspaper. I didn't tell you but there were unauthorized copy changes in the paper before the mob hits. I think they are looking to see if we can identify any smoke in advance of a major crack down. You better come clean. The mayor and the governor are determined to do what's necessary to root this out. Mob hits in public are bad enough, but taking three dozen people with you is way beyond what anyone will stand for. You got any guys with violent criminal records? Talk to me about guys involved in any of these syndicates."

"Well, yeah, we have a few guys with records for violence, but it's all domestics or youthful car theft or knocking over a convenience store. Not good stuff, sure, but nothing that suggests a recent walk on the wild side. The syndicates leave us alone for the most part though I do hear rumors that they talk to the big bosses - those connections, if they exist at all are not on the shop floor," said Desroches. "Nor are they at my level within the union. Frankly I don't even know what the attraction is other than some violence for hire, and we're pretty much past that these days."

"I'm going to be talking to some other guys. Just be warned if I find anything else, or anything that suggests there is more to the story here, you're going to get a thorough dressing down by the authorities. It's out of my hands. I just have to report anything I come up with to Carrington and I'm sure he's going to pass it on."

"Hey, we've known each other for years. You've always been honorable with me. I am trying my best to return the favor," said Desroches. "Hey, I did notice a typo in your column the other day, just an 'ie' when their should have been an 'ei' nothing big. It made me wonder if the copy editing cuts were affecting quality."

Lardner hit the phones, wandered the floor at the printing plant and in the delivery bays. He talked to anyone he could not hiding the reason for his questions and the seriousness of the situation. He couldn't get the transposed letters out of his head.

He ran into a couple of police detectives running a parallel investigation. They shared notes. Well, Lardner told them most of what he knew and the two detectives make some general noises that fit the facts. It did not appear that the union had any involvement nor any knowledge of the mob attacks.

"Well, if the union wasn't involved in the computer breaches, who did it and why? asked Inspector Marginot.

"Exactly what were the minor changes that have you concerned?"

"They were minor stuff. The result of a horse race was altered only to show the payouts as different than what was official. A weather report for Miami was altered to show rain when it was hot and humid. And on the last day a story about holes in airport security was altered to suggest the vulnerability was in a different part of the airport," said Carrington. "You tell me what it means. Code?"

"Yeah, that's what we thought too. I'm thinking we have an arms shipment coming in under our noses, so the story was altered to keep us off the track," said Marginot. "You wouldn't have found the weather thing or the horse race alteration if we hadn't been scanning after catching the terminal change. My boys only cottoned on to that after we put two and two together due to a tip from the airport authority. They saw some funny business on their security tapes. Nothing specific just some odd behaviour and an unauthorized personnel."

"So you are investigating us? I'm told our union guys simply don't have that level of violence in them."

"Yeah, but were also told there are some tenuous connections with the union and the syndicates. Maybe the union is involved without knowing it. The truck receiving the shipment at the airport looked a lot like one of your delivery trucks, though it appeared to have no markings. Got a truck with a fresh paint job?"

Carrington looked scared. "I'll, I'll have the plant manager look around for me."

Lardner completed his column on the aftermath of the hits. He pulled no punches, saying that all the city's resources were being put into finding those responsible and crushing any violent criminals before they perpetrated such wanton acts.

The letter transposition gnawed at him. He pulled his columns for a week before the hits and combed through them. Sure enough there were several mistakes in the copy, spread across three days prior to the attack.

He looked at them and then jotted them down on a blank page. He stared at them a while. First the 'ei' then the next day a small 'g' where there should have been a capital letter. Finally the day before the attack 'ht' used as a short cut for height where newspaper style demanded the word be written out in full.

It clicked 'ei-g-ht'. Eight. A code. Or a co-incidence. "The next day the attacks had commenced," thought Lardner. "There were only three locations, the attacks started after 11 p.m. What was the connection to the number eight?"

Chapter Twenty-three

"Jerry, I hope that anything I did, did not contribute to those explosions. Tell me they didn't," said Ash.

"I can't say for sure. Anastio was filling a contract for goods. It's out of his hands what happens to them after the contract is fulfilled," said Jerry as he handed Ash an envelope. "Let's just say there are fewer unsavory characters on the streets today."

"I don't want to be involved in that. What if we get caught? I don't want to go to prison. I'm just a computer guy. I like video games."

"I notice you play some of the heavy ones. They're pretty violent. Violence is usually the last resort with these guys. They aren't all bad you know. Sometimes they resort to violence to keep the peace. Anyway, I'll be back Friday," he said, nodding at the envelope before closing the door behind him.

Ash looked inside. Again there were packets of $100s and a short note. The things he was asked to do were innocent enough, except for the large order of arms and the delivery instructions.

"I can't do this," he thought. "I know what's going to happen. Ash started to run escape scenarios through his mind eventually thinking he had to fake his own death to keep Jerry and Anastio off his trail.

Ash decided to tell Jerry the dark web was shut down.

Jerry laughed. "Look bud, you're in now. One phone call and I can implicate you in 42 deaths. Or I can simply let the Russians know who ordered the arms. Either way you are done. You're with us now and your best bet is to stick close. Anastio takes care of his people. I haven't heard any complaints about his thanks," he smirked, gesturing at the bundles of $100s.

Ash knew he was right. He arranged the next arms deal without trying to pay too close attention to the stuff that was being brought it. At least they were just dealers, not the actual users of the stuff, thought Ash.

He was exploring the dark web after placing his order for goods when a message popped up on his screen.

"Want out? I can help. Meet me on fourth floor elevator in 5 minutes."

Ash was stunned. He did want out. He knew his place was guarded 24/7 and so did his apparent helper. However he was nervous. Was it a plot to catch him? Who could possibly help him and know where he was?

Ash decided not to go. But he wanted out. As the clock wound towards the five minute deadline he bolted. Any chance to get out was better than nothing. After all what would they do. They needed him and could only make his jail a bit tighter. He went to the elevator and pushed the fourth floor button.

The door opened. Jerry was there. Ash's heart jumped - it was a set up.

"Hi, Jerry. Just taking a bit of exercise around the building," you know. "Can't be sitting down all day and night. Maybe you could stop holding me prisoner. After all you know where I live."

He roughly pushed Ash back onto the elevator, telling him loudly that he needed to get back to work. Once the doors had closed he towered over him menacingly.

"Ash, the note came from me. I want out too. I'm moving my arms to show the cameras that I'm giving you a dressing down. Continue to look scared."

"That's easy."

"Anastio has set off a turf war that's going to get us all killed. Complete the next job and use the reward money to help us both get out. I can hold them off so you get away and in the confusion I'll just disappear, with a bit of the cash of course. Got a new life to set up somewhere. We can help each other . . . " Jerry was almost pleading.

Ash was deciding if it was a set up.

"Okay Jerry, how are we going to do it?"

"When the next envelope comes through just fulfill the terms of the job.

That will keep them off you for a few days."

"Then make a break for it. I'll make sure there is nobody watching. If you have plane tickets arranged you are clear. I'm going to bolt after I announce you've escaped. That'll buy me a few days clear. With all the carnage, the word out there is that Anastio is being targeted as the instigator. If he is then his whole organization is too."

Days later Jerry arrived as if he had never spoken to Ash about the escape. He handed Jerry an envelope, this one especially full. Ash opened it and bundles of 100s fell out.

Jerry smiled. He scooped up about half the bundles, then threw one back into the pile.

"You might need it more than me," he said. "I know how to take care of myself. Whatever you do, deposit it slowly into a few different banks. Then use it to buy a business. Something small and quiet like a dry cleaners. Then it's all legit."

Ash set up the final arms deal. Usual channels, usual terms.

Two days went by. Ash had a single bag packed with his essentials including two portable hard drives - no evidence of his activities but knowledge that might prove useful in a future that looked very uncertain. He looked around the apartment - he hadn't lived there long and most of the stuff was Anastio's but he had a few things which he had put together in a trunk and posted for delivery to a storage unit in Kansas City which he had booked and paid for on-line. The trunk just contained the detris of his life, things he'd like to keep if he could walk away unscathed. He could try and recover the trunk whenever it seemed safe, he thought.

Jerry arrived. "This is it bud. He looked at his watch. You ready, 15 minutes to go time."

Ash was nervous. His stomach in knots. He was glad he had decided to eat nothing as he was sure it would come out. He just wasn't sure which end.

"Let's go," said Jerry. "You got plane tickets?"

"Yeah. I need to get to JFK, right away."

They went down in the lobby and Jerry ushered him out of the building with a nod to the security desk. They went out and immediately grabbed a cab that Ash was sure pulled away from the curb 100 yards down the street only to respond to their hail.

They both got in and Jerry said, "The Met on Fifth."

Ash looked at Jerry confused. He still wasn't sure he wasn't being set up. Jerry mouthed - trust me - and held his hands out palms down. They exited the cab at the Art Museum and crossed the park to pick up a cab on Eighth. Jerry explained he was trying to break up the trail. They entered the cab and Jerry said, "Yankee Stadium."

Ash was not fully convinced but at least they were moving in something like the right direction.

They exited the cab and started into the stadium before moving away from the entrance and catching a cab as two baseball fans exited.

"JFK" said Jerry.

The cab pulled up to departures and Ash got out.

"Thanks, I guess. Good luck to you."

The cab, with Jerry still in it, pulled away.

Ash moved into the airport and immediately caught a shuttle to LaGuardia. He wasn't above playing the misdirection game himself. Upon arriving at LaGuardia he caught a shuttle for Newark and then a plane bound for Edinburgh. He could melt in there and decide how and where to complete his escape.

Jerry left JFK and went to Anastio's condo.

"I lost him," he said. "He jumped out of the cab midtown and immediately grabbed another. I couldn't find him in the rush. I thought he jumped out and into the subway but he was gone. He moves pretty quick for someone confined to his computer for 6 months."

"Jerry. How could you let this happen. I thought he was on-side with us."

"He had me fooled. He only balked at filling the orders you gave him, but he did it after I reminded him that he was involved and could be outed. I had no more trouble from him after that . . . until today."

"Well, check the airports and the train stations and where ever else you think he might go. Get a few of the boys to help. Fan out. You take charge and report to me every 6 hours. We'll decide what to do if you can't trace him by noon tomorrow."

Jerry left. He knew he had better throw Anastio off his trail by reporting back through the night. He'd bail out first thing in the morning after his morning report. He already had his plane ticket to Atlanta and a second flight from there to Salt Lake City. He blessed his mother's genes which gave him a decidedly northern European look and meant he could blend in with the Mormons a bit better than many of his Southern European cousins.

"I can't find him, boss. I did trace him to JFK but from there he could have gone anywhere. He seems to have blended into the crowds. Without our computer hacker it's difficult to get anything reliable. I did ask a few airlines if he was on board - said he was my brother-in-law and I'd missed picking him up. Most refused me outright but a couple said they had no record of him. It's a start."

"Keep on it boy. Let me know what you find."

Jerry shut off his phone. He sat for several minutes waiting for his flight and then slipped the phone into a newspaper and casually tossed it all in the garbage. He figured it would end up in landfill before Anastio could trace it.

When Jerry arrived in Atlanta he saw the headline, 'Mob war engulfs Big Apple'.

He watched the carnage on CNN while waiting for his connecting flight. More than 200 people were dead after a series of timed attacks throughout the city. The FBI were investigating a carbon monoxide poisoning of a high end condo building in Brooklyn to see if there was a connection. More than 100 people had died as the CO flooded the building in an apparent deliberate act. Several people on the lower floors were unaffected suggesting that the attack was aimed at upper floors of the building, according to the report.

Jerry noted the building in question, pictured in footage of emergency vehicle responses, was Anastio's. He was likely dead. He fought off a momentary thought of going to the airport to claim the last arms shipment. The profits it represented could be huge but so were the likely logistics of getting possession of the shipment. He shook his head, determined to drop the thought, and simply be thankful he had escaped. His hunches were correct.

Syndicates in New York all suspected each other of the co-ordinated attack on the Russians and appear to have picked similar times to take a pre-emptive approach to their future business prospects.

Police were appalled at the size of the carnage and its public nature.

"People are scared, but I can't say this publically, the mobsters just took care of the organized crime problem in New York, at least until the inevitable shake out between criminal factions settles back down again," said Marginot.

"And the criminal element will slither back into the city, once they realize its empty of competition. That should take about a week," said Lardner. "Once the addicts can't get their hits all hell will break loose with new suppliers battling for market share - the complete opposite of oligarchic or monopolistic practices that have previously existed. Essentially the criminal market had carved out their areas of influence and the addition of large quantities of armaments upset the balance."

"Yeah. So my guys are now ready for smaller running gun battles and a large number of small but violent incidents as the new normal is being established," said Marginot.

Chapter Twenty-four

Ash found a small hotel in the Edwardian center of Edinburgh. He used it as his base as he searched for a place to live. He eventually decided to move to Inverness in the north. From there it was easy to get to Edinburgh, but far enough off the beaten path that he would not be surprised in a crowded city - he was justifiably paranoid.

He too had seen reports of the carnage in New York. He had immediately purchased a laptop and accessed news reports on the web. The British press had breathlessly reported on the killings for two days and then entirely dropped the story as the river of gory photos and lurid revelations dried up.

Ash was at first confused by the reporting as they got so many basic facts wrong. He soon realized it was due to non-New Yorkers filing reports, people who were not conversant with the city and its geography. Ash started to correlate the photos with shots from Google Street View to determine exactly what had happened.

It appeared among the significant carnage that his apartment building had been broken into and ransacked. While he had not seen the location, the building in Brooklyn that had been poisoned was most likely Anastio's headquarters, he figured.

It didn't take long for him to enter the dark web in search of information. He stayed away from his previous correspondents and looked around for any stray bits of information.

Ash made regular runs for supplies. Generally he was ignored but his accent triggered a few odd looks from locals. He tried to limit his public exposure, until he had more information. He was hoping that his existence had died with Anastio, assuming he was dead. Ash trolled obituary sites in New York and surrounding areas looking for some sort of match.

A month after his escape he caught the eye of an apparent tourist in Inverness when he ordered a pint in a local pub. The barman looked at a woman sitting at a table alone and nodded at her before nodding again toward Ash. Uncomfortable, he left.

A few days went by without incident and Ash was thinking less about the encounter when a knock at his door froze him cold. He didn't want to answer it but rationalized it would be odd to avoid contact - and besides what type of master criminal knocks?

"Aye," he said as he opened the door, trying to put a bit of Scots lilt in his voice.

"Mr. Clifton Ash?" said a woman, the same one in the pub. "I must speak with you. I am not the police. I am aware of who you are. It is in your best interest to listen to my proposal."

He hesitated. The last time he listened it hadn't turned out so good. Well, if she knew who he was, and it was bad, the jig was up. He'd listen."

She made her way inside. Ash offered her a cup of tea. Something he had come to enjoy in Scotland.

"Mr. Ash, I represent a company which would like to make use of your knowledge and unique talents," she said.

"Well you know how that worked out the last time."

"I assure you Mr. Ash we are not engaged in criminal activity. My employer has been able to track you through our already very capable computer department by matching your searches and web site activities with those you displayed during your time in New York. It was simply a matter of looking for the patterns, something computers are quite good at."

"What do you want me for?"

"Truth be told, a bit of outside-the-box industrial espionage. My employer will pay generously and requires you to do nothing that is criminal in nature. He is interested in you because of your ability to alter copy at The Daily Times, and your apparent experience in various levels of the web."

"I thought there was nothing criminal required?" Ash raised his voice.

"And there isn't. My employer owns The Daily Times and would also like you to monitor computer patterns at various businesses - something requiring specialized knowledge but nothing criminal - more of a collating of facts which you can strip from the web."

"Tell me more. Do you work for Mr. Carrington?"

"I will report your findings to my boss and he will provide information to the board," Christine said. "Are you interested? I am able to provide you with a deeper cover than you have managed yourself - though I applaud you on your choice of hidey-hole, what's left of the syndicate would not likely find you here, and they have more on their minds than finding you. However I advise you drop your usual searches as they gave you away."

Ash considered briefly. The proposal appeared benign. It was work and she provided him with assurances of his freedom to move on and to come and go as he pleased.

"I will warn you though, continued use of the sites you have been using with eventually get you noticed by people you might rather avoid. To be safe, I think you would be better served to find another place to call home. We can help with that when you desire."

She left with an agreement to return in two days with details of his assignments and financial support. Ash promised to consider her offer to relocate.

Ash was visibly shaking after she left. He didn't realize he could so easily be traced but it made sense he thought. She must have traced his searches to his IP address and then just started to look for him in the area. Eventually she found her quarry in the pub.

He decided to stay the remaining few weeks of his holiday lease and then move. he didn't want to attract attention by running away. He thought through the possibilities. He only spoke English so that would somewhat determine his scope of living arrangements - or would it? Perhaps he should widen his world a bit.

He thought about trying to disappear into the vast armies of people in California, where his accent and appearance would make him disappear. He thought about South America and thought that perhaps Chile or Argentina were sufficiently European to hide him as long as he learned enough Spanish to get by. He thought of the south of France or one of the smaller European enclaves like Malta or Majorca or even the Canary Islands.

He considered Christine's offer. It seemed ideal; a source of income and resources to hide and move around as required.

When she returned he glanced at the papers she brought outlining his pay, methods for providing it to a Swiss bank account, a company credit card in his name for most of his expenses and details of the assignment.

He nodded to all but wanted to talk about his location. He asked her advice.

"Israel," she said without hesitation. "It's Europeanized, modern, accessible and most of the population are from other places. You can melt in there and if you want, you can move again. I would also suggest you ditch that computer and start fresh.

Ash agreed. He would leave for Tel Aviv in two weeks.

"It appears that the expected violence in New York, as new crime groups move into the city, has not materialized," said Christine. "It appears that existing syndicates simply got together and agreed to wipe out the Anastio family as they had instigated the violence. It appears there was even an agreement on how to carve up the Anastio business dealings once they were eliminated. All's well in Gotham, but I wouldn't go there if I was you."

Chapter Twenty five

James Noble Harris sat by the pool. An attendant brought him a telephone. He thanked the man politely and took the call.

"Yes."

"Our man has agreed to everything. He will be on the ground in a fortnight. His reports should commence shortly after that. He may require a second relocation at some point."

"Good. And your report on Carrington?"

"Complete in your in box by this evening."

"Excellent. Please take some time off."

"Thank you sir, I shall."

"Just remember to remain available. And I shall try to remember you are on holiday. If you receive anything from me please only respond if I ask you to directly, otherwise everything I send is FYI - I shall try to mark it as such."

She hung up. Scotland was as good a place as any to start a holiday. From here she would go to York and then perhaps London. The London Eye has always been a fascination of hers as a way to get a bird's eye view of all the new construction that was remaking the city from east to west.

Chapter 26

It was dark and moonless with the only light coming from streetlights. Two large trucks pulled up to the gate - the lead trucker provided the necessary pass code and the two trucks rolled into the compound. There was a low level whine of jet engines coming from some distance away - where airline planes were being serviced for use the next morning.

First of the two large white transport trucks maneuvered into position between the loading dock and the gatehouse. The second truck backed up to the dock and disgorged several men and a forklift. They quickly loaded their goods. The two trucks switched positions and the second truck was quickly filled with the remaining boxes and crates.

The pair of truck rolled away into the night.

The next evening the same procedure was completed - two large freightliners were filled with boxes and rolled away.

"Got it sir - transported and stored."

"Wonderful my boy, now please execute our plan. I can feel the tension in this city and it must be dissipated. What better way to eliminate it?"

"Please report to me any part of the plan which is not completed. It is there that our greatest concern lay."

Across town in an old warehouse by the East River, near Hell's Kitchen, a group of 50 men were distributing their new arsenal.

"Hell, Jimmy how does this stuff even work?"

"Look if it's too much for you, change places with Albert, he can fire the weapon, you can go in and complete the job."

"Oh here's the firing pin. I'm good."

"You better be, there is no second shot at this. Once begun the battle will rage until one side is complete in its victory."

The men dispersed to take up their positions.

Four hours later a voice crackled across a cell phone, "Jimmy, there is nobody here."

In several other spots around town the same message was being relayed.

"Okay, I got their warehouse and command center, but it looked like nobody was around," Albert's voice came from the phone.

"Shit. Shoot now and then go looking for them. They have the same plan."

Jimmy calmly put the phone down, quickly grabbed some papers, his gun and a small strong box and ran, calling out a warning. He flew down a flight of stairs into the empty storage area below, through a door to the outside and heard the low thump of a powerful round. The building behind him exploded and caught fire. He knew no more than the ambush was complete when several shots sounded and tore into him. As he lay on the broken pavement, his consciousness fading, his last conscious seconds allowed him to see a few others mowed down as they ran for cover from the burning building.

Albert, unleashed his anti-tank weapon. The huge round ripped into the building and exploded, then continued through the empty warehouse where the second part of the round penetrated the neighboring building before exploding.

Albert had been knocked backwards 15 feet, but he held onto the rocket launcher. He scrambled away to get some time to think, quickly entering a van located just around the corner from his shooting position.

Once in the van he gave instructions to go to a certain East Side restaurant he had previously conducted business in. He reloaded. He tried Jimmy but there was no response just a message that the line was not available.

Albert opened the sliding door of the van. Propped himself against the side wall and told the driver to slow down as they passed the restaurant. Albert didn't hesitate and sent another rocket into the building's main floor. The heat from the resulting explosion was intense and was only partly blocked by the van walls.

They moved on. Albert gave another address, this time of an old movie theatre just off Broadway. It was under renovation. Albert stepped from the van. Set up and fired another rocket into the construction site causing a huge boom, with the resultant rush of air racing into the concussed space. A few fires broke out. Albert stationed two of his guys at either side of the building site and waited. Sure enough a few minutes later some people came out of the rubble. They were gunned down immediately.

Similar scenes were playing themselves out across town. Across the river and in several cities in the northeast. Philadelphia experienced a high level of carnage. Jersey City, Atlantic City and Newark collectively took more hits than Manhattan. There were isolated incidents in Atlanta, Hilton Head, New Orleans. Miami was shot up pretty good.

Once Albert realized their organizational equivalents were doing the same thing to them as they were trying to do - it became a bit of a running battle. There was no home left to return to. No safe place they could use to consider their next moves. Obvious targets were destroyed on both sides, residential blocks took hits and known locations of syndicate members were also attacked. Knowing their own places were being targeted Albert doubled back on them as quickly as he could to go after those who were targeting him. He succeeded in killing a dozen before they figured it out as well. In the wake of the carnage the city emptied itself of syndicate members, all looking for refuge.

They all regrouped in the most likely, unlikely place they could and then made arrangements to keep their tattered remnants together in even less likely locales.

The scattered hills of western Pennsylvania were riddled with remnant groups of organized crime syndicates.

Chapter 27

"Well, there are more dead mobsters than you can count. There are also a lot of collateral damage. The city looks like a war zone," said the Mayor, holding his head in his hands.

"There is going to be a reckoning," said his police chief.

"You mean this isn't the reckoning?"

"Strictly speaking it is the fallout from the battle two weeks ago, back on the Eighth. What I gather is that the Brooklyn bunch started selling weapons to one of their rivals, hoping the rival would knock out some of the other families and they would look innocent. They did the dirty work. But when everyone figured what was going on, the remaining syndicates got together and committed the ambushes of a couple of weeks ago to wipe out the Brooklyn Morelli gang and restore balance to the city. However, I'm told that balance is difficult to find and another family was offered large arms for a song, to encourage retribution for the destruction of the Brooklyn gang. Problem is more than one family got that offer so they subsequently tried to knock each other off and do it on the same night - and the result is the war of last night."

"And you are saying it isn't over. Just what now?"

"The rivals have to see who survived and will have to knock out a peace treaty of sorts. At the end of the day, contraband and organized crime are going to exist - it's our preferred policy to insist it be done outside of the main and only within acceptable terms. Generally that is followed and our enforcement is only applied when they get too far out of line - holding people against their will, shooting innocents to defend their turf and when their activities infringe on the normal enjoyment of the city."

"The problem now is that peace will take some time to achieve as nobody really knows how many were killed, what hierarchy remains and what organization can continue. There will be a huge hole to fill in terms of what those shadowy groups did and others might try to muscle in - none too peaceably."

Chapter 28

Ash read the news reports. New York was a war zone. To read the British newspaper reports, most of the east coast was a war zone. He didn't know much about it but he secretly hoped that Jerry was dead - one less person who knew of his connection to the whole bloody mess.

Ash had checked his Isle of Mann bank account. His balance stood at $2,500,001 after wire two deposits for $1,250,000 were posted four days ago. He made arrangements to transfer $2 million to a bank in the Channel Islands. He would forward the remainder in the next two weeks and then quietly close the Isle of Mann account.

The thieves had been very honorable as Ash had trusted them to pay him by wire and they delivered without a hitch. Of course they were both very anxious to get a hold of the arms they were promised and likely more. But for Ash, there would be no more of this activity. He had accepted the Daily Times offer and was trying to distance himself from the events in New York.

Ash's holiday rental in Scotland was ended and he moved to a small apartment block in Tel Aviv where he had been set up by the Carrington Group. He had begun to do some work for them on the cutting edge of app development, payments and video streaming. Of course the Carrington Group would not know of his activities but he wanted to clean up all the loose ends before jumping on board with them whole heartedly.

That meant also closing the contract for the Morelli storage units at the airport in Nashua. He hoped that the units were empty now.

Poolside in Scotland a phone rang.

"Yes sir, the New York business definitely has Mr. Ash's fingerprints on it. I expect he was getting rid of excess stock and trying to cover his tracks at the same time. I am hopeful he is not engaged in a continuing operation. I will speak to him about it."

Lardner was down to police headquarters early in the morning.

The police chief gave him the straight talk. Told him that nothing was off the record and told him that police hoped that the battles of control of organized crime would be fought elsewhere and be concluded without further loss of life or damage to property.

There were more than 500 dead now and several blocks of buildings had been destroyed. Most of the destruction was in older neighborhoods and in the old industrial waterfront but the damage was extensive.

"Who is supplying the weapons? Some of this stuff is industrial, military grade material, according to forensics. How are they getting it into the city? Could it be terrorism?"

"All the targets are organized crime. It doesn't appear to be terrorists. More likely they are just capitalists with some goods for sale who have managed to create a market. Forensics tells me that the stuff is American made, some of its Russian and some of it is Chinese knockoffs of Russian and American arms. Essentially it is all black market stuff."

"Warehousing facilities are being searched all through the tri-state area but with the large number of trucks that roll through the city on a daily and nightly basis, and the amount of coastline available to smugglers it is almost impossible to figure out how it came in. It's not terrorists so the feds are not wetting themselves."

"The newspaper's offices were not damaged but a little place some of the staff used to go for lunch a block and a half away was shot up pretty good."

Once Lardner had put down his pen. The chief opened up.

"Have you seen your columns lately?"

"No. I rarely read my stuff once it leaves my desk."

"We noticed that in advance of the first shoot up and the last, there were a few odd errors in your column. they appeared to be editing mistakes. Of course the editors have been cleared. They showed their copy as clean, so the mistakes were introduced at the printing plant or at least some time after the copy left the editor's desks."

"Really?"

"Yeah, and those mistakes when taken in total appear to be some sort of code."

"What does it say?"

"The first collection spells out the letter 'EIGHT'. That was in just before the initial attack on the Russian syndicate. And then just prior to the latest carnage the collection of 'mistakes' spell out 'ALL IN'. It's obviously an instruction of some kind. Some kind of a code. Our computer guys say the edits came from an internet connection in a seaside area north of Edinburgh, in Scotland."

"Given the instruction we figure that this attack is likely the end. However, we'd really like to piece it together so we can stop this from happening again. Do you have anything to add, Mr. Lardner? Have you received any more ransom letters?"

"Now that you mention it, one of the union guys noticed a mistake in my column just before the Russians were hit but both of us didn't put any stock into it. It seemed random and was only a single mistake."

"That would have been part of the original code word. Of course the FBI are all over this, as are a number of other law enforcement agencies. However, we've been asked to investigate locally, especially any newspaper connections. I'll be blunt Mr. Lardner, you haven't been home for almost two weeks. That seems rather unusual. That and the code appearing in your column and you receiving the ransom note, which the Daily Times mailroom has no record of receiving."

Lardner started to laugh. "You think I had something to do with this? I'm the master criminal kingpin of all New York - of the East Coast?"

"No Mr. Lardner we don't believe that. It's just awfully strange that everything seems to funnel through you. Can you think of any reason for that."

"Other than I am a daily fixture here at the Times. Other than other pages were targeted for edits and mine is a regular feature? Other than my girlfriend is a great cook and I hadn't run out of toothpaste? No, I can't think of any other reason."

Chapter 29

"I just told them where to collect the stuff, I wanted it gone, the warehouse closed and any connection to me to be dust."

"You realize that you are now a target of every mobster in New York, as they know you set them against one another and heavily armed them all."

"I only gave them what they asked for. The determination to use the stuff was not my idea. Anyway I'm pretty sure they don't know me or care as I am gone. Only Jerry Morelli knows me and I don't even know if he's alive."

"Mr. Ash this whole incident is making our continuing relationship very strained. You are toxic. In fact I will not be speaking to you for perhaps a year, to let the heat die down and the dominoes in New York to fall into place. We will honor our agreement and suggest you let us know your movements. After sufficient time has passed I will contact you to renew our acquaintance."

She left. Ash was left with the four walls of his apartment and his computer window into the world. Perhaps he should disappear more, moving around between places to keep any trail he left difficult to find. He decided to play off line video games - but the violence bore into him. He began to shiver even though it was over 90 degrees where he sat.

Chapter Thirty

He returned the letter to the envelope. He didn't want anything to do with this but it was falling in his lap. He knew he would go to police but wanted to roll the contents of the letter around in his mind before handing it over.

The letter read . . .

"The person behind the carnage is Clifton Ash. He is the Daily Times hacker and he managed the arms shipments that started this war. I bugged out before it started because I could see the future that has unfolded."

The letter was postmarked Atlanta, Georgia.

Likely a member of the Morelli family, thought Lardner. Though it was said on the street that they were all dead. Mob connected businesses were unsure of how to proceed as their organizations had been disrupted. Some of those who operated the businesses thought they were blessed, some thought they were cursed as they didn't know when someone would come back to reclaim their deals. Many were just figuring out the connections they thought they had with benefactors were really connections with shadowy figures who had not survived the mob war.

"Clifton Ash, whoever that is," thought Lardner. He decided to do a bit of background checking on this guy before turning over the letter to police. He couldn't hold it for too long though as even the US Postal Service could only be counted on for a few days between postmark and delivery. He tore a bit of the envelope's flap off and carefully dropped it in a plastic bag.

He decided right then to take it to police.

They asked him how much he had handled it. "Quite a bit before I knew what it was. I receive a fair bit of crank mail. It's hard to know it's criminally cranky until after I've opened it."

"I checked for you, the Times never had a Clifton Ash as an employee. However I haven't checked other media companies nor local universities to see who this guy might be. Though I intend to."

"You might want to stay clear Mr. Lardner. I know these cloak and dagger things seem pretty interesting to outsiders but this stuff can be very mundane and then rapidly very dangerous. We will be doing some of the local investigating and then turn it over to the FBI as it's obviously something they'll want to know."

"Don't worry Inspector, I will give you anything I find and anything that comes back to me after I mention Clifton Ash in a column."

"Please don't do that Mr. Lardner, we don't want Ash or anyone Ash knows to figure out that we are on to him."

"Okay, fair enough, but I want an exclusive once the name becomes public."

The detective nodded. "And I'm still going to look around. Quietly."

"I've warned you about that. You don't want to get charged with Obstruction of Justice, do you."

"No I don't but you must want a little bit of free help - I don't have much time to put into this and it might make your job a bit easier."

Lardner did put some time into finding out who Clifton Ash was, or is, if he was still alive. Inquiries at hospitals and on the web didn't get any hits. There were a few Clifton Ash's around but none of them fit the profile. Well, one was a university student studying statistics, another was a warehouse manager in Jersey City. Then he hit pay dirt.

Columbia had dismissed a Clifton Ash from its computer program three years before. He had apparently hacked into the faculty system and altered a bit of information on various professors which had them answering embarrassing questions for a while. He hadn't covered his tracks too well and had been found out and expelled.

"Yeah, well thanks for that," said the detective. "He's a disgruntled former computer hacker who isn't terribly concerned about getting caught doing the high tech equivalent of high school pranks. We already knew about that. As I said Lardner, please back off."

Lardner couldn't quite let it go. He did a little computer stalking and found that Ash had stayed in Scotland for a time before his trail went cold. That squared with what police had told him. He didn't bother to inform the police of his discovery. He couldn't bring himself to write about the wanted man. He was a bit afraid of the police and what might transpire if he broke the code of silence. That was enough to keep him quiet.

A few months later Lardner received an email.

"I am being dangled by the FBI and by my new employer who has abandoned me until the heat is turned down. Please let me know what is happening between the syndicate families - I did not expect this to happen. I hacked The Times for a lark and got cornered by the Morelli family to arrange for dark web purchases of heavy weapons. I had no idea what would happen and once I found out, I ran. I'm not sure you can help me but you are my only lifeline."

Lardner sat on it for a day and then told police - he had no choice, as failure to pass on the information, should his negligence become known, would certainly trigger the obstruction of justice charges he had been threatened with. He also figured his mail was been screened.

"You need to contact him. Sympathize, try to draw him out so we might be able to find him. You might even suggest a plea deal and the witness protection program," explained FBI investigator Brian Stone.

"Okay, I'll see what he says."

Lardner told Laura. Laura sympathized with Ash.

"He never meant for this to happen and now his life is ruined."

"He should have thought of that before he decided to prank the newspaper."

"You've never pulled a prank? Come on, people might know they are risking a nasty response but they certainly don't expect to go into hiding after cellophaning the toilet."

Lardner smiled, "I never expected you to be the pranking type. Who's toilet did you sabotage?"

"Nobody, the boys at university did it to the girl's floor in first year. It didn't affect me, except for having to check every time for the rest of the year. I thought it was pretty clever actually. Mind you, my friend Emily Davidson was not so charmed," she giggled.

"I'm not sure that's an apt comparison, mind you he did foul his own nest, so to speak," said Lardner.

"Emily Davidson wasn't too happy, but she did get over it; especially after she pennied the fifth floor boys into their rooms a few days later."

"Hah, so you all got even and nobody got hurt."

"Well we took quite a bit of heat from the dean as three of the boys missed a chem mid-term because they couldn't get out of their rooms. They fixed it and nobody on our floor ever let on we knew how it had happened."

"How did it happen?"

"Emily woke us all up at 4:30 am and we went upstairs and used the pennies as shims in the doorframes. You can't open the door if its jammed shut. Some of the boys climbed down the outside balconies from the fifth floor. One guy twisted his ankle but made it to the mid-term. There was definitely an uneasy peace after that. More so as the dean was watching very closely."

Lardner laughed, "I'm guessing the FBI is watching for Ash every bit as closely. They asked me to offer him witness protection if he turns himself in and is forthcoming with the whole story. Haven't heard back from him yet."

"I'm sure he's weighing his options. Staying hidden and unfound by those looking for him for the next 20-50 years or being put through the wringer by the FBI who nobody entirely trusts."

Chapter Thirty One

"Okay put me in touch with the FBI. I have arranged a lawyer to act as a go between," said Ash in an email.

Lardner dutifully tapped out the FBI contact's email address, wished Ash the best result and signed off.

Thinking about it he quickly tapped out a second message asking for an exclusive so he could write a column to coincide with the news that Ash has surrendered to the FBI.

Ash agreed but said he would have to run the idea past his lawyer.

Two days later Lardner closed up his lap top, grabbed a notebook and a couple of pens and left the Times office for a coffee shop a block and a half away. He managed to get a coffee and sit down only moments before a dapper young man appeared at his table. "You look almost exactly like your picture."

"Not sure that's actually a complement. It's printed black and white every day."

"It's just an observation. I'm Glen Johns. We spoke on the phone. I represent Clifton Ash."

Johns handed Lardner an envelope. This is Mr. Ash's statement to the press. I fully expect you will twist these statements so I ask two things, that you print the entire statement and that you remain fair in your judgment of Mr. Ash and his actions."

"I always work to be fair. I couldn't have lasted in this business for as long as I have if I wasn't fair. However you must understand fairness, and that sometimes a person's actions make even the fairest judgment appear harsh."

"Mr. Ash was caught up in a series of events he had little control over. He was blackmailed, threatened with death and never understood the consequences of what he was doing under duress."

Lardner began to scribble down Mr. John's statement.

"Hey don't do that. This is all off the record. Only the statement I gave you is authorized for publication."

"I'm sorry Mr. John's but you cannot be assured of getting a conversation with a reporter off the record after you have had it. You have to ask in advance or make sure you haven't said anything you don't want public. However, I don't see anything too damning in your statements thus far," he said looking over his notes.

Mr. Johns began to object but thought the better of it. It was obvious to Lardner that Ash had hired a very raw, inexperienced lawyer. He put two and two together.

"When did you and Ash go to school together?"

"How do you know that?"

"It's obvious. You are young, have referred to Mr. Ash as Clifton a few times and who else would Ash get but a friend, someone he could trust?"

Mr. Johns, rocked his head back and forth, adjusting his tight collar without touching it, he didn't like dealing with someone so attuned to the details. Details were what they taught in law school - that and a way of thinking that cut right to the chase.

"Observant of you. Yes, we were roommates at Columbia for two years. We knew each other before school."

"Your boy is in a heap of trouble. If I were you I'd make sure every possible 'i' is dotted when you speak to the FBI. If his evidence doesn't bring in a number of people involved with the domestic terror that was visited upon this city, then Mr. Ash will be the fall guy and his witness deal could evaporate."

The young lawyer thought for a second. "Good advice," he said.

"Do you have any suggestions on the extent of Mr. Ash's requirements in the witness protection program?"

"He needs to be buried very deeply as there are multiple groups that want him dead and others that might do it simply to curry favor with newly built syndicates in the New York area. I'd look to have him resettled in another country and that is not an easy task given most countries don't like importing criminals. You might have to suggest a reciprocal agreement bringing someone non-violent to the States in return for settling Ash."

"I'm sure you understand all this has to be in place and ironclad before you even bring Ash in," said Lardner. "The FBI has more than one way of disappearing people."

Chapter Thirty Two

"Christine, how can we make this work for us?" asked James Noble Harris. "Mr. Ash is going to slip through our fingers as a possible operative, I mean employee."

"Sir, we could instruct Griffiths to offer Ash a job in computer security through the FBI. They might go for it as Ash's future living expenses would be off their plate and internally it would look good for the criminal to work on the right side of the law. The FBI is going to want to know everything about the dark web and Ash's connections. They might even set up a sting with Ash's suppliers."

"Remember the FBI wants to keep this all quiet. That might be part of their reasoning. He will probably mention our contact with him, and while we may be called in to explain ourselves, there is nothing we did that would cast any incriminations upon us. They may want to know how we traced him though."

"I prefer to keep our secrets to ourselves. You can provide a proper line of mumbo jumbo to satisfy them, I trust."

"Yes, your name should not even come up. I spoke to Ash only referencing the corporate level. Once the FBI clear him for the Daily Times job we have him back . . . under contract."

Two weeks later Ash was flown to Washington via Frankfurt under the name Herr Teufel, a none too subtle FBI joke. He was driven directly to Quantico, the FBI compound, where he was housed, interrogated and processed for witness protection.

Eventually he was moved to Strasbourg, France, a city with a significant German population, after he was given several months of French and German language lessons.

The whole affair slipped quietly away. The public was still concerned about the carnage but official reassurances that there was no public danger coupled with a vastly reduced crime rate in the city, had its effect.

Jerry disappeared as nobody real knew of him or his connection to the whole affair. Ash took on remote location computer work for the Daily Times after unloading his entire story to the FBI. On the advice of his lawyer he left out no detail, except one, one that even the lawyer didn't know about.

He didn't mention the $2.5 million in a numbered account in Switzerland. He lived in fear of a knock on his door. His own efforts at trying to hide had been futile. He had little faith in the FBI's program and he spoke very poor German and pretty rough French.

He wanted to go back to Tel Aviv but anyone involved in the case knew he had been there. And the arms dealer knew about the money and Jerry Morelli was still out there somewhere, likely having figured it out. It appeared to Ash, that bad decisions would never go away, and even his insurance policy . . . the money in the bank was only that . . . a distant insurance policy available only in the most dire circumstances.

-END-

Touch them all

He knew.

He just knew. Years of experience, the situation and the pitcher. He knew.

College World Series, his team had squeaked into the tournament, and their pitching got hot. With two players who were rapidly gaining the attention of pro scouts they had bullied their way into the final.

He was a slick fielding shortstop, and they couldn't stop talking about some of the plays he made. However his bat wasn't there. Not a surprise really, it never had been and he had moved up the local baseball ranks with his glove and arm. He was a youth baseball fastball king. Find the strike zone, find a win.

In college his lack of control hurt. Without it he couldn't even try to throw off speed stuff with any success. Without a range of pitches he had settled in as a defensive anchor. He held the defense together and near the bottom of the order, he held back offensive rallies.

But he was here today, in the bottom of the seventh, his team down by one in the College World Series Championship game. He had a few defensive gems in other games in the tournament and had made all the routine plays today.

There was one out and two guys on. He had taken a strike to allow the runner from first to steal second mostly uncontested. They hadn't even made a throw over, but they looked at him menacingly before he trotted down to second with the pitch. The next pitch was a failed curve in the dirt to even the count and another fastball away to get ahead.

He knew a slider was coming. It was the pitcher's best pitch and had been commented on during the tournament. He also knew the pitcher could not afford to walk him so he would throw the slider over the plate. He was so sure of the pitch that he backed out of the box to run it through his mind again as it had come to him whole - the situation, the pitch and the high probability of its intended location.

He stepped back in and waited trying to remain calm and fighting the urge to over swing.

The pitcher looked in, nodded imperceptibly, confirming his foreknowledge of the slider and fired.

He held his weight back, followed the pitch in on the inner part of the plate and started his swing getting the fat part of the bat out over the plate and a bit lower than the pitch's trajectory indicated.

Just as a smidgen of doubt flashed in his head, the ball hopped away over the plate and cut down meeting the bat head perfectly and leaping off it with that perfect crack that indicates a well struck ball. He couldn't feel anything as the ball intersected with the sweet spot and trampolined out over second base. Only the sound and trajectory suggested anything special and he dropped the bat and ran hard toward first base. The centerfielder took a step in and then sprinted back giving the hitter hope it would go over his head for extra bases.

As he rounded first at a full sprint the ball disappeared over the centerfield wall with the fielder still trying to catch up but knowing it to be impossible and unnecessary. He dropped his head to his chest in resignation.

He was elated. The three run homer gave them the lead. It presented his team with the College World Series Championship for the taking. A two run lead with only two innings remaining - just six outs.

The grin on his face started with a smirk as one side of his face smiled before it spread ear to ear. He had only hit one other home run in his entire college baseball career and that was into a short porch against a Tier II team in a rout. He hadn't spoken to any scouts and frankly didn't expect to. His numbers were just not there, the scouts all knew that his entire college career indicated he was no prospect.

His teammates were whooping it up before they thought of approaching home plate to wait for his arrival. His shot came out of nowhere. Getting significant offense from him was a big bonus. Even members of the bull pen could be seen jumping up and down high fiving beyond the left field fence.

As he approached second base he realized that this was the most significant moment of his baseball career, better than the shutouts he pitched as a kid in state tournaments, better than the five hit game with two defensive gems he had when his team qualified for the Little League playoffs, better than anything.

He touched second and turned toward third and he deliberately slowed down. He was going to enjoy this, he thought - this was likely the highlight of his whole life. He had heard the stories from his father of sporting glory, and heard his father's acquaintances speak in glowing and sometimes even reverential terms of his father's sporting accomplishments from decades old games and contests.

"This is it. This is the greatest moment of my life. I don't want it to end," he thought. He tried to think of something he could do while rounding the bases to make the occasion more memorable. He thought of running from third backwards - but that wasn't legit. He thought of throwing his hands in the air to whoop it up a bit - but that wasn't his style. He thought of just stopping and looking around the stadium, kind of willing time to stop for a few moments - but that would likely start a fight and that was not what he wanted to happen to his great moment.

He looked skyward for guidance but he had no dead family members to seek out. Even all four of his grandparents were will alive, in fact they were in the stands. He took a quick look for them but couldn't see them in the mass of cheering fans.

He reached third having rejected all the thoughts that had gone through his mind. He did a little hop, switching from one foot to the other while running through the base. In that instant, that small portion of a whole second of time, he glanced around the stadium, willing himself to remember, to take a mental photo. He looked at the pitcher, angrily rubbing up the ball. the opponents dugout where their manager had popped out and started toward the mound. He looked at his own dugout where several of his teammates were high-fiving.

As he put out his hand out to touch the third base coach who greeted him with an "Attaboy," he took another mental photo of the greeting at the plate. He grinned a big grin and turned toward home. His teammates had formed a horseshoe around the plate and were looking to his arrival.

He couldn't help but see the happy faces there. His closest friends on the team would be the first to greet him. The back-up infielders were hanging around the outside of the group. The relief pitchers were still in the bull pen beyond the left field wall.

It was the most significant moment of his life, one that would live in his thoughts every day and one that he would be reminded of in small ways and large for years to come. And it was almost over. The grin disappeared from his face. As he entered the horseshoe and felt the back-slaps his face had changed from the face covering grin of pure joy to an almost painful neutrality, even in the face of his teammates joy.

And then it dawned on him - it was only beginning. He would have this memory forever. it couldn't be taken away from him. His face lit up and he jumped up and onto the plate emerging from the leap with his joy restored. And then he was surrounded by happy teammates, and it struck him that he wanted the celebration over and just wanted to breath.

The glory of the moment was yet untarnished. Only subsequent moments could reduce the luster. Not only was it the most significant moment of his life but it's value to him was dependent on his care of it.

Sure, other events could overwhelm and overshadow it. Some of those events would occur in the next few minutes as the game continued and his team was forced to play out the remaining six outs. His glory was fleeting or not - it was largely out of his hands now.

A million events had provided the moment, his experience had produced the moment and the flow of time would determine the importance of it. Glory might be fleeting. It might be forever. It would never go away, but it would change.

Perhaps even the scouts would take a second look at him - he thought before smiling to himself - "Yeah, right," he said aloud, that wasn't going to happen. He was the hero of the College World Series as long as nobody else stepped up. In fact maybe he would cement the win with a brilliant play. And then which moment would be the biggest - his huge and unexpected homer or perhaps a game saving dive and double play with the tying run on second.

Maybe, he thought, sporting glory doesn't hit like a thunderbolt but only became enshrined by subsequent events.

"Damn," he thought, "it really felt like the biggest moment of my life."

There were six outs left to enshrine his moment. What could go wrong? and a lifetime of other moments large and small to jig saw together into a life.

His fleeting moment had ended but the clock still ticked relentlessly forward revealing new opportunities for success and failure, or a pall over events great and small, good and bad.

-End-

F. Bradley Reaume has written six books. A graduate of the University of Guelph, a former newspaper columnist and reporter, he has been involved in government and public policy issues on both sides of the aisle. He has also taken an active interest in sport both as a participant and as a coach.

He lives in Burlington, Ontario with his wife Judy and two children, Holly and Bill.

Books by F. Bradley Reaume

The Spiral Aim - (2001) a treatise on the nature of truth

Amusadorus - (2003) a collection of verse

Wogs - (2014) an illustrated children's book

The Rhyme of History - (2014) a survey of current affairs

A Picture of Distance - (2015) a novel of the 20th century

Other Skylines - (2015) a collection of short fiction